BENEATH THE SURFACE

BENEATH THE SURFACE

Terrence Brock

Writers Club Press
San Jose New York Lincoln Shanghai

"The true measure of a man is not the levels of testosterone which course through his veins, but the fearlessness with which he opens his soul to those who dare enter."

R.R.Rodriguez 04/1997

"I'm really glad we decided not to go up to Miami tonight." Nick said, as he caressed Donna's long blonde hair.

Slightly tilting her head to have her eyes meet his as she reclined in his lap, she smiled and said. "So am I, this has been a perfect night." Donna curled her hand behind his neck and pulled his face to hers for a gentle kiss.

The two sat on the beach looking out over the ocean as the moonlight highlighted the tops of the waves in the distance. A faint glow began showing on the horizon, hinting that the sunrise was not far away.

"Are you sure you're not mad? I know you made reservations and all, I just didn't feel like going back up to Miami after spending three weeks there on this case." Nick said.

"Sweetie, I just wanted to spend some time with you all to myself; I thought it would be the easiest way to get you away from everybody at the Shack." Donna sat up looking him straight in the eyes to get her point across. "I've missed you, and I know how much you like being with our friends, and I like it too. But I work there all week, and when you're not on a case, you're there running the place. I just like being alone with you once in a while, and tonight couldn't have been more perfect."

No more words were spoken. The two merely sat embraced and enjoyed the sunrise as they had so many times before.

The alarm sounded. Nick rolled over to turn it off and check the time. As he did, he realized that Donna was not in bed with him and he smelled the aroma of her famous French toast cooking from the kitchen. He sat up and stretched as he saw the late morning sunlight streaming through the window. Nick pulled on a pair of shorts and went to the kitchen to find Donna putting the finishing touches on the table. "Good morning gorgeous, you seem to have a lot of energy this morning, considering…" Nick did not finish the statement, he simply let the smile on his face stand for the words.

Donna turned and placed a glass of orange juice in his hand. "Well I guess I don't want to waste any more of this day." She leaned forward and kissed his cheek. "It's just one of the perks of dating the owner. Since you finished the case you were on, I got Carol to work for me so that we could spend the whole day together."

"Sounds great Babe, what do you think about taking the boat out to one of the lower keys and having a picnic, just the two of us?" He took a drink of his juice as a sheepish grin began to come over his face. "But I would like to swing by the Dive Shack and say hi to everybody, you know, just to make sure the place is all right."

"As long as you promise me that we're not going to wind up spending the whole day there. Besides, they've all been asking when you would be back. This has been the longest you've been away since you opened the place five years ago." She led him to the table and sat down as well. "Now lets hurry up, the sooner we get out of here the sooner we get to that picnic you promised me."

Nick, like many of the inhabitants of the Florida Keys, was a transplant from another part of the country. A former police officer from Chicago, he had made many trips to the Keys to go scuba diving, and had fallen in love with all the Keys had to offer. The lifestyle in the Keys was laid back, and every one seemed to be far more at ease than in Chicago. When Nick's parents died in a car crash four and a half years earlier, Nick was left one million dollars in insurance money, and decided to move to Key Largo.

Within a couple months he had found the perfect place to open his bar. It had been a dream of his to own one since the time he tended bar part time while going to college. Now at the age of thirty, Nick had his bar and a small investigation service that had started with a favor for a friend. Who, knowing he had been a cop, had asked him to look into a business venture for him that turned out to be a con.

Donna and Nick drove into the parking lot of the marina where his boat was moored, and which the bar also shared. The area in front of the bar was full of cars he recognized, since it was only the first week of March, and the spring diving season had not yet begun.

The Dive Shack was the favorite hang out for most of the area divers and fishing guides, although some tourists were beginning to hang around more and more. The bar was styled like a typical sports bar from Chicago, with pictures from the Bears to the Blackhawks, and especially the Bulls.

"Hi Nick," Came the greetings from around the bar as Nick and Donna entered. Being around the same age as the bar's staff, they were all like Nick's surrogate family, and most had been there since the bar opened. They were a tight knit group, more friends than coworkers.

"Hi Carol, how about two BloodyMary's," Nick called across the bar as he and Donna pulled up a couple of stools and sat down. "By the way, thanks for taking Donna's shift so we could spend some time together."

"Actually, I'm surprised to see the two of you out today. Considering how long you were up in Miami, I thought you wouldn't leave the house all weekend." Carol said as she winked at the two, obviously not as well rested as she had seen them in the past.

Nick smiled at the remark and said, "Well we spent a great quiet night alone last night, and we thought we would take the boat out and find ourselves a beach to have a picnic on."

"Hey Stranger, where have you been hiding all my life." The voice came from over Nick's shoulder as a pair of arms reached around his waist and he felt a kiss on his cheek.

Nick turned to see Julie, his best friend. "Hi sweets, it's nice to know I've been missed." He returned the kiss.

Julie was one of the first people Nick had met upon moving. She was a waitress at Coconut's next to the Best Western in Key Largo where he had stayed. Although she was a beautiful woman, about 5'10" tall, thin, and very athletic, the two of them never were more then friends. With her thick auburn hair, and eyes as emerald green as the leaves of a tropical rain forest, all types of men were always pursuing her.

The first night they met, Nick was sitting at the bar in Coconut's around five in the evening having something to eat after a day of diving. A group of guys also in the Keys for some diving were at a table next to the bar getting rather drunk and hitting on Julie. At first it was just playful flirting and all were enjoying themselves, but with the passage of a little time and a lot of beer, things began to get a bit out of hand. Nick had been watching the situation, mostly because being an ex-cop; he tended to try to keep an eye on what was happening around him. Julie had also taken notice of him watching, and once the grabbing of her by the men at the table was more than she could put up with, she decided to put and end to it. Hoping Nick would follow her lead and realize what she was doing.

"All right you guys, that's just about enough." Julie scolded the man who had just grabbed her bottom, as she looked up at Nick, locking her eyes on his.

"Awe come on honey, you know you're going to wind up with one of us by the end of the night anyway," said the man next to her. He was obviously the leader of this group of forty something men going through their mid life crisis.

Nick began to size up the group, wondering if this might turn into a physical confrontation, or if it would be resolved quietly. Three of the men were around five-ten, and thin. Office types that probably stayed in shape by jogging a couple of times a week. But the fourth, he was about 6'2" and 240 pounds, just as tall and 20 pounds heavier than Nick, however not in very good shape. Nick at 26 years old felt none at the table was a match for him, should it go in that direction. He also sensed that the largest of the group seemed to be the calmest, and not likely to initiate a fight.

Julie looked at the man who had just spoken, and said. "Well I doubt that very much, you see, my boyfriend might have something to say about that."

"Maybe, but first he has to get here to say anything at all." Replied the leader of the group.

Recognizing the queue Julie had just given, Nick stood and took two steps towards the table so that he was directly across from the big one, and directly above the loud one at her side. "Well that's where you're wrong, I'm already here." He said, laying his hand on Julie's shoulder. "Is everything all right Honey?"

"Well guys, what do you think my answer should be?" She asked with a slight smirk.

The most aggressive of the group was directly below Nick. As he looked up, his eyes showed that he was backing down quickly. "Hey, I'm very sorry. We were just joking around, I guess we just had a little to much to drink."

Nick immediately looked to the larger man across the table to see what he was going to do. He just grabbed his beer and took a drink, looking at Nick while doing so. Nick could see he had no intention of creating an incident on account of his friend's mouth, so Nick escorted Julie over to the waitress station.

From that day on the two were very good friends, and Julie was the first person he had hired when he bought the bar. Although both had been told on numerous occasions how cute a couple they made, they just remained close friends.

"So Julie, where's Frank today, does he have a charter out?" Nick asked her about her husband.

"No, he went down to Key West on some business yesterday, and I really don't want to talk about it."

"What's wrong, Jules?" Nick inquired, noticing that her usual happy demeanor had changed.

"Oh, nothing really, I guess I'm just mad that he didn't call me last night, and that's the first time since we've been married that we haven't talked all day."

"You've been married for one year and he doesn't call. I guess the honeymoon's over." He said with a smile.

Just then from out of the kitchen came Tony, the man Nick had hired to manage the bar when he decided to start the investigation service. "Hey boss, how's it going?"

"Good, how do the numbers look?"

"Compared to last year, we did about twenty percent better this winter. I just hope it lasts through the spring, because I have a feeling that this summer won't be as good as last year."

"Oh, why is that Tony?" Nick asked with a slight look of concern.

"Nothing really, I guess we've just had two exceptional summers in a row and I'm being the pessimist." Tony said with a smile

Just then Nick felt Donna grabbing at his elbow. "Come on Honey, you promised we wouldn't spend all afternoon here, and we both know if you start talking business and getting wrapped up in what has been going on around here, we'll be here all night."

"Your right." he said as he leaned forward to kiss her on the cheek. Then Nick turned back to Tony. "We'll go over all this on Monday when I come in, I promised her a picnic and a day out on the boat."

Donna and Nick said their good-byes and made their way to the marina.

Nick truly enjoyed the time he got to spend in his boat. Except for his, all the boats at the marina were cruisers set up for fishing or scuba diving. Nick however, enjoyed fast boats, so when he decided the year before to buy one, he went up to Miami. Once there he made his way to "Thunder Alley", known as the place to go for high performance, offshore race boats, and named for the sound from the engines used to power them.

While visiting a company called Hawk, he saw a boat on a trailer out back of the building. The boat was a forty-foot Baja, painted a deep cobalt blue with custom silver and red striping. Nick asked one of the salesmen about the boat and was told that it had been a special order for a man who was currently awaiting trial on drug trafficking charges.

After being told about all the options the boat had, and that it was probably one of the fastest boats in all of south Florida, Nick just had to have it. He went to the bank, got the loan, and spent the next few weeks proving how fast it was. He had even joined a group of people who had a club, much like many sports car clubs. Getting together on weekends partying and even putting together informal, friendly races among its members.

About an hour after leaving the marina Nick and Donna approached the secluded beach they had discovered a few weeks earlier. It was a small patch of sand about a hundred feet long and thirty feet deep, flanked on both sides by lush thick mango groves. As Nick tied the boat to a palm tree, Donna unloaded the picnic basket.

The two of them spent the next several hours nibbling at the picnic, and laying on the beach. Very few words were exchanged, they just enjoyed each others company, and the privacy this place had to offer.

As they watched the sun going down over the horizon, Nick turned to her and said, "Honey, I think it's getting kind of late, we should probably start packing up to go back."

"Nick…would you mind if we stayed out here tonight?" Donna asked.

"What do you mean? It's still the beginning of March, and it's going to get down into the fifties tonight."

"I don't mean here on the beach, I just thought we could leave the boat tied up and spend the night on board."

"I guess we could do that. If that's what you really want?"

"It's what I want." She whispered into his ear.

The sun gently came up into the eastern sky as the two slept deeply in each other's arms, after a night of passion. The sound of the breeze in the leaves of the mango groves, and the swaying of the boat in the gentle tide.

Suddenly, a beeping began at the foot of the bed, awakening Nick immediately. He sat up, wiped his eyes and crawled to the edge and grabbed his shorts from where they landed the evening before. Reaching into the pocket, he grabbed his beeper and stopped the annoying sound.

Checking his watch, Nick saw that it was almost eight a.m., he wondered who was trying to reach him this early on a Sunday morning.

"Honey, what is it?" The groggy voice came from over his shoulder.

He turned to see that his movements in the bed had awoken Donna, her long blonde hair covering half her face. She was still one of the most beautiful women he had ever seen, he thought to himself. "I don't know, my beeper just went off." He said as he pressed the button to check the number.

"Well, who's the nut calling at this hour of the morning?"

As the number flashed across the display, Nick's stomach tensed. It was Julie's home number. He didn't know how, but he knew that something was wrong. Was it that Julie would never call this early, knowing that he had just finished a case, and he would be with Donna? Or was it that Julie had worked till close the night before, and she would not have gotten home until almost three in the morning?

"It's Julie." He said with obvious concern in his voice.

"I wonder what's wrong." Donna was also worried, she and Julie had become very good friends since she had started seeing Nick, and working at the bar.

"I don't know, but I had better give her a call."

Nick got out of bed and threw on his shorts as he opened a compartment overhead. He pulled out a cellular phone and hurriedly dialed the number of his best friend.

The phone barely rang once when the frantic voice on the other end answered. "Nick, is that you?"

"Yeah Jules, what's up?"

"I don't know what's going on Nick. I haven't heard from Frank since he left Friday morning, so I called everyone we know in Key West, but nobody has heard from him!" Her voice trembled with fear.

"Okay Julie, calm down a second and tell me what you know. Why was Frank going there?"

"He said he had to go down on some business, and that when he got back he would have a surprise for me, but he didn't tell me what it was. It's not like him not to call, Nick."

"Julie, calm down and make sure you called everyone you can think of. I'll be there as soon as I can." He tried to sound calm, even though he knew she was right. Frank would never be out of contact with her this long if he could help it.

As he finished getting dressed Nick told Donna what he had just heard; she too was very worried now.

Within thirty minutes Nick and Donna pulled in the driveway. Nick's jeep sliding to a stop on the gravel. Julie met them at the door. "I called all the dive shops a second time. They haven't seen him."

"Julie, maybe he's down there working out a deal with someone new to get some more business?"

"Frank doesn't need any more business. He's already booked from next week through the end of July."

Frank Marks owned a custom charter service, arranging special diving trips for those who didn't want to go to the usual places and could afford his rates. He could take up to four couples on a one-day outing, or on a week long live aboard cruise anywhere in the Caribbean. And when he had an open day or so, Frank would take referrals from some shops in Key West, or send some of his clients to them if he were to busy himself. Frank and Julie had met at the Dive Shack and started dating about two and a half years earlier, and had been married almost a year now. Frank, like most of the other local divers would hang out at the bar during the off season, or in the evenings after a day of diving.

Being as close as Nick and Julie were, Nick had also become very close with Frank. Both of their parents were dead and neither had any brothers or sisters. Franks father had died of a heart attack when he was young, and his mother had died of cancer just a few years earlier. Like Nick, Frank had moved to the keys after his mother passed, with enough money to start his business from what he made selling three liquor stores they owned in New York.

"Julie, I don't want to worry you or anything, but I think we should go to the police and file a Missing Persons Report," he said as he gently took her by the hand and sat her down on the sofa.

"Why, what do you think has happened?" Her eyes searching his as if he held the answer she so desperately sought.

"I don't know Julie, but like you said, it's not like Frank not to keep in touch. Plus this way we can make sure he hasn't been in a car wreck or anything." Nick was trying to hide the fact that he was getting a very bad feeling about this. His stomach was now in knots, and he was usually right when it came to instinct about bad situations.

"If you think we should Nick, lets go now." Julie stood and went to the door.

"Before we go you should grab a picture of Frank. We can give it to the police so they know what he looks like." Nick was now trying to approach this as he would have when he was still on the force, trying to remain objective. Although seeing how distraught Julie was, made it hard.

Donna went with Julie to the bedroom to get the photo album. When the two returned she said, "There isn't anything I can do by going with you, so why don't I stay here in case Frank calls."

Nick knew that Donna was trying to stay optimistic for Julie's sake, and he appreciated the effort on her part. "That's a great idea, and when he does call, tell him he has two very angry people to deal with."

Julie smiled, mostly in appreciation of their effort to keep her thinking positively. "I'm ready if you are Nick."

They drove to the station in silence. It was difficult for him to just sit there and not say anything, but he knew that she was in no mood to discuss what was happening. Nick found this so different from any case he had worked on before; he had never had to work a case that involved a friend. He hoped the authorities would find out what was going on quickly so that he would not have to get involved. The little voice inside him told him more and more that this would not be easy, or turn out well.

"What do we do, who do we talk to?" She asked as they walked into the Monroe County Sheriff's station.

"I figured we'd speak with a friend of mine, he's a detective. I think you've met him at the bar before, his name is Steve."

"Yes, I know who you mean. Will he help?"

"Of course he will." Nick walked over to the officer at the desk. "Excuse me, is Steve Jenkins in today?"

"Yes he is. May I tell him who you are?"

"Sure, tell him it's Nick Thomas, and tell him it's very important."

The woman behind the desk picked up the phone and dialed, he could hear her repeat his words. Then he heard her say, "I'll send them right up." She then turned to Nick, "Go up those stairs to the second floor, first door on the left. Detective Jenkins will meet you there."

"Thank you." He took Julie by the hand and led her up the stairs.

"Hey Nick, how's it going?" The detective extended his hand to his friend as they approached, "What's this big problem you need my help with?"

"Steve, this is Julie Marks, I'm sure you know her from the bar."

"Of course, how are you?"

"Detective, it's my husband…he's missing. Can you help?"

Steve noted the desperation in her voice. "Why don't we go to the conference room over here." He led the across the squad room to a smaller room with a table and a few chairs. He reached for the coffee machine in the corner. "Can I pour you each a cup?"

"Please." was the response from the two as they sat at the table.

Steve placed the cups on the table and excused himself for a moment to get something to take notes on.

As he returned, Nick spoke softly to Julie, "Would you like me to stay with you?"

"Yes, please don't leave, I don't think I can do this without you." She turned to the officer and said, "That's all right, isn't it, he can stay with me, right?"

"Yes, what ever makes you feel most comfortable, I know this can't be easy for you. Now, tell me what you know."

Julie took a deep breath to steady herself as she took the picture from her purse. "This is my husband, Frank Marks. He left the house early Friday morning. He said he was going to Key West on some business, and that he would be back that night or the next day. He hasn't come back, or called, or anything, and that's just not like him. Even when he's out on the boat for days, he still finds the time to call and check in."

"So he took his boat down to Key West?" Steve asked as he took down the information.

"No, he drove. That's why I gave you that picture. It's him with his new truck, I also wrote down his plate number on the back."

Steve turned the picture over and copied the number on to the report. "You haven't heard from him at all since he left Friday?"

"No, and I spent all this morning calling everyone he does work for down there. You see, Frank takes some referrals from shops that don't run dives in the upper keys, and sends them people who want to dive in the lower keys. Nobody I spoke with has seen or heard from him, nor were they expecting him on any business." She said, trying to get the detective to understand how out of character this was for her husband.

"Could you get me a list of the shops he has done work for in the past?"

Nick leaned forward to join the conversation. "I'll bring you Frank's address book later today, I didn't think to grab it when we were at the house. If that's okay with you, Julie?"

"Of course Nick, whatever you need to do. Just find him." her voice trembled.

"We'll do everything we can Mrs. Marks. I believe I have enough to get going on, for now. If you could just leave a number at which I can reach you, we can get started."

"Actually Steve, you can reach her through me. I don't want Julie to be alone right now." Nick took her hand as he saw it trembling on the table.

Steve stood up and walked to the door. "That's fine Nick, I have your pager number if I need anything else." He then gestured for him to follow him outside for a moment.

"Julie, I'll be back in a minute, I need to use the washroom."

"Okay, I'll wait here for you,"

The two men rounded the corner to be sure she could not see or hear them. "So Nick, you agree with her that there is something strange about all this?"

"I know the two of them as well as I know anybody. The kind of marriage they have, it's almost sickening at times. It's like they're joined at the hip, or something. There has to be something wrong for Frank not to at least have called her."

"Fine, you know I just had to ask. I didn't want to get her any more upset than she already is."

"I know, thanks."

"Don't forget to bring me that address book so we can check it out."

"I'll have it for you as soon as I get a copy made of it."

"Why do you need to get a copy made?"

"That girl in there is like a sister to me, I'm going to be looking into this myself. Have you got a problem with that?"

"No, just don't get in our way. I think you're a good guy, but you know the chief has no place in his life for P.I.'s."

"I'll stay out of your way, you just make sure you keep me informed of what's happening."

"I'll do what I can, you just be sure to do the same."

As Nick drove Julie home, he couldn't help but notice how lost she seemed to be in this whole situation. This lively, friendly person he knew so well, was slowly withdrawing, and there was nothing he could do except find her husband.

"Julie, I think it would be best if you weren't alone right now." He wasn't sure how she was going to take this suggestion. "I want you to stay at my place until we find Frank."

"I thought you were going to go look for him yourself. If I'm at your place, won't I be alone anyway?"

"I was thinking Tony and I could work out something at the bar to give Donna and Carol some time off to stay with you."

She considered both women friends, and it was obvious that she did not want to be alone. "I think I'd like that."

"Good, then I'll let Tony know what's going on, and have him make the changes in the schedule." He was glad she had agreed to the idea. Besides not wanting her to be alone for the reasons he had told her, he would also feel safer with her at his home since there was always the possibility that foul play was involved, especially knowing that Frank had never done anything like this before.

After retrieving Donna and the address book from Julie's house they all returned to Nick's place. Julie was so exhausted that she was easily convinced to go into the guestroom and get some rest. While she rested Nick called the bar to let Tony know what was happening, and was assured that all the employees would do what ever they could.

Nick had expected that response, he knew everyone at the Dive Shack would come together to help one of their own, and prove it whenever needed.

As he began to go through Frank's book he saw that he knew, or at least knew of, every name it held. Although the keys were a very wide spread group of islands, divers were a tight knit group. They worked and partied together, and usually shared related information about what areas had the best conditions at any given time. That had been one of the things that Nick liked about the Keys, and one of the reasons the Dive Shack had a steady clientele of divers and locals alike.

Although most of the names were those of divers, only five were of shops in or around Key West. Just as he finished writing down the names,

Donna came from Julie's room and told him that she finally closed her eyes.

"I promised her that I would do whatever I could to find Frank, so I won't be around too much the next few days." He told her as he took her hand. "I've got my pager with me, so let me know if you need anything, or if the police call. I told them she would be here."

"Don't worry Honey, I'll keep an eye on everything around here." She said as she leaned forward to kiss him.

Nick drove to the station to drop off the list of names he had promised Steve. As he drove, he tried to separate himself from all that was happening so as to remain objective, he had learned that being to close to a situation only served to cloud one's judgment.

He entered the station and saw Steve standing over his desk talking on the telephone. Steve saw Nick and motioned for him to come and have a seat.

"I was just on the phone with Dispatch, I'm putting out a locator for Mr. Marks, and every officer will be getting a copy of the picture you gave me. Is there anything new from you?"

"No, I just came to give you that list of people he did work for. Here, but like I told you, they were already contacted by phone, and no one has seen or heard from Frank since he left."

"I know, but just the same we're going to have a talk with all of them. Just as I'm sure you plan to do as soon as you leave here."

"That was the plan." Nick looked him squarely in the eyes, waiting for what he was sure to follow.

"I don't suppose I can talk you into waiting for us to speak with them first?"

"That depends on when you plan on getting around to it."

"I'm leaving as soon as I speak with the captain, and ask him to let me handle this personally. He should be here in a half hour or so."

"I'll tell you what, I'll give you till noon tomorrow before I start poking around. It's two o'clock now, that gives you almost a full day's head start, but you promise to let me know if you find out anything. That way I should be able to stay out of your way, and you out of mine."

"Deal, but remember, I'm not going against policy if there is something else going on." Although they were friends, Steve was a good cop who always followed the rules.

After leaving the station, Nick decided to go to the bar and have some lunch, while he thought of where he would begin looking. The bar was full of the usual crowd and he wanted to be alone, so he entered through the back and went straight to his office.

A few minutes after calling to the kitchen to order some food, there was a knock on the door. "Yeah, come on in."

Tony entered the room carrying his sandwich and drink. "Here you go boss. I thought I'd bring it myself so I could ask what was going on."

"Right now there's nothing new. I told the police that I'd stay out of their way for a day." Nick said as he took his beer off the tray.

"How's Julie taking all this?"

"Not well, as you'd probably expect, and I don't know what to do to make this any easier for her."

"All we can do is be here for her, and I know that it helps knowing that you'll be looking for him too. She knows that you'll do everything you can to find him. Even though the police are looking, it helps to know that you won't treat it like just another investigation, which they might." Tony placed his hand on Nick's shoulder, trying to give him some show of support.

"Being so close to a case isn't always a good thing; sometimes it can cloud your judgment and you wind up missing something that's staring you right in the face. Seeing the fear in Julie's eyes makes it that much harder. I just hope I don't have to deliver any bad news, I don't know if I could handle it."

Tony could see this was tearing Nick up, and knew that he was in his office to get his thoughts together. "I'm going to get back out front. Everything is covered here so don't even think about it."

When he returned home, Nick found Donna sitting on the sofa in the living room, reading a magazine. Looking out the back door he saw Julie sitting on the back porch, staring out over the ocean as the sun was beginning to go down. "How's she doing?" he asked as he sat next to Donna.

"She slept for about three hours after you left, I got her to eat a sandwich a little while ago. But other than that, she just sits there and jumps out of her skin whenever the phone rings."

Hearing their voices, Julie turned and entered the room with Nick and Donna. "I guess since you didn't come straight to me, there isn't any news yet."

"No, the police are down in Key West now, talking to some people. If they don't find anything out by nine a.m., I'm going to go down myself and do some poking around."

"I appreciate this Nick, and I want you to keep a record of the bills and expenses so I can pay you back."

"Don't be silly, Julie. I'm doing this because you're like my sister, and there isn't anything to be paid back."

Knowing that there would be no arguing with him, Julie let it drop. "I think I'm going to go into work tomorrow, maybe it will take my mind off what's happening."

"If you think you'll feel better, it's up to you, but I don't want you over doing it. I also don't want you to be alone until we find out what's going on. By the way, do you have keys to Frank's boat? I wanted to take a look around it if you don't mind."

"Of course I don't Nick, but if you tell me what you're looking for, maybe I can tell you where to look."

"I'm not sure, maybe he has more names of people he does work for, or a list of clients, anything might help."

Julie got up and went to her purse on the coffee table. "Here you go, the keys to the house are on there too. Frank keeps most of that stuff at the office in the back of the house. Go through whatever you need to, Nick." She tossed the keys to him.

"I'm leaving very early in the morning, and Carol said she'd be here by nine, so why don't you try to get some sleep?"

Nick spent the whole night going over what he knew so far, trying to come up with something that would explain what was happening. The more he thought, the more he had the feeling that something was missing in the information he had about Frank. The man he knew was just a regular, likable guy who spent his time taking tourists out to reefs and wrecks to enjoy for a few days what they didn't have at home. He was a loving husband to Julie and a friend to everyone.

By seven in the morning, Nick had already gone through a pot and a half of coffee, and was about to climb the walls. He decided to go to the marina and have a look at Frank's boat before driving to the end of the keys. The house could wait till he returned.

The marina was already bustling with activity. Besides being the diving capital of the country, the Florida Keys also had more than their share of fishing enthusiasts. There were all sizes of boats. Everything from ten-foot rowboats, to fifty-foot convertibles rigged for deep sea.

Nick walked half way down the dock till he came to Frank's boat, the "JULE OF THE SEA". It was a thirty eight-foot cabin cruiser, the aft deck lined with racks to hold scuba tanks, and some additional lockers built in for more storage.

He made his way on board looking for anything that might appear to be out of place. There was nothing, it was just as it always was. He entered the cabin of the boat and began to look around; again there was nothing that caught his eye as irregular. Opening some cabinets he came across some maps rolled up and tucked away under the sink in the galley. Although Frank knew the waters around Key Largo as well as anybody, Nick figured the maps were there because he took trips to many other islands, and some tourists also liked to be shown where they would be going ahead of time. Again nothing. He thought to himself, "Where the hell are you Frank, and what's going on?"

As he left the boat to return to his car, he saw one of the regulars from the bar, loading some equipment onto his boat, a couple of slips away. "Hey John, got a minute?"

"Morning Nick, taking your boat out today?" He asked as he secured some tanks in their racks.

"No, actually I was over on Frank's looking around. Do you remember the last time you saw him?"

"Sure, it was a few days ago, Thursday I think."

"It's really important, can you be more specific?"

"Sure, it was Thursday afternoon, about three p.m. That's when I came in with a group I took out to Davis reef to feed the morays." He began to wonder what was wrong.

"Do you remember who was with him?" Nick asked with a hint of urgency.

"Nobody, it looked like he was just working around the boat and drinking a beer."

"So there wasn't anything strange you remember. How was his mood?"

"There wasn't anything weird going on that I saw, and he was in a great mood, smiling ear to ear and whistling. Why, what the hells going on?" John finally asked.

"Frank's missing. He told Julie he was going away for a day or two, and hasn't been heard from since. No phone call, no nothing."

"Sorry to here that, must be tearing his wife apart. Do the police know what's going on?"

"We filed a report yesterday, but they still don't know anything yet. Let me know if you think of anything out of the ordinary that I should know about."

"I sure will. I hope it turns out all right."

"So do I John, thanks. I'll see you around."

Although he still wanted to check out Frank's office, Nick decided to head on down right away. He figured there would be no new information in Key West, but it was where Frank said he was going, and the only place Nick had to begin. Even if he found nothing, it was better to get it out of the way now, than to have it in the back of his mind that he had over looked something. Julie had called everybody on his list, but face to face people sometimes offered a clue that they didn't think important when asked over the phone. It was also easier to tell if they were lying, or hiding something.

Finally arriving in Key West, Nick saw the sidewalks teaming with tourists. The streets were loaded with cars and hundreds of mopeds that many rented, since it was easier to find a place to put them, than to find an actual parking place in this zoo.

As he entered the first shop, Nick saw Steve off in a corner. He appeared to be waiting for something. As Nick approached, the detective turned and looked at his watch.

"Hey, I thought you were going to give me till noon? It's barely half past ten."

"I guess I'm just not very good at waiting around."

"I know how you feel, the owner's in back on the phone. I'm just waiting for him to come out now, so I can hear the same answers I heard from the other four."

"You already went to the others?"

"Yup, and everybody said the same thing. They didn't see Frank, he wasn't expected, and there was no reason for him to be on his way."

"Here your man comes now. Do you mind if I listen in?" Nick said, recognizing the owner.

"Go ahead."

As Nick listened to Steve question the man, he heard exactly what Steve had told him…nothing. There seemed to be no explanation as to why Frank had come down here on "business". At least none they could find.

Steve thanked the man for his time and turned to Nick. "Well, are you going to go to the rest of the shops and check for yourself?"

"I heard you ask the same questions I would have asked, and I assume you asked the others the same questions. I don't see any reason for me to waste my time too."

"Well if Frank Marks was on his way here, he didn't see any of them. So the next question, assuming he was on his way here, is did he get here? And if not, where did he get stopped?" Steve pulled a little notebook from his pocket to check his notes. "To that end I'm having patrol cars check every gas station, restaurant, and rest stop between here and his home. Have you got any suggestions?"

"No, but I can tell you that I checked his boat and the marina this morning, and didn't find anything there either. All I got was that he was there the day before and in a quote, "great mood", while working on his boat that afternoon."

"Well you just saved me another wasted trip. That was going to be my first stop when I got back." Steve took out a pen and scratched the marina off his list. "I'll let you know what the patrol cars turn up. You let me know if you get any new leads."

"I'll do that. Thanks again." The two went their different ways, with Nick continuing to feel that tightening in his guts that told him there was more to this than anyone knew.

Upon his return home, Nick noticed that only Julie's car was in the driveway. He thought that perhaps Donna had taken her home to get some things for her while she stayed at his home. As he entered, he went to the refrigerator to get something to drink. When he sat down at the table with his coke he saw a note. He took a drink and began to read.

> Dear Nick,
> Julie was getting very restless, and thought it might help to get her mind off things if she went to work.
>
> Love, Donna

He began to feel better knowing that Donna was with Julie. Whenever things went wrong, or got out of hand, she was always calm and reasonable. She was the perfect picture of stability. Nick decided to take a long hot shower and change, before going to the Dive Shack to face Julie, and tell her that there was still no news.

He stepped out of the shower feeling a bit more relaxed than when he had entered. As he wiped the steam from the mirror, he noticed that he hadn't shaved in the past two days, and was showing the same signs of concern that he had noticed on Julie the night before. He knew he had to at least try to look calm, for her sake, so he took the time to shave and do his hair as well.

Nick entered the bar and saw Julie as she went into the kitchen with a tray full of dishes. Over by the bar he saw Tony sitting down having something to eat. "Hey Tony, how's everything going around here?"

"Okay, I guess. We didn't expect you back so soon."

"Well there isn't anything down there that we didn't already know from Julie's calls the other day." He said as he motioned to Donna behind the bar to bring him a beer. "How are the girls doing?"

"Well, when they showed up they said it would help to keep busy. So I told Julie she could take section three, and I let Tasha go home since she covered last night and had to open this morning." Tony paused and took a bite of his sandwich before going on. "Donna told me that I looked like hell. And when I told her how many hours I was working to cover the open shifts, she basically kicked me out and told me to go home and get some rest. I hope it's not a problem?"

"Not at all Tony, I was just asking. I really appreciate all that you and everyone are doing to make this easier for Julie, and for me." Nick reached over and patted him on the shoulder.

Just then, Donna brought over his beer and inquired as to any news.

As he was about to answer, Julie appeared at the table as well. "Still nothing?"

"No babe, I'm sorry. I got the same answers you got by phone. I saw Steve down there and he said the police are checking everything between here and there to see if anyone has seen or heard from him. Unless something new turns up, I don't know where else to look."

"I know you're doing all that you can, and so are the police. It's just so frustrating." Without saying another word she turned and went to check on her customers.

Donna must have seen the look in his eyes. She took his hand in hers and said. "We all know you're doing all you can Nick, don't beat yourself up."

"I just feel so helpless…there's nothing to go on. It's all so out of character for Frank to disappear like this."

"How about something to eat? I bet you haven't eaten all day."

"Sure, order me a cheeseburger. I came to grab something before going to check out Frank's office."

"Donna, don't bother. I'm going back there to the office anyway. I'll have them whip it up." Tony said as he stood to leave. "Oh, By the way Nick, I'm going to make up the food and liquor order for tomorrow, anything special you need me to order?"

"No, whatever you think we need will be fine. Don't forget, I haven't made a deposit all week, so make sure there is enough in the account to cover the check."

"Already taken care of, I saw the bank bags in the safe when I closed last night, so I made a drop this morning."

"Great, remind you to give you a raise when this is all over with."

"Don't worry, I will."

An hour later Nick found himself sitting in Frank's home office. Sitting at the desk he began looking through the papers, right on top, he found the client and reservation books, along with the financial records for the business. He went through the books and found basically what he had expected. As he returned the books to the desk, he began to realize that something there seemed very strange. Suddenly he noticed that he was staring at a bunch of maps, rolled up and in a pile over in one corner of the room, and he saw that there were some more maps on the desk, and yet more across the room on a large table with some books and a lamp on it. Nick first looked at the ones on the desk. They were of the area containing the Cayman Islands, Cuba, and Puerto Rico. Since he ran a dive charter service, it didn't seem unusual for Frank to have maps around the office, just as he had had on the boat. And even though they were not of the usual places he dove, it was possible that he was planning a vacation for himself and Julie, or he may have had a special request to plan a trip there for a client. But what did strike him as odd was the sheer number of maps throughout the room. Nick then lifted the map to look at the one underneath; there he saw what appeared to him to be a map of basically the same area. Only this one was different, it was a copy of what looked like a hand drawn map, not as accurate as the one before. It also seemed to have routes to and from different ports of call drawn all over it.

As he checked more and more of the maps in the room, he found that they were all in pairs. New, modern maps, and their older counterparts. He began checking the books on the table against the wall, and found that they all pertained to sunken ships. Almost exclusively, Spanish sunken ships that had gone down, or at least rumored to have gone down all over the Caribbean. In one of the books he found a scrap of paper with two names written on it, Jake Phillips, and Craig Michaels.

The first name he knew, as would most divers in the Keys. Jake Phillips was well known, for he had found a sunken Spanish galleon almost fifteen years ago. After finding it, and bringing up all sorts of gold doubloons, jewelry, and other artifacts, he had opened up a small museum in which he displayed much of what he had recovered. Phillips even took groups of tourists to dive the famous wreck and on occasion, stories of one of the tourists finding gold coins or other memento would float around the islands.

Nick had taken one of Phillips' tours on one of his trips before moving down to the keys, but alas; he didn't find any gold for himself. He had wondered if anyone really had, since he was sure Jake's expedition had made a thorough search years earlier, and hundreds of divers since had poked around in the years that followed. Although possible, he thought maybe Jake would occasionally replace a coin found years earlier for someone to re-find. It would after all be a pretty good publicity stunt, and it made for added interest for his customers to think they just might be the lucky one to find it. The second name, Craig Michaels, was unfamiliar to Nick, but he assumed it had something to do with sunken treasure as well.

Looking around at all this, he wondered what else he did not know about his friend Frank Marks. It was obvious that this was something Frank studied in depth, but why was the mystery. Everything else in the room made sense, and was what Nick had expected to find, so he locked up and returned home.

On his way back, Nick couldn't shake the feeling that had come over him minutes earlier. He had just found out something about Frank that he had never known, and although it probably had nothing to do with his disappearance, it showed Nick that he didn't know Frank as well as he thought. Which also brought him to wonder what other areas of Frank's life he would discover had led to this sudden vanishing act.

As he pulled into the drive, he saw that all the lights were off. Nick checked his watch and saw that it was nearly three thirty in the morning, much later than he had realized. He decided to go for a walk. He enjoyed walking around his neighborhood late at night when the cool ocean breezes were rustling in the palm trees. Within a couple of minutes he found himself at the end of his street, where it ended into the ocean. There was a small pier, where he often went to listen to the waves as they crashed into the pilings below. Nick just stood there and looked at the reflections on the water, the lights from the street lamps across on the next island, or the moon as it shined on cloudless nights. He could just sit there and let his mind wonder off, it was all so relaxing to him.

Suddenly he was startled by the touch of a hand on his shoulder. He turned quickly to see Donna standing at his side, her long blonde hair pulled back, wearing a tee shirt and shorts. "You startled me. What are you doing here at this hour?"

"Well I went to the kitchen for a glass of water, and as I passed the front door I saw your jeep out front. I looked around the house, and since you weren't there, I figured you were here. Remember, I know how much you like it here, we've spent many a morning watching the sunrise."

In his thoughts he could remember those times. How great it felt, watching the sun come up, and starting the new day with her by his side. "Yes, I do remember."

"Did you find anything that could help at Julie's?"

"No, nothing. I did however find out something I never knew about Frank. Apparently he is into sunken ships in some way."

She looked at him slightly puzzled. "What do you mean…sunken ships?"

"Well, I found a bunch of books and maps on the subject all over his office. I just never knew that he was into that sort of thing."

Donna decided not to ask any more questions, she knew he had come out there to think, or to just get away and relax. She moved around behind him and placed her hands on his shoulders. She could feel the tension in his back, and began to give him a massage.

Nick leaned forward onto the rail and sighed. "That feels great, thanks."

"Shhh, quiet, just relax." She could feel the stress slowly beginning to lessen and leave his body.

After awhile, he turned and put his arms around her. "Thanks, you have no idea how much I needed that."

"Oh, I think I do." She said as she stared into his eyes.

"Well, are you ready to head on back to the house?"

"No, I think I'd like to stay here awhile longer." She motioned over his shoulder with her eyes.

He turned to see the horizon beginning to turn orange, and said. "I think I'd like that too." The two just stood there holding one another, not saying a word, just enjoying the moment.

Upon returning to the house, Nick decided he was going to go lay down for a couple hours and get some much-needed sleep. In the mean time Donna was going to take Julie back to her place to get some things, since it seemed she would be staying a while longer.

He rolled out of bed and looked at the clock on the dresser, it was just past eleven. He had been asleep for nearly five hours, and that seemed to enough, he felt better than he had felt since this whole thing had started. A long shower and some breakfast, and he would go to the bar since he had nothing to go on as of yet.

As he sat in the kitchen with a glass of juice, the phone rang. "Hello, Nick here."

"Hi Nick, its Steve. I just wanted to touch base with you and let you know what was going on."

"I appreciate it Steve. I feel like there's nothing for me to do till you turn something up, and it's driving me nuts."

"All we've found out so far, is that around ten minutes after Julie said he left the house, Frank stopped at a gas station and filled up along with a car wash. The clerk was positive it was him, because he went there at least once a week for a wash, and was in all the time for cigarettes."

"The clerk didn't see anything strange in Frank's attitude or anything?"

"All he said, was Frank was in a good mood, and saw him turn south out of the station. So at least the last person we know saw him, puts him heading in the direction of Key West."

"For all the good that does us."

The next several days were hard on all of them, especially Julie. She was becoming more and more despondent, and Nick knew that there was nothing he could do, short of finding Frank. Everybody seemed to understand how difficult it was for him to be with her, without being able to help, so they were able to spend time with her by shuffling their schedules so she would not be alone. Nick spent most of his waking hours at the bar, While checking in with Steve on a daily basis, waiting for even the smallest clue.

Tuesday afternoon, eleven days since Frank had been seen. Detective Steve Jenkins came walking into the bar, he saw Nick sitting at a table going over some papers. "Nick, we need to talk." His tone was serious as he sat across from Nick.

"What is it, what's wrong?" Nick asked the expected question, even though his little voice inside him already told him what the answer would be.

"I just got a call from Metro Dade County. They found a body on a dirt road in the everglades. They also found a truck near the body, and when they ran the plates our report popped up on their computer."

"Have you told Julie?"

"No, I thought she would be here. Besides, I figured that you would want to be there when I told her."

"I appreciate that, she'll be in, in about an hour. Are you sure it's him?"

"The plates match, it's his truck. And the descriptions of size, hair color and approximate age all fit. But they want her up there to make a positive ID"

"Can't they just send one of their guys down here with a picture for a photo ID?"

"You know the drill, they want her up there in their jurisdiction for questioning. Remember, this is a murder investigation now, and they don't know anything about her or the missing persons case."

Nick stared at the table and took a drink of his beer. "This is going to destroy Julie. I suppose they want you to transport her for this questioning."

"No, they wanted to know where to find her since they couldn't reach her at home. They were going to send someone down to notify her, and take her back themselves. I told them I had an idea where to find her, but they had to let me handle it since it was my case first."

"Well, I guess we better get going, it's not going to be easier if we put it off." Steve followed him back to his house, he knew this wasn't going to be easy, it never was. But it was always harder when you know the people involved on a personal level. The two men entered the house and found Julie, Carol, and Donna sitting on the back deck drinking coffee.

It may have been the looks on their faces, or just seeing the two of them enter together, but Julie could tell it was bad news instantly. "What is it, did you find him, is he hurt?" She came towards them, waiting for an answer.

Nick met her half way and led her to a seat at the kitchen table as the others joined them. "Here Julie sit down, we need to talk. It seems they found Frank's body up in the everglades along with his truck."

"No." She cried as she pounded her hands on his chest. "It can't be him, there has to be a mistake. Frank was going to Key

West, not the everglades." Tears now streamed from her eyes.

"I know it's hard Julie, but the truck is his and the body they found matches his description." He held her close, not knowing what else to do.

Steve stepped forward and placed his hand on her shoulder. "I'm very sorry about all this, but the Dade county sheriff wants me to drive you up to Miami so you can identify the body, and answer some questions."

Julie looked up at him as she began to calm. "I understand. Is it O.K. for Nick to come with me?"

"Of course it is."

Nick took her hand and said, "I'll be there with you."

As they all rose to leave Donna pulled Nick aside to speak with him. "I think it might be best if I stayed here, you'll be with her and I don't think we should all mob her with our support just now." She put her arms around him and gave him a hug. "Take care of her, she's on the edge."

As they drove to Miami, the car was silent. Julie sat staring at the floor, and holding on tightly to Nick's hand in the back seat of Steve's car. Her crying had diminished to an occasional tear that trickled down her cheek. Nick attributed her silence mostly to shock, which was understandable considering what she had just been told.

Later, as they sat in an office at the sheriff's, a man in a brown sport coat entered. "Are you Mrs. Marks?" He asked.

"Yes. How did it happen."

"I'll answer your questions in a moment Mrs. Marks, but first we need you to identify the body. I realize this is hard, but the sooner we do this the sooner it's over." He reached into his pocket and pulled out a Polaroid.

With only a glance she quickly turned her head and began to sob once more. Nick and Steve had also seen the picture, although the face shown them was severely bruised and swollen, there was no question that it was Frank.

"How did it happen?" Steve asked.

"The coroner still has to perform an autopsy, but it seems he died of a gunshot wound to the chest at close range. Mrs. Marks, I do have some questions I need answered if you think you can."

"Can't this wait?" Nick stood placing himself between the officer and Julie. "Can't you see she's upset?"

"Of course I can, I only need to ask her one thing. Do you know what he was doing up here, the report I have said he was supposed to be in Key West."

"All I know is what he told me when he was leaving."

Steve was next to speak. "And we have a witness who saw him heading south on the highway shortly after that."

"Well than that's all I need for now, we'll contact you if we have any other questions, or if the autopsy turns up anything. Again I'm sorry for your loss, and thank you for coming up here."

Steve dropped the two of them off at Nick's, and promised to let them know the second he heard anything from Miami. As they entered Carol and Donna were sitting in the living room, they instantly rose and met Nick and Julie at the door. They could tell by the look in Julie's eyes that it was Frank that had been found, and the three women burst into tears and began to comfort one another. Nick walked slowly into the kitchen, grabbed a beer out of the refrigerator and went out back to be alone.

Both of Nick's parents had died years earlier. Even though he had lived through those two deaths, as well as the deaths of some friends in his thirty years, he still found it difficult to deal with, or to be around those who had just suffered a loss.

His way was to go be by himself, sort out the emotions he was feeling, and try to get on with his life as quickly as possible.

For the next several hours Nick could hear the sobbing, and the consoling words through an open window, while he sat at the picnic table where they had all shared so many afternoons just enjoying being together. The longer he sat and reflected on all that had transpired the past week, the more his grief turned exasperation for the lack of help he had been to his friends.

Then it began to turn to resentment for what Frank's death was doing to his best friend, the sweetest person he had ever known.

Finally Nick's mood became anger at whoever had done this. He would find the person or people responsible, this he swore to the heavens above. He would find out what happened.

Later in the night, Donna emerged from the house. Walking slowly towards him, he could see her eyes, red and swollen. She came and sat in his lap; She placed her arms around him and her head upon his shoulder and said, "Don't say a word, just please hold me a while."

He did as she asked, gently brushing his hand along her cheek, then placing his cheek next to hers. They sat there under the stars simply sharing their warmth.

After some time had passed, he asked, "How's Julie holding up?"

"About as well as anyone can expect her to. I think we all cried ourselves out. She decided to go to bed, but I don't think she's going to sleep, I think she just wants to be alone for some time. So did Carol, so I came out here."

"I'm glad you did." As he spoke she smiled slightly, comforted by the sound of his voice.

He soon noticed that she was asleep, obviously exhausted from the emotional stress of the night. He gently carried her back to the house, and into the bedroom, where he took off her shoes and placed her on top of the comforter.

As he turned to leave she took him by the hand and spoke.

"Please don't go, I don't want to wake up alone." She gently pulled him onto the bed as she moved over to give him room.

"O.K., I'll stay with you." He sat on the bed and kicked off his boots. When he lay down she placed her head across his chest as to take comfort in the sound of his heart beating under her.

Donna was soon asleep again as Nick stared blankly at the ceiling fan as it whirred away above.

Suddenly he felt Donna move, as he looked at her he noticed the sun streaming through the window shades, and realized he had been asleep. He looked at the clock on the dresser and saw that it was almost noon. The events of the previous day had also taken their toll on him. He gently lifted her arm from across his body so as not to wake her, and carefully got up from the bed. She looked peaceful, and he remembered the delight he always felt in her face being the first thing he saw when he opened his eyes. He quietly left the room and headed for the kitchen were he saw Julie and Carol seated at the table. He also noticed that their things were on chairs next to them. "What's going on, why do you have your stuff in here?"

"Nick, I appreciate your having me stay here while he was missing, but now that I know Frank is gone, I feel like I should be at home, like it would help being by his things. I'm going to have to go back there sooner or later."

"I know, but I would feel better if I knew you weren't alone right now."

"I won't be, I have asked Carol to move in with me, at least for a while and she said yes. Besides, I always have you, and Tony, and all my friends only minutes away if I need you." Julie stood and took her things in hand. "We were just waiting for you to wake up. Tell Donna I said thanks, and I'll call her later this afternoon."

"I'm not sure about this, but if you think it's best for you I'll go along with it, as long as you promise me that if you need anything, or decide you want to come back here you won't hesitate."

"I promise." She gave him a hug and a kiss on the cheek.

Carol also stood and gave him a hug as she whispered in his ear, "Don't worry, I'll keep an eye on her and let you know how it's going."

"Thanks, I'm glad you'll be with her." He stood and watched them leave, not knowing if she was handling it better than he thought she would or if she was in shock over the loss of he husband.

He wondered how it must feel to lose one's spouse, the person you have chosen to spend the rest of your life with. He knew what it was to have a member of his family die, but a family member is blood, a love that has to do with who you are born to. He thought some how that it must be different to meet some one, fall in love with them, and consciously make the decision that this is the one you want to spend the rest of your life with. He could only imagine how she felt or what she must be going through.

A little while later, Donna came from the bedroom. He told her about Julie's decision, to which she seemed to think was the best thing for Julie to do.

Nick decided to spend the day out on his boat. He went to the marina and climbed aboard his "SEA CZAR". The name had no significance other than he thought the pun amusing. SeaCzar was a forty-foot triple engine speedboat, and where Nick enjoyed spending as much time as he could. As he left the marina and headed out to open water, Nick wasn't sure where he would go. Then as an after thought he found himself heading south, thinking about what he had found in Franks office. Although it would probably prove to be nothing, he decided to check out the two names he had found in the book about sunken treasures.

Since he knew more about Jake Phillips, that would be where he would begin. Nick made the short walk from the marina to the small museum Jake had built to house some of the treasures he had recovered, everything from cannons and cannon balls, to gold coins and jewelry.

After looking around a little, he found a young woman who appeared to work there. "Excuse me, but could you tell me if Mr. Phillips is around?"

"Yes he's in his office. Is there something that I can help you with?"

"No, actually I need to speak with him directly." Nick reached into his pocket and handed the young lady a business card for his private investigation firm. "My name is Nick Thomas, and I'd appreciate it if you would tell him it's kind of important that I speak with him."

As she looked at the card, the woman turned towards the back and began walking to a pair of double doors. "I'll let him know you'd like to see him."

Within a minute or so, she returned. "Go right through those doors, he said he could spare you a few minutes."

"Thank you." Nick said as she passed him on her way back to the front counter where she sold souvenirs.

He entered the doors to see a man in his late fifties seated at a desk piled high with books, and maps similar to what he found at Frank's. The man stood to greet Nick as he approached.

"Jake Phillips. My daughter tells me you'd like to talk to me about something or other. Have a seat and tell me what this is all about."

"Thank you for seeing me Mr. Phillips,"

"Please, call me Jake, every one does."

"O.K., Jake. A friend of mine's husband disappeared last week, and yesterday his body was found up in the everglades. I'm here because the last thing he told his wife was that he was coming down to Key West on some business, but every one we know he does work for has no idea he was coming, nor have they seen him in a couple of weeks."

"You mean Frank Marks?"

"Yes, do you know him?"

"Well at first I didn't think so when I read about it in the paper this morning, but for some reason I felt the name was familiar to me. So when I got here this morning, I asked my daughter Karen if she knew the name, and she reminded me of the guy who was here a few months ago asking my advise about the treasure hunting business."

"So Frank hasn't been here in a few months then?"

"No, actually Mr. Marks has come by every couple weeks, according to Karen. You see, I've got a reference library I put together back in the days when I was active in the wreck finding business. Mr. Marks came down to do some research and to speak with me. Since then, if he wanted to borrow a book he talked with Karen because she handles all of that for me. But when I told her about his death she told me that Mr. Marks had been here about three weeks ago to return some books he had used."

"Well, then I guess your daughter is the one I need to speak with. But I do have one other question for you. I found your name on a piece of paper in Frank's home, along with another name I don't recognize, Craig Michaels, does that name ring a bell for you?"

"Sure does, Craig used to work for me about ten years ago. I told Frank to look him up for additional research, you see he's the new breed of hunters since I've retired. He has all the new fancy equipment, and all the financial backing he needs. He approaches wreck finding as a business, not as a historian like I do. Although I'm not going to tell you I mind making all the money I made from the gold on the wreck I found." Jake stood and shook Nick's hand as he led him to the door. "I hope I've been of some help to you. Take care."

Nick began to tell himself that he knew he was looking in the wrong place, that this sunken ship stuff had nothing to do with Frank's disappearance. Yet and still he decided to follow it to the end since he was already here. He looked around the museum for Jake's daughter until he finally found her in what he presumed was the library Jake had mentioned.

"Excuse me, your father told me that I should talk to you instead of him."

"Is that right? And what is it that you should speak to me about?"

"Your father said that you knew Frank Marks, that you were the one he dealt with when he needed something from the library."

She instantly stopped what she had been doing and turned her attention solely on Nick. "Yes, and my father told me about reading in the paper that he was found dead in the everglades. So what is it you need to ask me?"

"I just need to know if you'd seen or heard from Frank Marks the early part of last week? You see, he told his wife that he was coming down here on business last time she saw him."

"No, I haven't seen or heard from him in about three weeks. Now do you mind if I ask you a question or two?"

"Go right ahead."

"Well, I just wanted to know, if Frank's body was just found yesterday, who has already hired a private eye to check out what happened?" Her voice had a quizzical tone about it.

"Actually, nobody has hired me. Frank's wife works for me, and the two of them happen to be very dear friends of mine."

"Then I guess you're the owner of the Dive Shack?" She asked, now with a friendlier demeanor.

"Yes I am. How did you know that?" It was Nick's turn to have the attitude of disbelief.

"Frank told me that his wife worked there, and that the owner was a good friend. He also told me next time my father and I were in Key Largo to stop in and he would buy us dinner." She answered very matter of factly. "I've never met his wife, but please give her my condolences, and if you would let me know when and where any services will be held."

"I'll do that, and thank you for your time. By the way, do you know where I can find Craig Michaels' office."

She told him it was in the marina, so he left and proceeded to walk back the way he came.

Once back at the marina he easily found the offices of Mr. Michaels. The office took up the better half of one of the strip mall sections, and had the name MICHAELS SALVAGE across the front. It was much larger than he had expected; though he remembered Jake saying something about financial backing of some sort or another. He entered to find a receptionist waiting to assist. When he asked to see Mr. Michaels, he was told that Mr. Michaels was checking something out in the boat, but if he would wait in the office she would see if he were available to speak with him.

As Nick looked around the office while waiting he noticed that just like Frank's, and Jake's offices, there were books and maps everywhere. He looked at some papers on a table and saw an intricate sketch of a cross; it appeared to be a piece of jewelry with a chain at the top. He then saw that a book next to it was opened to a picture of a man dressed in what looked like an old Spanish naval uniform. As he studied the picture closer he saw that the man in it was wearing a cross just like the one in the sketch. Nick then went over to have a seat on the sofa across the room to wait.

A few minutes later a man in his late thirties entered, his face deeply tanned by the sun. "My secretary says you'd like to ask me some questions, Mr. Thomas."

"Yes, I would like to speak with you about the disappearance of Frank Marks, that is if you know who he is?"

"You mean the death of Frank Marks don't you? This mornings paper said they found his body up north, and yes I do know him."

"Well then maybe you can tell me when you last saw or heard from Frank Marks?" Nick watched the man closely as he answered, maybe it was just the arrogant air about him, but Nick did not like this man.

"Frank came by about a month ago to return some electronic equipment he borrowed. I haven't seen or heard from him since." Craig Michaels sat back in the chair behind his desk and placed his feet up on the corner.

"Isn't the equipment you use awfully expensive to be loaning it out?"

"Yes, that's why Frank is the only one I would loan it to. Besides which, I let him use the old electronics that were taken off the boat last year. I keep it around as back up to the new stuff we're using, and in case we decide to search a large area of ocean floor, we can equip a second boat so it doesn't take as long. A couple of months ago Frank let us borrow his boat for three days, and he even came along as an extra diver, that's why I let him use some equipment on occasion." Michaels did not try to hide the fact that he did not like answering to anybody, especially some one he just met.

"Well is it possible that Frank was coming down to borrow something last week?"

"In the past Frank always called ahead to make sure it was O.K., but I suppose he could have come here, only I wouldn't know since we were out on the water last week and just got back last night. Now if there isn't anything else I can do for you I need to get back out to the boat. We're still unloading."

Nick stood, he knew he was being dismissed. "No that's all, I do want to thank you for your time though." He shook the man's hand and showed himself out.

Walking back to his own boat, Nick felt a little relief. He now knew that even though he had the names of these two men before Franks body was found the fact that he had not followed it up made no difference in the outcome since they had not seen or heard from him either. He also thought to himself that he was now back to not knowing anything, at least until he got a copy of the autopsy report. He decided to head back home and talk to Detective Jenkins.

By the time he got back to the marina in Key Largo, Nick decided that Steve would probably be gone for the day, so he would go to the Dive Shack for some dinner and to see how it was doing.

"Hey Tony, how's everything around here." Nick asked as he approached the table in the corner.

"It's going all right, where have you been all day?" He asked as he put down some papers he was reading.

"I was out on my boat, I didn't realize I had to keep you informed now that I made you the manager." He made sure his tone reflected the fact that he was just kidding. "By the way, Julie and Donna haven't been in, have they?"

"No. They called to let me know they weren't coming and I told them they didn't even have to call, and for Julie to take as much time as she needs. I figured you wouldn't mind."

"Of course not, that's fine. Have you eaten yet?"

"No, I was just figuring out the food order for the week and I was going to eat after I finished. Why?"

"I have a taste for pizza, feel like splitting one?"

"Sure sounds good. Oh I almost forgot, Steve Jenkins called for you awhile ago and said he beeped you but you hadn't answered. Also he said he'd call or come by later to see if I'd heard from you."

The two of them sat and watched the basketball game on the television. It seemed odd that they were barely speaking, but both of them wanted to avoid the topic of Frank's murder.

After a while Nick saw Steve enter and make a beeline directly towards him. "Hey Steve, Tony told me you were looking for me. What's up?"

"Nick, we need to talk in private, now."

"Fine let's go to my office." They both excused themselves to Tony and quickly headed to the back.

"Nick you have to tell me everything you know about what's going on" There was a nervousness in Steve's voice that Nick was not accustomed to hearing from his friend.

"Steve, I don't know what you're talking about. I've told you everything I knew, right from the beginning. What makes you think I have any other information?" He was sincere in his reply.

"Well, Nick something is going on. Earlier this afternoon I called Metro Dade to see if the autopsy had been done so that they could fax me a copy. I was told that it was finished but they wouldn't release it to me yet, so I went to the chief to have him call. While I was in with him, we got a call telling us to expect a D.E.A. agent along with some one from the FBI first thing in the morning. They would be bringing it with them and to have me, and Julie available for them to speak with." Steve stood up and began to pace while he finished. "Now I don't know about you, but all that tells me is there's something going on that we don't know about, and I for one don't like it."

"Neither do I, but nothing I know about Frank would explain his being killed. Other than a random act of violence, there had to be some reason, but I have no idea what it could be." Nick stood and walked over to Steve. "And I can guarantee you that Julie doesn't know either."

The policeman looked squarely at Nick and said, "I'm not trying to imply anything, I just don't like being blind sided by the fed.'s, and then having them keep me in the dark too."

They spent the next few hours trying to come up with a theory, but to no avail. They decided not to say anything to Julie until Nick went to pick her up tomorrow morning, there was no reason to have her up all night wondering what was happening. The two left for their homes agreeing to meet at the police station at nine in the morning.

By the following morning, Nick still had not come up with any explanation for the federal agents getting involved. He had also decided that he would not tell her why she was being taken to the station, but simply to say that Steve had called and asked him to bring her. Nick called Steve to let him know that this would be how he wanted to handle it. Steve agreed, he felt it might be a good idea for her to have some genuine shock to the situation so the feds would not know that Steve had been keeping Nick informed, as it were.

By the time they reached the police station, Nick was beginning to get frustrated with having to lie to Julie every two seconds when ever she asked him what was going on. They went right up the stairs where they had met with Steve Jenkins before. At the top of the steps they could see the detective in a conference room with three other men. Nick recognized one of them as the Chief of Police, and assumed the other two were the federal agents down from Miami.

As they approached the door to the room, the men inside noticed them and motioned them inside. Steve was the first to greet them. "Mrs. Marks, thank you for coming, these two men are with the D.E.A. and FBI respectively and they would like to ask you some questions about your husband."

Julie looked back and forth between Nick and Steve, obviously wondering what was going on. "Of course I'll answer any questions you have, I'll do anything to help find whomever killed my husband. But I already told officer Jenkins all I know, and I don't understand why the FBI or the D.E.A. would be involved in my husband's murder."

The older of the two agents stood and went to Julie, "Please Mrs. Marks, if you'll just have a seat we'll explain what we can and get this over as quickly as possible. I'm agent Collins with the FBI and this is agent Bradshaw with the D.E.A. We'd just like to go over what you told the police in the initial report and ask you a couple of questions."

Bradshaw took a piece of paper from the file before him and asked, "You said that your husband told you he was going to Key West on some business, is that right?"

"That's what he said, yes." Julie replied.

"So you have no idea what your husband was doing up where he was found?"

"There is no reason I can think of for him to be anywhere north of our home if it has to do with business. Frank dives the upper keys, and takes referrals from shops in the lower keys."

"Well can you think of any non business reason for him to be there?"

"No, actually he didn't like going up to Miami, or any where around there. He liked the easygoing life style of the keys, not the city. It was like pulling teeth to get him to bring me shopping, the only time he didn't mind was if a bunch of us would go on Nick's boat." She said as she motioned towards Nick.

The agent turned to Nick and asked, "Who exactly are you and why are you here?"

"I'm Nick Thomas, and Julie and Frank are very good friends of mine. I'm here to help support her any way I can." He stated firmly. "Julie Marks has worked for me at my bar for almost four years now, she's like family to me."

"He's also a local P.I." The police chief decided to ring in.

"And we all know your opinion of us, so why don't you give it a rest, Chief." The disdain between them was obvious.

"As a matter of fact, I have other duties to attend to. Jenkins, I want to see you in my office when this is finished."

The chief turned and left the room with one last sideways glance at Nick.

The FBI agent now spoke to Julie. "Mrs. Marks, what about your husband's family, do you know anything about them?"

Looking puzzled at the question she replied. "Frank is not from Florida, he moved here from New York a few years ago. As far as his family goes, he never liked to talk about it. You see, both his parents are dead, that's why he moved, to get away from the memories."

"Mrs. Marks, does the name DiMarko mean anything to you?"

"No, should it?" She replied, obviously curious as to the significance of the name.

"Yes as a matter of fact it should." Agent Collins picked up another page from the file before him. "This is part of the autopsy report from your husband's case. As regular procedure the fingerprints are run through the computer in Washington. When his were run they came back as belonging to Francis Gianni DiMarko."

Her eyes widened in genuine shock as she looked to Nick and then back to the FBI agent. "That's impossible, there has to be some kind of mistake."

He could tell that she truly was lost in all he was saying. "I don't know where to begin. First of all, your husband's parents are not dead. They still live in New York. His father is Angelo DiMarko."

Suddenly the name meant something to Nick; he remembered it from when he was a cop in Chicago. "The Angelo DiMarko, the mobster?" As he spoke the words he could feel Julie squeeze his hand.

The agent looked to Nick. "That's the one. What do you know about him?"

"Not much, I used to be a cop in Chicago, and I remember he was in the news as being linked to some mob bosses that were being indicted on racketeering charges a few years back."

"Angelo DiMarko been linked to everything from gambling, to prostitution, to drugs, but there has never been enough to bust him. And I've been working on him for over ten years." There was bitterness in the FBI man's voice.

"What does this have to do with my husband?" Julie asked.

Bradshaw now decided to get involved. "Well, his organization has been linked to Miami's cocaine trafficking, and your husband was found outside of Miami with a bullet in his chest."

"Frank had nothing to do with drugs." She stood and glared directly at the agent.

Collins took Julie by the arm. "Mrs. Marks please, calm down. We have to look into every possibility, and since you didn't even know his real name, isn't it a chance he was into something with out your knowing?"

That statement rocked Julie to the core of her being. She sat back down next to Nick and tried to compose herself. "If it's true what you say, I suppose it's possible, but the man I was married to was totally against drugs."

"If I can continue. As I said, I've been investigating DiMarko for a long time, and from what we know his son was never involved in the family business, but it's still a possibility. It could also be some type of retribution, a man in his business has a lot of enemies, and they have been known to go after family if they can't get to him." Collins went back to the file on the desk. "We do know that about three years ago the son disappeared. At first it was thought that he might have been killed back then. Angelo DiMarko had his people turning the city upside down looking for him and we thought it might erupt into a war if his suspicions turned out to be true. A couple months later an informer we had in his operation told us that a letter from his son came saying that he wanted to be left alone, and that he wanted nothing further to do with his father."

"That was about the time he moved here, so you see, Frank changed his name and wasn't involved in any of that." Julie's tone was one of both conviction and hope in what she was saying.

"Right now we don't know, but we're going to find out either way. You see, shortly after the letter came they found our man out and he was killed. We haven't been able to get anyone back inside so we don't know if it was leaked to him to throw us off that direction, or if it was true." The FBI man went to her side once again. "Mrs. Marks, I realize this is all difficult for you, so for now I think we're through. But I need to ask you to remain available in case we need to speak with you some more."

Without saying another word, the two agents left the room with Steve. As Nick watched the federal agents leave, he had a feeling of bitterness towards them, even though he knew they were just doing their job. Nick took Julie by the hand and led her to the car not knowing what to say. He felt as though he was in shock, but it could not compare with what she was going through. He drove her home in silence and walked with her to the door.

"Nick, if you don't mind, I just want to be alone right now."

"Are you sure?" He said.

"Yes," She took his hand and looked into his eyes, the pain was evident. "I just need to think this through. I'll call you later"

"Okay, I'm going to the bar, if you need anything give me a yell. I mean it…anything." He knew there was nothing he could do to ease the shock, so he went to his car and drove off.

Once back at the Dive Shack, Nick began to tell Tony of the events of the day. Tony was as shocked as he was about the revelations of Franks past. They sat together wondering how they could know so little about a man they considered such a good friend.

Nick saw Steve Jenkins walk through the front door and come over to them. "Steve, what else did they say after we left?'

"Not much. They're taking over the investigation, and are playing it close to the vest. They said they would keep me posted on any progress, but we both know that's not likely to happen." Jenkins turned to a passing waitress and ordered a beer. "I'd like to know what you've gotten me into…whatever it is it's big."

"I don't know either, but I can guarantee you that I'm going to find out."

"Nick, you better stay out of this. You don't want to get caught screwing around with a federal investigation."

"I don't care if it's federal or not, I'm going to get to the bottom of this for Julie, she's being torn up by all this. With or without your help I am involved." Nick paused to make sure his point got across to his friend seated with him. "The first thing I'm going to do is find out if Frank was involved with drugs coming into Miami."

"How the hell are you going to do that? The feds don't even have a clue yet."

"I have an idea where I'm going to start, but I need you to find out where Frank's father is, and how I can get in touch with him."

"Well that I can help with. I overheard a call to Collins, and when I asked him about that, he told me that another agent had gone to notify and question Angelo DiMarko about his son's murder. Collins said the old man flipped, and told the agent he was flying into Miami personally to find out what was going on. They found out he's flying in tomorrow evening and is registered at the Omni Hotel in Coconut Grove. Now tell me where you think you're going to start to check into his drug involvement."

"Steve, you're still a cop, and it's better for your career if I don't get you in on this just yet. At least until I know something anyway. I'll tell you everything I can, I promise."

"Nick, I guess there's nothing I can do to stop you, but DiMarko's big time, so don't get in over your head."

Nick stood and turned to Tony. "Keep an eye on Julie, I'm going up to Miami tonight. Beep me if you need me." With that he left to go home and pack a bag.

During the drive up, Nick began to think about the man that he was going to see. Jose Garcia was a friend of sorts. He belonged to a group of men who formed an informal boating club, with which Nick was also associated. They got together mostly on weekends and took trips to Bimini, or the Bahamas. The men involved ranged from restaurant owners like Nick, to doctors, lawyers, and assorted businessmen. They had all met around the Miami area, mostly at "Sundays", the bar where Donna once worked. That is where Nick had met Jose after racing him on the return trip from Bimini. They sat around that night and joked about whose boat was faster. Jose had introduced him to some of the other members and they had asked him to join, which he did. It was a casual group, just formed to relax and socialize. Everyone had an understanding that work was not to be a part of what they were about.

Nick was about to break that unwritten rule with Jose. For a long time he had no idea what type of business Jose was in, only that he was very good at whatever it was. After a few months, Nick had heard rumors that Jose was probably involved in drug trafficking, but as long as he kept it out of their group, nobody seemed to care. Jose Garcia was a nice, very likable man. The more Nick had thought about it, the more he knew it was true. Jose was always with his two "friends" which everyone knew were his bodyguards, but they generally kept to themselves.

Nick drove into an exclusive area of Coral Gables, to Jose's home. It was very large and modern, circled by a brick wall with an iron gate. He pressed the intercom and awaited a reply.

The box crackled with static, and then he heard a voice. "Yes, what is it?"

"It's Nick Thomas, I need to speak with Mr. Garcia." Nick wasn't sure, but the voice sounded like that of one of his bodyguards.

"Hello Mr. Thomas. Is Mr. Garcia expecting you?" The voice from the box asked.

Nick looked at the clock on his dash; it was almost nine in the evening. "No he's not, but please tell him it's rather important that I see him."

A minute later the gate swung open and he drove up to the house. As he got out of his car the front door opened with a woman standing in a maid's uniform waiting to greet him. "Please follow me Mr. Thomas." She said as she led him to the library.

As he entered, Nick saw Jose sitting in a chair reading a book, across from him on a couch were his two guards. "I'm sorry to come unannounced Jose, but it is important."

"Don't worry about it Nick, you're always welcome. What can I do for you?" He asked as he went over to the table to freshen his drink. "Would you like one?"

"Sure, whatever you are having will be fine." Nick looked at the two men watching him. "Jose, if you don't mind I'd like to speak to you in private."

"Okay," He handed Nick the drink. "Why don't we take a walk out by the pool."

They walked out through the sliding doors that lined the entire back of the house, and went over to a table next to a waterfall that streamed into the pool. Nick paused as they sat and took a long drink of the Scotch in his hand. He wondered how Jose was going to react to his questions that were to follow.

"Jose, I know we always keep our relationship social, and none of us get involved in the others' business life."

"Yes, that's how the club usually handles itself, but it sounds as if you are thinking of crossing that line. Are you, Nick?" Jose leaned back in his chair and stared at Nick.

"I guess I am. I need to ask you some questions, because I'm trying to help a friend find out what happened to her husband."

"Nick, I consider you a friend, and your being here seems to say you feel the same. Ask me what you need to, and I'll see what I can do." There was a cautiousness to Jose's words.

"Let me start by saying that I do think of you as a friend, but over the past couple years I've heard rumors that you are involved in the drug trade around here." Nick watched carefully for any sign that he was going to far. "And very powerful in that trade. Now I've never said anything or really thought about it since you never brought it around us, but now I need to talk about it."

"I'm not admitting to anything, but lets proceed with this conversation in a hypothetical context." Jose seemed to be curious as to where this was all going.

"Let me start at the beginning. You have met my friends Julie and Frank Marks. I've brought them out on my boat several times. Well about ten days ago Frank told Julie that he was going to Key West on some business and just disappeared. A week later his body is found in the everglades and the police think it's drug related."

"I read about that in the paper, but I didn't know their last name so I didn't make the connection. I'm sorry to here about it; they were a nice couple." Jose said, still not seeing why this would involve him.

"There's more. This morning I took Julie to the police station where we were told that the FBI and the D.E.A. were getting involved and taking over the investigation."

"They must know something to be taking over from the local authorities. So what do you want from me?"

"Does the name Angelo DiMarko mean anything to you?" Nick instantly saw the look of recognition in Jose Garcia's eyes.

"Angelo DiMarko basically owns New York, and everything that goes on in or around it. Why? What does he have to do with your friend being murdered?"

"Well, Jose, as it happens, Frank was Angelo DiMarko's son. They think he was either involved in the family business, or someone found out who he was and did it to get at the father."

Jose listened quietly before responding. "They would be really stupid if they did it to get to the old man, you don't mess with people like that unless you want to start a war." Jose obviously meant what he said.

"Anyway, I was hoping you could use your position to see if Frank Marks was involved, or if you heard of someone going after him.

"Look, Nick, off the record, I have done some business with DiMarko's organization. Everyone that moves anything into that area has to. Come back tomorrow night, and I'll let you know if I find anything." Jose Garcia stood, letting Nick know that this discussion was over for now.

"Thank you Jose, I really appreciate this." Nick extended his hand to his friend.

"I'm going to let you know what I find because you're a friend, but I'm checking this out for my own reasons."

"I don't get what you mean."

"Angelo DiMarko is a good person to have as a friend in my line of work, and if I can help find out what happened to his son, he just might feel like he owes me some gratitude. And that could be worth…something in the future." In Jose's answer, Nick saw a cold calculating side he had never seen before, but always knew was there.

They walked back to the house where the maid showed him out as Nick heard Jose begin barking orders to his two men.

It was now past eleven at night and Nick had been going all day. That and the stress of the day made him decide to get some rest for the night. He went to the Mayfair hotel in Coconut grove and checked in. As he settled in for the night he began to think about what he would do the next day, since he knew the elder DiMarko would not be arriving until late in the day.

First he thought he would pay a visit to the supply house where Frank had purchased his equipment for the dive business. Nick had gone with

Frank to buy his own gear there since they only dealt with dive shops or guides, and Frank had told him he could save him a lot of money.

Next he would go to the boat dealer that had sold him his boat, where he had taken Frank to return the favor, and saved him some money by using the fact he had spent so much there before.

Seven a.m., as the morning sun came in through the window of his room, Nick opened his eyes and began to rub the sleep from them. He reached for the phone on the nightstand and dialed his home.

"Hello, who is it?" Donna's voice answered on the other end, obviously just having been woken.

"Hi honey, it's me. I'm sorry I woke you." He said gently.

"No problem, I'm glad you did. Is anything wrong?"

"No, I just wanted to check in with you and see how things were down there."

"Okay, I guess. I think the shock is starting to wear off of Julie though, she spent the night here with Carol and me. I think the fact that the reality of her life with Frank being shattered by what she heard at the station today is sinking in, and it's going to get worse before it gets any better." She paused for a moment and Nick could hear her take a drink of water. "Anything new up there?"

"No, I just stopped by Jose's place to talk to him when I got here and then I checked into the Mayfair."

"Why did you do that?" There was a sudden concern in her voice; she had been the first to tell him about Jose's rumored background, and to warn him not to ask to many questions.

"You know why. Being who he is, he's the best way I have to find out if Frank really was involved in any drug trafficking here in south Florida."

"I don't like the idea of you getting involved with Jose Garcia. He's a dangerous man with a lot of secrets." She said nervously.

"Hey, I know what I'm doing, I've dealt with his type before, remember I used to be a cop. Besides, it's not like I'm going after him or anything, I'm just asking a friend for some help in getting some information." Nick hoped he was hiding the fact that he held some of the same concerns Donna was stating.

"People like him have very few friends, Nick, and what if he decides that you owe him something in the future for his help?"

"I'll have to deal with that when the time comes, but for now I'll do whatever it takes to find out the truth for Julie."

Donna knew that statement to be as true as any he had ever made before. She would not change his mind and decided not to try. "Fine, just do me a favor and be careful, and keep in touch while you're up there."

"I will. I should get going, I have some other things I want to check into this morning."

"I'm not even going to ask what. Take care, I love you."

"I love you too." With that he hung up the phone and prepared to go to the supply shop.

As Nick arrived at the supply house he wasn't sure what he was going to ask or even what he was looking for, he just knew he had to start somewhere, and this was as good a place as any. Looking around, the walls were lined with all sorts of diving equipment. Racks of wet suits, rows of tanks, and bins filled with masks and weights of every color imaginable. A couple customers roamed the aisles, and two men worked behind a counter at the rear of the store. He walked up to the counter and the man nearest him came over to greet him.

"Hi there, I'm Tom. Is there something I can help you with today?" The man asked.

Nick pulled a card from his back pocket and handed it to the man. "Well if you can spare a few minutes I'd like to ask you a couple questions about one of your customers."

The man looked at the card as he replied. "Sure, I'll answer what I can. Who is it?"

"His name is Frank Marks, he has a diving tour business down in Key Largo."

"Sorry, the name doesn't ring a bell."

"Undersea Tours, right." The second man behind the counter interrupted. "That's my account. Frank dealt with me, unless I wasn't in. I'm Jim, how can I help?" He too looked at Nick's card as Tom handed it to him. "You're a private investigator? What's going on?"

"I'm checking into the murder of Frank Marks. His body was found a couple days ago in the everglades with a gunshot to the chest."

"His murder…what does that have to do with us here?" He asked, his eyes wide and questioning

"Probably nothing." Nick answered, trying to put the man at ease. "But he was found up here, when he was supposed to be in Key West. So I'm just checking everywhere we know he did business with in the area. I don't have much to go on, so I have to start some place."

"I only knew Mr. Marks from here, but he seemed like a nice enough guy. I'll help anyway I can."

"Do you remember the last time you saw him?"

"I think it was about two months ago. He brought some equipment in for some routine maintenance and certification. But I can tell you for sure if you'll follow me to the office, I'll pull up his account on the computer." He stepped around the counter and led Nick to an office around the corner.

Nick watched over the man's shoulder as he began typing at the computer keyboard. A few moments later the screen showed Frank's account, listings of equipment purchased, and services performed. "Do you keep a record of all transactions that go on here?"

"Sure, ninety percent of our business is with professional divers. We service and maintain their equipment, so we need to keep detailed records for the certifications. Most equipment has to be re-certified every year." He continued to work at the computer as he spoke. "Here it is, that's what Mr. Marks was here for two months ago. I was doing routine work and certification on his tanks and regulators."

Just then the next page to appear on the screen was the balance for Frank's account, at the bottom of the page it read zero. "That shows that he was all paid up in his bills with you, is that right?"

"Of course. I just thought I'd double check, but he always wrote out a check for all the work around here." He looked at Nick wondering what all this had to do with a murder.

"Is that normal? I mean don't most of your customers at least have you bill them at their business? You have to admit the items you sell aren't cheap."

"Yes, most have us bill them, and we even offer financing to established clients. But there are some like him that prefer to keep their balance at zero. They don't like buying what they can't afford." He cleared the screen and turned back to Nick. "Is there anything else I can do for you?"

"No that's it. Thanks for your time." Nick walked out of the office and went to his car.

As he drove to the boat dealership where Frank had purchased his boat, he began to think about Frank's business. Frank didn't run the usual type of dive guide service that would take large groups of divers on generic dives to the same reefs or wrecks day after day. His specialty was setting up dives that had the specific interests of his clients in mind. They would contact Frank in advance of their arrival and he would design an itinerary for them. Whether it was a one-day dive, or a week staying on his boat traveling throughout the keys. In a short time Frank Marks had built a good reputation and had many repeat clients, along with the referrals that he got, Frank was as busy as he wanted to be. And since he offered a customized service, he was able to charge premium rates for that service.

Nick drove into the dealership that he knew so well. He had bought his boat there. However, Nick's boat being basically an offshore racer, it required far more maintenance than the average leisure crafts. Regardless of what it cost, Nick derived so much pleasure from it that he felt that it was worth it. He had purchased the best about a year and a half after opening the dive shack. The bar had taken off so well and become profitable so quickly that he decided he deserved it, and hadn't really regretted it once.

The moment Nick stepped through the door he saw George, the sales rep he usually dealt with. "Nick…hey Buddy, how's everything going." George's eyes lit up like a Christmas tree. He worked on commission and Nick often meant a big one.

"Take it easy George, and you can get those dollar signs out of your eyes, I'm not buying anything today." Nick always teased him, even though he knew George had often saved him quite a bit of money by giving him good deals.

"But Nick, my daughter's going to need braces soon." He replied as he took Nick's hand with a smile.

"Sorry, but today I'm just looking for some information."

"About what?" He asked curiously.

"You know my friend Frank Marks, don't you."

"Sure, I sold him that thirty eight footer for his dive business a while back. What do you need to know?"

"I need for you to tell me if Frank has been in lately, specifically about two weeks ago."

"Well, I can tell you that he hasn't been in to buy a new boat, or any electronics for his, but I wouldn't know if he came in for parts or service."

"Is there any way you can find that out for me, George?" Nick asked with certain urgency, so that he was taken seriously.

"Sure, lets go to my desk and I'll punch it up on the computer."

The two men walked over to George's cubicle, and once again Nick watched as Frank's file flashed on the screen. Again, it was a shock for Nick to see that Frank owed nothing, not for the boat, not even for any of the expensive electronics he had purchased for the boat.

"George, am I reading that right, Frank Marks doesn't owe anything?"

"That's right. But that isn't necessarily out of the ordinary, a lot of people finance their purchases with their own bank. They can usually get a better rate there if they have good credit, or some type of business account."

"Is there a way to check on that?"

"I can see if we have anything in his file that might tell us, would you like me to check it out?"

"Yes, it would really help if you could do that for me."

After a couple of minutes, George returned with a file containing copies of the transactions in question. As Nick watched on he began to look strangely at the papers.

"What is it George, what do you see?"

"I'm not sure. It seems that Frank brought a certified check for the entire amount of the boat, and just wrote personal checks every other time he's been in to buy anything." Nick could tell that it was puzzling to him.

"What are you trying to say, is there something strange about that?"

"Well, had he taken out a loan from a bank, they would have just issued him a bank check for the amount. The fact that he had a certified check, would lead me to believe, that he had the money taken out of a personal account."

Again, Nick had gone in search of answers and come away with more questions. He was beginning to believe that it was possibly that Frank had been involved in something illegal to have access to so much ready capital.

He decided to go to "Sundays" to have some lunch and think about not only what he had learned so far, but how he would handle his meeting with the elder DiMarko. Assuming he would be able to get in to speak with him…

Upon arriving at the Omni hotel where Mr. DiMarko was staying, Nick entered the lobby and went to the front desk. Standing there was a young woman in her early twenties. "Excuse me, could you give me the room number for a Mr. Angelo DiMarko?"

"I'm sorry, I'm not allowed to give out the room number of our guests. If you would like to speak with him you'll need to go to one of the house phones and ask the operator to connect you." She stated in a friendly voice as she motioned him towards a bank of white phones over against the wall.

He picked up the receiver and heard a click on the line followed by the operator. "Guest name please."

As he waited for the answer on the line, he began to feel some apprehension. He began to remember the feelings of being a cop, the dealing with criminals. Nick had been a patrolman, and had never dealt with anyone on Angelo DiMarko's level.

"Mr. DiMarko's room, who's calling?" The voice on the line was that of a young woman. Nick had been expecting it to be one of his bodyguards, just as it would have been at Jose's.

"My name is Nick Thomas, I need to speak with Mr. DiMarko."

"I'm his secretary, and I don't believe you have an appointment."

"Well, if you'll just tell him it has to do with the murder of his son. I think he'll want to see me."

"Just a minute please."

As he waited on the line to get permission to see Frank's father, Nick could see the bank of elevators across the lobby. People of all types were coming and going, then he saw two men in suits get out of one of the elevators. Something about them told him that they were federal agents, as they made their way through the lobby towards the door, they stopped and spoke with a third man. Not surprisingly, the government had decided to put the elder DiMarko under surveillance.

"Mr. Thomas, Mr. DiMarko will see you. Please come up to the presidential suite." Came the voice from the phone.

"Thank you, I'll be right up."

As the elevator rose to take him to his meeting, Nick's stomach tensed with each floor he passed. Not knowing what to expect, or what the real reason for Frank's death was, he was at a heightened sense of awareness.

The doors to the elevator opened, revealing two men in dark suits standing on either side of the door. The man on the right approached first. "Mr. Thomas?"

"Yes, and you are?"

"We're Mr. DiMarko's security, if you don't mind?" The man held up a small metal detector.

"I guess I don't have a choice, at least not if I want to see Mr. DiMarko." Nick opened his jacket, revealing a Berretta nine-millimeter pistol in his belt.

The second man quickly reached for the weapon and asked. "You haven't identified yourself as a police officer, so why are you carrying a gun Mr. Thomas?"

"I'm a private investigator, investigating a violent murder. I think it's just safer to be armed until I find out what's going on." Nick directed his words to the man holding his gun, obviously the senior of the two.

"Of course Mr. Thomas, but if you wish to speak with Mr. DiMarko, I will hang on to this until you are ready to leave." He placed the weapon in his jacket. "You can go on in now."

Nick stepped past them to the door and went in. He saw a young woman sitting at a desk speaking on the phone, and two more men sitting on a sofa.

The woman hung up the phone and made her way to Nick. "Mr. DiMarko will be with you in a moment. Please have a seat." She said as she directed him to a pair of chairs around a coffee table with a pair of empty cups on it.

As Nick took a seat he noticed the two men across the room watching him closely, apparently they too were bodyguards.

Just then the door to an adjacent room opened, emerging was a man in his late fifties. He was dressed in a dark gray pin striped suit, which obviously was custom tailored to him, and he had an air of authority to him. "Mr. Thomas, I'm Angelo DiMarko. I've been told you wish to speak with me concerning my son." His tone was cold, and unmoved.

"Yes sir. I'm a private investigator, and I'm looking into why he was killed."

"Please have a seat." He said gesturing towards the chairs and pouring each a cup of coffee. "I've been contacted by the authorities, and given very little information about what has happened. Would you tell me who else is so interested in this case as to have hired you?"

Not knowing how much the man across from him really knew, Nick decided to start with very little information and see where it took him. "Actually sir, nobody has hired me. I don't know if he ever spoke of me to you, but your son and I were close friends for the past few years. I'm looking into this for personal reasons." Watching closely, nick could still see no response.

"I have not seen or spoken to my son in several years Mr. Thomas, I would think that you would have known that if you were truly close to him." The mobster obviously knew he was being tested in some way or another.

"Sir, Frank had told me and others that his parents had died years ago, but now knowing who you are, I assumed he merely wanted to keep it quiet, but would still have been in contact with you."

"He hadn't." DiMarko replied, hesitating as if deciding whether or not to tell more to this stranger. "Mr. Thomas, being my son was difficult for Francis throughout his life. A few years ago it must have become too much, because he disappeared. A couple months later, my son wrote his mother a letter telling her that he loved her, and that was the last we had heard of him, till the FBI showed up to tell us that Francis had been killed."

For an instant, Nick thought he saw a glint of emotion. Just enough for him to give this man the benefit of the doubt for now. It also may have been that Nick wanted to believe his friend had not totally deceived him and Julie.

"I heard that when he first disappeared that you had your people looking all over for him."

The look in DiMarko's eyes changed to one of distrust. "You seem to have me at a great disadvantage. You have access to information about me that only the authorities should have."

Knowing that he needed to not loose this line of information, Nick decided to give some information. "Actually, I have a friend on the Monroe County sheriff's department. He's the one I took Frank's wife Julie to when she called me to say he was missing."

"Frank's wife…" The surprise with which he replied seemed genuine. " I did not know Francis was married."

Nick began to see a thaw in Angelo DiMarko's cold exterior. "Well he was. She is actually the one I was closest to, but Frank and I became good friends after they began dating. As a matter of fact, I stood up at the wedding at the request of both of them. I was with her when the federal agents shattered the reality of what she knew to be her life with the revelations of Frank's past."

"And that is how you heard of the search for my son?" This time he asked with less doubt.

"Yes, although they seemed to think that it was merely a trick to make them think that Frank had disappeared, when in truth he was somewhere else working for you and your organization." Nick was still testing him to see if he could strike a nerve, which he did. Only it was not the nerve he had expected.

"Francis was never a part of my business," He replied with conviction. "I would never allow it, and he would never have done it!"

Nick heard the words of a caring, protective parent, and suddenly believed him. "Okay, I believe you, so please don't take what I'm going to ask next the wrong way, I just need to know so that I can find out who killed him and why."

"If it helps find the killer, I'll answer what I can. But I want to know why you don't just let the police handle this?" DiMarko asked.

"I told you, Frank and Julie were very close to me. They were the closest thing to a family I have, and I take it personally when a family member is hurt or needs help. There is nothing that I can do for Frank now, but Julie needs answers." Nick's reply was more emotional than he had wanted, but it seemed to have the desired effect on DiMarko.

"Mr. Thomas, I can tell that you were close to Francis. I am glad to know he had good friends who cared about him. What is it you need to ask?"

Nick took a drink of the coffee before him, trying to compose himself, and wishing it were something stronger. "Well, first of all, so far I have found that Frank has little or no debt. His boat and all the equipment for his business seem to have been paid for out of his personal accounts. He didn't take out any loans, which sounds kind of odd, don't you think."

"Not if you knew the whole story about his leaving. You see, when Francis disappeared, he also took with him five million dollars."

"Is that why you had all your people looking for him?"

"No, that had nothing to do with the money. I loved my son, I was afraid something had happened to him. As I'm sure you can understand, my business puts my family and me at some risk. When Francis was missing along with the money, I was worried that someone had gotten to him, and forced him to access the funds."

"So the fact the he took several millions of dollars from you, didn't upset you." Nick had a tone of incredulity in his voice.

"Mr. Thomas, I am telling you that if I had known that Francis wanted to get away from me so badly, I would have given him that much and more, if only he would have kept in contact with his mother and myself." His words and the conviction with which he spoke them were very convincing.

Nick could feel himself beginning to believe Mr. DiMarko's story, and decided to end this meeting for now. He wanted to check into a few more things and get back to Jose to see what he had learned. "Mr. DiMarko, I think I've taken up enough of your time, but I hope you will see me again, should I need some more information."

"Just a moment please." He stood and went into the other room.

Nick had expected to be dismissed, he didn't know what to make of this development.

A couple of minutes later the mobster emerged holding an envelope. "Here, I want you to take this." He said as he placed it on the table.

Nick took the envelope and opened it; inside was a stack of hundred dollar bills, several thousand dollars worth. "I'm not sure I understand why you're giving this to me?"

"You said you are a private investigator. In that envelope is ten thousand dollars, a retainer for your services. Should you need more to cover expenses or costs, just call and let me know."

"I told you, I'm looking into Frank's death for his wife Julie, and because he was my friend. Not because I'm being paid to."

"I realize that, I just want to make sure that you tell me everything you find out. And having spoken to you, you seem to be a capable man with some access to information I do not. Like your friend at the sheriff's office."

Nick wasn't sure if he wanted to be on this man's payroll, but to keep him placated he would take the money for now. After all, he could decide for himself what information he wanted to pass on, and this meant he could get in to see him as he needed.

Nick placed the package in his jacket pocket and extended his hand. "Okay, I'll keep in touch and let you know if I find any new information." The two shook hands and parted with no more words between them.

As Nick exited the suite he turned to the man outside the door. "If you don't mind, I'll have my gun back now."

The man did not speak; he simply removed the weapon from his belt and handed it to Nick. Never once removing his gaze from Nick's own. The magazine had been removed, and was handed to him separately.

Nick took the gun and replaced it in his holster. "See ya around."

Back in his room, Nick wasn't sure if he believe the tales told him by DiMarko, but he hoped they were true. It would be nice to be able to tell Julie that the reason Frank had lied to all of them, especially her. Was it to protect her from a part of his life he was ashamed of, and not to use her as a cover for illegal activity as the D.E.A. agent had implied? Even if Angelo DiMarko had been telling the truth, it was still possible that some how someone from the past had found his son and killed him as an act of retribution.

Nick decided to call down to the Dive Shack and check in. The voice on the other end was Tony. "Hi Tony, its Nick. Have you seen Julie around?"

"Yeah, she came in to work a couple of hours ago. Do you want to talk to her?"

"Sure, put her on."

"Nick, have you found anything out?" Her voice seemed calmer than he had expected, but still seeking the truth about her husband. It seemed she had begun to come to terms with the fact he was dead, but not knowing the how or the why was difficult.

"A little, I met with Frank's father. According to him, he had not seen or heard from Frank in several years, and what the authorities were thinking that Frank was working down here, was totally wrong."

"And do you believe him? I mean, he wouldn't tell you if it were true would he?"

"No, he probably wouldn't. But I was there with him, and if I'm any judge of people, he doesn't know why his son was killed." Right about there Nick should have told her that he took the money to keep DiMarko informed of where the investigation led him, but Nick wasn't sure how she would take it. "I'm not saying I believe him completely, just that I am leaning in that direction."

"Is there anything else you found out?" She asked.

"Sort of, but I wanted to ask you something first. What did you know about the business finances?"

"Not much, Frank handled all the bills, home and work. Why?"

"Well, it just seemed kind of strange that he didn't take out any loans for the boat or equipment for the business."

"Not at the time it didn't. Remember he told us that he had sold his parents chain of liquor stores in New York, he told me that after the legal fees and taxes he still had about 1.5 million remaining. That's why he didn't even take out a loan for the house Nick. I guess looking back now there were signs that something was strange." There were hints of self-doubt in Julie's voice.

"Don't think like that Julie, after all, if somebody were to look into my finances they could start to draw the wrong conclusions too. Think about it, I'm thirty years old, and if it weren't for the insurance money I got when my parents died, I wouldn't have the bar or a lot of other things." He felt that he was saying this to her, not only to alleviate her doubts, but his as well.

"I guess so. When are you going to be back?" she asked.

"Probably in a day or two, I still have a few things to check out up here. But I think the answers I'm looking for are going to be down there." He did not know why, but his little voice inside told him that the answers were indeed in the Keys.

"Okay, but promise me that you'll be careful. I already lost my husband, I don't want to lose the only other person in this world that means anything to me."

"I promise. You're stuck with me in your life for a very long time. Take care."

"You too."

Checking his watch, Nick saw that it was almost seven, and he realized that he had not eaten all day. Nick decided that he would go down to the hotel restaurant and get some dinner before going over to Jose's tonight.

As he sat off in a corner by himself, Nick's mind wandered between the facts of this case, which were few and far between, and the memories of the past few years. His mind was so far away that he had to occasionally look down at his plate to remember what he had ordered.

Nick also began to have another uneasy feeling, the one of being watched. As he continued to eat, he began to look around the room to see if anybody was taking special notice of him. He could see no one, not so much as an extended glance. Although none stood out in his mind, he began to study the faces around the room so as to have a reference for comparison the next time this feeling came over him.

As Nick drove to Jose Garcia's home, he took a less direct route than usual, just to make sure he was not being followed. The only car behind him for any length of time, was a small sports car, several cars back. And that was not strange since they were on Eighth Street, "Calle Ocho", the main drive through the Cuban area of Miami and Coral Gables. Even though all of Miami could be known as the Cuban area.

At the gate Nick pressed the intercom and asked to see Jose. This time there was no hesitation the gate was immediately opened for him to pass, and as he was told he was expected by the voice at the other end.

Nick was met at the door by the housekeeper, which somewhat surprised him. Usually it would have been one of Jose's security people. She led him directly to the library where Nick saw Jose over at a desk speaking on the phone. Jose motioned Nick over to the sofa, where he sat and waited for him to finish his call.

"Nick, my friend, has your investigation turned up anything new?" he asked.

"No Jose, it hasn't. Have you, or your people been able to find anything at your end?"

"Not yet," Jose said, "I'm sorry to say. But I did not expect to have any news for you this soon. You see, not only is it going to be hard to find out who may have the information we seek, but also once we know who, it will take…some convincing…to get them to talk. The people of whom we speak, are not accustomed to being…open and forthright…with anyone outside their organization."

"I understand." Nick stood and went to the bar. "Do you mind if I pour myself a drink?"

"Not at all. Please pour one for me as well"

"So Jose, where are your usual people? I don't think I've ever seen you without them around."

"No, I don't suppose you have. I still have a couple in the television room monitoring the cameras and the property. But the rest are out asking questions, with the two you are used to seeing, handling the more delicate areas."

"Of course. I'm sure they are your…more trusted associates." Nick said as he took a drink of his Scotch. "Well, Jose, I must thank you for the drink, and for having your people look into this for me. But I really should be going, I just wanted to touch base with you, and let you know to call me at home if you come up with anything."

"You mean you're going back to Key Largo?"

"Yes, I want to see how Julie is doing and check out a few things down there." Nick wanted to avoid telling Jose that he had spoken with DiMarko.

"Fine then, if I have any news, I'll call you at home or at the bar." He rose and placed his drink on the table, then he escorted Nick to the door where the two shook hands, but did not say another word. Both could feel that something had changed between them, it was no longer a social friendship.

Back in his hotel room, Nick picked up the phone and dialed his home.

"Hello." Donna answered.

"Hi Honey, it's me." Nick replied as he lay down on the bed, kicking his shoes off.

"Hey, what's going on? I was beginning to wonder if you were going to call tonight, Julie told me that you had called her earlier at the bar." Donna seemed rather tense.

"I've just been poking around up here, seeing if I could find anything to help."

"I don't know what you told her, but what ever it was, Julie seemed to be in a little better spirits after your call."

"I just told her about my meeting with Frank's father. And that at least on the surface, he seems to be telling the truth about not having heard from Frank since he disappeared a few years back. Of course, it's hard to tell if someone like that is lying, especially the first time you meet them."

"Nick, I know you're capable of taking care of yourself, but I get worried knowing that you're dealing with that kind of people. Promise me you'll be careful."

"I will. Besides, I'm probably going to be home some time tomorrow. I really think that what ever happened to Frank, the answers are going to be down there."

"What makes you think that?"

"Just a feeling I get, along with his words to Julie that he was going to Key West, not to Miami." Nick said trying to alleviate her fears.

"Well, I'll just feel better when you're home. I've got to get going, I have Julie and Carol coming over for dinner."

"Fine, tell them I'll see them soon." With that he hung up the phone and just lie there waiting for sleep to come.

Morning came too early for Nick. The whole night was spent tossing and turning, trying to put the pieces together. Nick also began to wonder if his believing the story told by Mr. Angelo DiMarko had anything to do with his wanting to believe in his Frank, or was it Francis. He decided that all he would do before heading back home would be to see DiMarko one more time to try and get a feeling for him.

After showering and packing his things from the room, Nick went down to the lobby to check out. Standing at the front desk he again began to feel as though he was being watched. Looking around the lobby he saw a few faces that looked familiar from the restaurant the night before, but none seemed to be taking any notice of him.

At DiMarko's hotel, Nick went directly up to the suite. The door was only being watched by one guard this time, the younger of the two. "I'm here to see Mr. DiMarko."

"I'll see if he's available."

Within a minute or so the guard returned and showed Nick in, this time not bothering to take his weapon. Looking around the room Nick saw that only the secretary was anywhere to be seen, and he sat at the table where he had talked with the mobster.

"Mr. Thomas." The voice came from the adjoining room as Angelo DiMarko entered. "Do you have any news for me?"

"No Sir, I just came to let you know that I would be heading down to the keys today." Nick said.

"So you believe me that Francis had nothing to do with my business affairs?"

"I'm still not sure. But either way, I think the best place for me to start is back where this all began. If it leads me back to Miami, I'll come back and look around some more. Regardless of the fact that you have retained my services, I plan on getting to the truth, no matter what that may be." Nick was almost surprised by his own frankness with this powerful crime boss, but he wanted it known that he would not be compromised.

"Good, I want you to be diligent in your efforts, nobody wants more than I to know what really happened to my son"

"You're forgetting his wife, Mr. DiMarko."

"I suppose she has as much interest in the truth as I. Speaking of which, I too believe that the answers are down in the keys, so I am making arrangements to stay at the Sheridan on Islamorda. Unless you can suggest a better hotel in the area?"

Nick became uneasy at the thought that DiMarko would be in the same area as Julie, as well as the possibility that he could interfere with his efforts to get at the truth. "No, I guess the Sheridan would be most comfortable for your needs."

"I also wanted to know if you could arrange for me to meet with this Julie. I would very much like to meet my daughter-in-law, and let her know that I will do everything in my power to find out who has taken Francis from us, and let her know I am here should she need anything."

Nick's mind raced between the reasons for DiMarko wanting to meet Julie. Could he be trying to make sure that she knew nothing of the business the son was doing for the father, could he be trying to get something Frank had at the house that could incriminate him? Or was it true that he merely wanted to meet her, the wife of his son?

Nick looked deep into Angelo DiMarko's eyes before answering. "Sir, I'm not sure she's ready to deal with meeting you. All that has happened recently has been a great shock to her."

"I understand, I don't want to upset her any more than she already has been. Please just relay the message for me, and let…Julie…know that I would like to meet with her."

"I'll do that." Nick rose to leave, and reached into his pocket for a card. "Here, if you need to reach me while I'm down there. Both my pager number and office number are on this card. Also, let me know if your people find anything out."

DiMarko realized that Nick meant that as a way of letting him know that the absence of his guards was noticed, and the reason behind it understood. "Of course, and I'm sure you'll let me know of any developments you uncover."

"Yes, goodbye, Sir." Nick left to begin the drive home.

During the drive he varied his speed watching for any cars that made any effort to keep him in sight. The only direct route down to the keys was Highway 1. The only car that caught Nick's attention was a blue sedan, which had followed him for about twenty minutes, but when Nick slowed to about five miles below the posted limit, the car passed him the first chance it had. Nick tried to see who was driving, but like most cars in south Florida, the windows were tinted dark. Once past him, Nick stayed at the slowed rate of speed until the sedan was out of sight for a couple of minutes. He never saw the car again on his drive home.

Nick arrived in Key Largo around one in the afternoon, and went directly to the Dive Shack. Both Julie and Donna would be there working the lunch shift, and he wanted to let them know that he was back. He also wanted to get Julie's keys once more so that he could check out the boat and office. With the information of Frank's background, which he had not had before, Nick wanted to see if there were any indications of a connection to his father.

As Nick entered the bar he saw Julie and Donna wiping down the tables after the lunch rush. At this time there was only six or eight people other than the employees still in the bar. "Hi girls."

Donna turned to see Nick at the door and left the bar towel on the table as she made a beeline directly for him. "Nick, you're back." She threw her arms around him and kissed him firmly.

"Well that's a nice welcome home." Nick said as he walked with her over to Julie at the bar.

"Hi Nick." Julie gave him a hug and kiss on the cheek as well.

"How are you holding up, Kiddo?" he asked Julie.

"Okay, I guess. I don't think it has really sunk in yet. I mean, maybe it would have if it were just the fact that Frank was gone. But hearing that he had lied to me as well, I don't know whether to grieve for him, or hate him for tearing my life apart. My Frank was Francis DiMarko, son of a crime lord…"

"No matter what else there is to all of this, I truly believe that he loved you Julie. I used to see how he looked at you when he thought nobody was watching. There was something there more than just using you."

"Thanks, I'm lucky to have you as a friend, both of you." She said as she turned to Donna.

"And we'll always be here for you." Donna took her hand and gave it a squeeze. "You are going to stay at the house with us a while longer, aren't you?"

Julie looked at the two of them and relied. "I've been around you two too much as it is, I'm sure you want some privacy."

"Don't be silly, you're family to us." Donna answered.

"Of course Julie. Besides, I would feel better if you weren't alone right now, we still don't know why Frank was killed."

"Okay, I think I'd like it too. I have to go check on an order in the kitchen. Thanks again you two, I don't know what I would do without you." As she left her eyes began to well up.

Donna watched as her friend left, then turned to Nick. "So what did you find out up in Miami?"

"Like I told you on the phone, not very much. I just did a little looking into Frank's business affairs, and talked to his father to see if there was anything to what the authorities believe he was doing."

"Well, was he working for his father in drug trafficking?"

"From what his father told me, and what I could read in his expression, no. But these are people used to being deceptive, and playing it close to the vest. I also went to Jose and asked him to check into the rumors for me." As he spoke the words, he could tell what Donna's reaction was going to be.

"You did what? I can't believe you went to Garcia for help. You know what he is, what he does for a living. I never liked being around him when we were with the club, where it was basically off limits to talk business. And now you go to him and ask for a favor that you know he'll expect to be returned someday."

"Actually, he's doing it to get in good with the DiMarko organization, not as a favor to me." Nick knew it was a weak defense to her argument, but it was the best he could do.

Donna knew that it did not matter to Nick what he had to do to get to the truth. All that mattered was that he was helping a friend, and for that reason she let the matter drop. "What ever Nick. So tell me, what did you think of Mr. DiMarko?"

"To look at him, it was obvious that he was Frank's father. The face was like seeing Frank thirty years in the future, but the personalities are totally different. He's a very guarded man, choosing his words carefully, not like Frank, saying exactly what's on his mind."

"Maybe Frank was just better at hiding it than his father is. After all, he spent the last few years living a lie around here." The statement was true, but even she wanted there to be more to it than that.

"Or, he was living the truth as he knew it. As far as he was concerned he wanted nothing to do with his father or his past life, and his father was dead."

"You know, if for no other reason than Julie, I hope that's the truth. It might make all of this a little easier for her to deal with." Donna held Nick's hand, and gave him a kiss.

Just then Julie returned from the kitchen with a steak and a bottle of beer, which she placed before Nick. "I hope you don't mind, but I figured you could use a good meal."

"Thanks Babe, you're always looking out for me." He grabbed the beer and took a long swallow.

"Just returning the favor."

"By the way Julie, do you think you can let me borrow your keys again. I want to go back to the boat and to Frank's office and look around some more."

"Actually, Officer Jenkins brought some of Frank's things by yesterday. That's what got me upset, so Donna had me stay with her last night. He gave me Frank's keys and his wallet, they are in my purse, I'll get them for you after you get some food in you."

"One other thing Julie, when I asked you if you knew anything about yours and Frank's finances, you said that Frank always took care of that stuff. Would you mind if I were to take a look at your papers?" Nick tried to broach the subject carefully so as not to let her know that he wanted to see if there was any drug money filtering it's way into their books.

"No, not at all Nick. Anything you need to find out why he was shot. Frank kept all the papers in a small safe in the bedroom, it looks like a nightstand, but if you open the doors you see the lock. The key to it is on Frank's key ring with all the rest. Are you going over there today?"

"No, I think I'm just going to stay in with the two of you tonight. I can start checking that stuff tomorrow."

Nick finished his meal as the girls went back to work. He still had not told Julie that the senior DiMarko had asked him to arrange a meeting with her, and decided to tell her later that night when they were all back at the house.

He told Donna and Julie that he would meet them at home after they got off work since he wanted to go home and unpack. What he really wanted to do was be alone and think about where to begin looking for answers.

Around seven o'clock, Donna and Julie came walking in the front door of the house. They saw Nick lying in the couch with his bags at his feet, but the sound of the door had woken him.

Donna leaned over him. "Sorry we woke you, Honey. Why don't you just go and lay down in the bedroom?"

"That's okay, I just needed to take a nap. What do you girls say to a barbecue for dinner?" He asked.

"Sounds good to me." Julie replied. "Did you have anything in particular in mind."

"I thought I'd throw on a couple of swordfish steaks I have in the fridge, unless you have a taste for something else."

"Yumm, I love your grilled swordfish. I'll make a salad." Donna said.

"And I'll steam up some vegetables." Said Julie.

It struck Nick as odd that this was how they had spent so many evenings in the past. Only now Frank was not with them, he would never be with them again.

Nick sat out on the back porch drinking a beer as the fish sizzled on the gas grill. He watched through the screen door as the two girls prepared their contributions to the meal, occasionally bumping into one another and giggling at something or another.

Julie came out onto the porch with Nick carrying some dishes and silverware. "How's the fish coming?"

"Take a look." Nick answered as he opened the lid.

"Smells terrific. How much longer?"

"About five minutes. Is everything else ready?" He asked

"Sure is. Donna and I are going to bring it out now. What kind of dressing do you want on your salad?"

"Bleu cheese sounds good." As he answered he watched her for a reaction.

She turned, cocking her head to one side. "You know, one of these days I'm actually going to get you to put something else on a salad."

"Give it up Julie, we're not going to change him." Donna called from the doorway. "We've both been trying for too long not to know how stubborn he can be."

"I agree, so why don't you two just give it up, and try to accept me for who I am." Nick replied, trying to feign righteous indignation.

While the three of them were eating, it was evident that there was a difference from their gatherings in the past. It was a strange silence, which was never a part of them. All were obviously avoiding any subject that might lead them in the direction of Frank's murder.

Just as the tension was about to make Nick burst, the phone rang. "I've got it." Nick said as he sprang from his chair towards the house.

"Hello, Nick Thomas here."

"Hi Nick, its Steve."

"Hey Steve, what's up. Have you got some information for us?"

"No, I'm sorry I don't. I was wondering if you could come by the station tomorrow, for a talk." There was a strangeness in his voice.

"No problem. Or you can come by here tonight if it's something important." Nick said.

"No, that's all right, it can wait till morning. I'm about to pack it in for the night anyway, but I would appreciate it if you could come by early, say about nine."

Nick couldn't place his finger on it, but there was a definite uneasiness to this conversation. "I'll be there bright and early."

"Okay, bye." Steve hung up without waiting for a reply.

Julie looked at Donna, and then back to Nick as he resumed his meal. "Was that something about Frank? Is there something new?"

"No, he said there is nothing new to report. Steve just said he needs me to come down to the station in the morning, there is something he needs to speak with me about." As Nick spoke, he could see that Donna was reading something into his words. Even if he didn't know what to make of the conversation, he could see that she knew something was making him uneasy.

"Are you sure you're not hiding anything from me, to try and protect me or something like that?" Julie asked.

Before Nick could answer Donna spoke for him. "Julie, you know everything he does. What more could there be for him to protect you from?"

Donna's words hung there over the three of them as they all realized how true they were. Frank was dead, the revelations about his past, what more could there be?

Nick decided this would be the best time to change the subject by telling Julie that Mr. DiMarko had asked him to introduce him to her. "She's right Jules, you know everything I do. But I do need to talk to you about something else."

"Sure Nick, and I'm sorry if I said anything out of line. I know you are doing everything you can for me, you're the best friend I have in the world. Both of you, you're all I've got now." Julie reached across the table to take each of their hands and gave them a squeeze and a smile.

"You know, I think that's the first real smile I've seen from you since all this started." Donna said, as she returned the look.

"And it looks good on you." Nick replied. "But as I was saying, I have to tell you something. When I went to meet with Frank's father, Mr. DiMarko, I told him that I was looking into Frank's murder for you, Frank's wife. I guess it was the look on his face when he heard that his son was married that got me believing that he really hadn't seen or heard from Frank."

Julie looked rather surprised. "You mean you don't believe what those agents said about him being down here doing work for his father?"

"The look on his eyes, along with the man I knew as Frank Marks, I guess I just find it hard to believe that they were both that good at acting. Plus, I remember the way Frank used to look at you, and I truly believe that was love."

Julie's eyes began to mist over. "Thank you Nick, I guess I didn't know how much I really wanted to believe that until I just heard you say it."

"Okay, so what does all this have to do with your having to tell her something?" Donna asked, always being the one to keep the group focused.

"Well, I didn't say anything to you at the bar earlier today, because I didn't know how you would react to it, but here goes. When I met with DiMarko before coming back, I told him that I believed the answers to Frank's death were down here and not in Miami. He told me that he thinks so too, and that he would be coming down here as well, and would be staying at the Sheridan on Islamorada." Nick watched as Julie and Donna's eyes widened. "That's another reason I'm leaning towards believing that Frank's murder had nothing to do with drug trafficking."

"What do you mean?" Julie asked intently.

"He knows that the federal and local authorities are looking into this, and if there was something going on, it would probably be based out of Miami. So if he were trying to keep a lid on it, he would stay up north to deal with it." Nick answered.

"But we all know that with the Keys being all spread out and all, there are always people smuggling drugs in here and driving them up to Miami to be distributed." Donna questioned.

"True, but if it were another organization that ordered it, it would be in Miami. Plus, if there was smuggling going on down here, I think DiMarko would try to distance himself from it. I just read his actions as one of a father trying to find out why his son was shot." Nick tried to explain.

"I still don't see why you're telling me all this?" Julie wondered.

"Because Julie, he asked me to arrange a meeting between the two of you. He says he just wants to meet the woman his son married, and I can sort of understand why."

Julie just sat there for a moment, staring at Nick. "I don't know Nick, I just don't know if I can deal with it right now."

"I told him I didn't think it was a good idea, but he asked me to ask you." Nick could feel Donna's eyes staring at him as well, although she just sat quietly listening.

"A part of me wants to, but another part of me is really scared to meet him. I want to meet him because he's Frank's father, but I'm afraid I might somehow find out that it's all true what the police said, that my life with Frank was all a lie, a front for him to smuggle drugs."

"If you don't want to meet him, you don't have to, I promise." Nick took her hand in his.

"I don't know, just let me think about it a while." Julie stood and cleared her plate from the table. "I'm going to go lay down for a bit."

As she left, Nick could sense that Donna was just waiting for her to get out of earshot to say something.

"I don't know how good of an idea it was to tell her that Nick. You shook her up pretty good." Donna said,

"At least I didn't tell her she was living off the mob's money, did I." Nick quipped.

"What, you mean it's true about him?"

"I do know. But if what his father told me is true, everything they had was bought with the mob's money either way."

Donna leaned forward and asked. "I don't understand Nick, what do you mean by the "mob's money"?"

"How much did Julie tell you about our conversation with the feds?"

"She told me all about it, about how Frank disappeared and his father had people looking for him, but that they think it may have been to throw them off or something like that."

"And if that is true, then everything they have, the house, the boat, and even the business are paid for with dirty money."

"And if it's not true?"

"Then DiMarko's version is true, and it was all paid for with his money anyway."

Donna looked bewildered. "I still don't get it, what is DiMarko's version?"

As Nick spent the next hour or so, explaining the story of the five million dollars Frank took from his father, and that his father was looking for him out of concern. He also explained that was why he had asked Julie for the keys to her house, to see if he could find some way to verify either story in the financial records Julie told him Frank took care of, and kept in the safe by their bed.

Now sitting out in the hammock in the back part of the yard, Donna began to ask Nick what he really thought was going on.

"So Honey, why do you think Frank was killed, and please don't sugar coat it."

"My heart says that it was probably a random act of violence. Not only because he was my friend, but because of what it will do to Julie if I prove he was using her. But little by little, the things we are finding out about him, make me believe it has something to do with his father's business dealings."

"And you don't believe there could be a third possibility?" She asked.

"I suppose it's possible, but I can't for the life of me figure out what other explanation there could be."

"Hey Nick." Suddenly came a voice from near the house.

Donna and Nick both turned to see Tony walking towards them. It was barely past eight o'clock and he should have still been at the bar.

"Tony, what are you doing here? Is there something wrong?" Nick asked as he stood and moved towards his friend.

"I don't know…here." Tony handed Nick an envelope. "Your detective friend Jenkins came by, ordered a sandwich, and told me to give this to you."

"When did this happen?" Nick asked, puzzled by this along with the call from Steve earlier in the evening.

"Just a little bit ago. Now I have to get back, the bar's jammed." Tony turned and walked away as quickly as he arrived.

"What was that all about." Donna asked.

"I have no idea." Nick looked at the letter in his hand. "Maybe this will explain it."

As Nick opened the envelope, Donna moved next to him to read it over his shoulder.

> Nick,
>
> I probably shouldn't be doing this, but you've been a good friend who has helped me in the past, and I feel I owe you.
>
> Do me a favor, and don't do anything else tonight, just stay in and wait until you see me tomorrow. Just know that you are being watched. I don't know to what extent, but I couldn't take the chance that they had you phone tapped. I couldn't say more earlier because I wasn't alone when I called you. Be careful, and I never wrote this letter.
>
> Steve

"Honey, what the hell is that about?" Donna asked as she finished reading the note.

"I have no idea, but I've felt like someone has been watching me for the past two days. If Steve knows about it, it means that it is the FBI or the D.E.A. The local cops wouldn't have any reason to be keeping an eye on me."

"But why would they be watching you? You're trying to find out what happened."

"It could be any number of things. For starters, they might think I know something that I haven't told them, or I could be getting close to finding out something that they haven't told me. They could even think that I'm somehow involved, either in Frank's death or in the drug dealing they claim he was part of."

"That's ridiculous, they can't believe that you have anything to do with something like that."

"Of course they could, they don't know me from Adam, so who knows what they might be thinking?" Even hearing himself say it, Nick could not believe that he was under surveillance. Nick began to wonder what it could be, what he had done to cause them to be watching him. He decided to wait until his meeting with Steve in the morning and not worry about it tonight.

The rest of the night he and Donna just lay in the hammock and watched the stars. She could tell that although he did not say it, Nick was irritated by the fact that he was being watched. What possible reason could they have? Was it that they suspected him of being involved with some illegal activity, or was he somehow, without knowing, closer to the truth than he himself knew? What did they know that he did not?

Nick was grateful to Steve for having let him know, but was also worried for his friend. What would happen if the federal agents found out that Nick had been warned? It could be the end of Steve's career as a cop, all because he felt he owed Nick for something that had happened a couple years earlier.

Shortly after the Dive Shack had opened, it became the place to be. One Friday night with the bar packed to the gills, Nick was sitting at the bar having a few drinks with the customers. Two weeks earlier Nick had hired Tony Del Valle to manage the place so he could have the freedom to run his newly started private investigation service, and enjoy some time away from both businesses. Sitting a couple barstools to Nick's right was a man Nick had seen in the place the past few nights. He always came in alone and just sat at the bar drinking and watching whatever sporting event happened to be on. He would rarely speak to anyone other than the bartender on duty, although one could tell that he paid close attention to whatever was going on around him. Nick had waited on him a couple of times, and from what he gathered from the other bartenders, the man was nice enough and tipped well. That was enough to have the staff take extra good care in making sure his glass was never empty and his drinks were never under poured.

This particular night, after about an hour and several shots on top of a few stiff drinks, Nick decided to play the good host and engage him in conversation. He began by remarking on the game at hand.

"Hey what do you think about the game, looks like the Heat are doing pretty well against the Bulls tonight?" Nick asked.

"Yeah, I guess so. I just wonder which team you're rooting for?" The man answered.

"I cannot tell a lie, the Bulls. It kind of shows with all the pictures around the bar, huh? By the way, I'm Nick Thomas, the owner."

"I know, that's why I made the crack. I'm Steve Jenkins, nice to meet you." The man extended his hand across the empty stools between them.

Nick took his hand and moved himself and his drink to the seat next to the man. "So you've been in here quite a bit lately."

"So, is that a crime?" Steve replied as he shot a look at Nick.

"No, I didn't mean it in a bad way. I was just commenting, making conversation."

"Sorry, I didn't mean to snap at you, I've just had a lot going on, and I'm kind of up tight." Steve offered as some sort of apology.

"Hey, no problem. How about accepting my apology by letting me get you a drink?" Nick asked

The next few hours were spent watching the game, drinking and talking. With more information than would usually be offered being exchanged due to the alcohol. The two also felt an instant bond when Steve told Nick he was an off duty county sheriff's deputy, and Nick informed Steve that he was a former Chicago cop.

As the night went on, Nick found out that Steve's sudden patronage at the Dive Shack was due to his wife's serving him with divorce papers. Nick could see that it was tearing him up, so they quickly dropped the subject and resumed their drinking. At the end of the night, Nick who had long before switched to straight soda offered to drive Steve home. Steve refused and made his way out to the parking lot with Nick in tow.

"Come on Steve, let me drive you home. I'll even pick you up in the morning and bring you back to your car."

"It's not necessary, I'm fine." He slurred.

"You are not fine. I've seen enough DUI's to see that, and you know it." Nick said as he grabbed Steve by the elbow.

As Nick turned around Steve, he swung wildly, and caught Nick flush on the chin. "Leave me the hell alone."

The punch was hard enough to put Nick on his ass, but as Steve bent over to see if he was all right, he passed out on top of Nick. Nick stood up and carried Steve back to the bar, where he took the man back to his office and laid him out on the couch.

About eight in the morning, a seriously hung over, and still slightly drunk, Steve Jenkins awoke. He began to look around, trying to figure out where he was. He looked over to see Nick, sitting at a desk with a cup of coffee, and a swollen jaw.

"Hiya Nick." He said timidly.

"Hiya yourself, deputy." Nick just sat there, waiting to see what Steve would say next.

As he sat up, Steve was obviously quite shaky. "I guess I owe you one, huh?"

"You don't owe me anything, I was just making sure you didn't get in an accident. I could have gotten sued, or lost my liquor license for over serving you." Nick said as he took another drink of coffee. "Want some?"

Steve knew that Nick was down playing what had happened the night before, and he appreciated it. Steve had found a friend during a difficult time in his life.

The next few months, although the two did not socialize away from the bar, they would sit at the bar and talk about nothing and everything. Steve would occasionally talk about his divorce, but mostly whatever game was on would be the topic, and the night they first met was never brought up again.

The alarm sounded next to the bed. As Nick reached over to turn it off he saw that it was seven thirty, he had set it so he would have time to shower and be wide awake for his meeting at the station.

It was five after nine, he had driven around the block several times, and just to make sure he was not early, showing that he was overly curious about the reason for this meeting, and to make sure he was not being followed. He wasn't, apparently they figured there was no reason to follow him since they knew where he was going.

As he entered the squad room he saw Collins and Bradshaw, the two federal agents, standing over Steve at his desk. When Steve saw Nick, he stood and quickly crossed the room to speak with him.

"Nick, in all the time I've known you, you've never been even one minute late, today is not the time to start."

"I didn't want to seem to anxious. Now are you going to tell me what's going on?" Nick asked his friend.

Before Steve could answer the two agents were next to them. Collins turned to Nick. "Why don't we go into the conference room?"

The four men went into the small room, Nick saw that Bradshaw was carrying a file of some sort. Nick sat at the table with Steve and the two agents across from him.

"So, is somebody going to tell me what this is about? Does it mean you have some news about Frank?" Nick asked, directing his question towards Collins. He had an unexplained dislike for Bradshaw; perhaps it had something to do with his treatment of Julie when they had first met.

"We'll be asking the questions here Thomas. Like what do you really have to do with Francis DiMarko's murder?" Bradshaw inquired.

"What the hell are you talking about?" Nick asked with genuine disbelief. Although it was one possibility for this meeting that he had thought of, he had not seriously considered it.

"We want to know what you had to do with DiMarko. Were you working for them, or did someone pay you to take him out?" Bradshaw was trying to push, and Nick knew it.

Collins interrupted, acting as a calming factor. "I think we can all be a little calmer, don't you?" He asked Bradshaw. It seemed to Nick that the FBI man also had a dislike for his D.E.A. counterpart.

"Fine, you want calm, I'll give you calm." Bradshaw opened the file before him and pulled out a picture, which he pushed over in front of Nick. "Care to explain this?"

Nick looked to see a picture taken through the window of DiMarko's hotel room. It showed Nick seated with DiMarko drinking coffee, it was their first meeting. "So...I found out he had flown in to find out about Frank's death. I wanted to know if what you told me about Frank was true, and I went to ask him about it."

"Then how about these?" He next produced a picture with Nick holding the envelope containing the ten thousand he took as a retainer.

Before answering Nick looked at the faces of the three men in the room with him. First, D.E.A. agent Bradshaw, he waited for Nick's answer with a look of conviction, as though he knew the conclusions he had drawn were right, and he was just waiting for confirmation.

Next, he looked to his friend. Steve was trying to look indifferent, but Nick could see the contempt in his eyes for the veiled accusations being leveled at his friend, and the compassion for Nick having to go through this.

Lastly, he looked to Collins, the man from the FBI. He was not a young, gun-ho agent looking to make a name for himself like the other man. Collins' experience showed in the small creases around his eyes, even as he watched every little reaction Nick had to the questions, and how he delivered his answers. He was there to find the truth, and he would be sure of the facts before he drew any conclusions, unlike Bradshaw.

Nick calmly, and with thought, looked the antagonist of the group directly in the eyes. "Well, as you know, I am a private investigator. When

Mr. DiMarko asked me for whom I was working, I told him nobody, that I was looking into this for my friend. She just happens to Frank's wife, and I was also his son's friend." Nick deliberately spoke in an obviously calculated and controlled manner. "When he heard that no one had hired me, he went into the other room and came out with that envelope. He told me that it was a retainer for my services, and that he wanted me to find out who did this to his son. I felt that if he at least thought I had accepted his offer to work for him, it would give me access to him whenever I needed, if I needed."

Before Bradshaw could vent some of his dislike for Nick, agent Collins jumped in to run interference. "Okay, suppose we believe all that you have said so far. You're just using DiMarko to get at the real reason for his son's murder, your friend, and the husband of a close friend." Collins reached in front of Bradshaw and withdrew yet another picture. "Would you care to explain this?"

Nick was truly shocked at what he saw before him. It was himself sitting on Jose's sofa having a drink with him. The photos of the DiMarko meeting had not surprised him, but they had followed him to Garcia's as well. Nick tried to compose himself, he was certain the shock he felt was evident to all in the room.

Before Nick could answer, Collins proceeded. "Let me tell you what we know first. Jose Garcia, one of the top two drug traffickers in Florida. Much of his drugs supply the eastern seaboard, including New York. To do business in New York, one has to work for, or deal with DiMarko. Are you beginning to see where we're going with this?"

Nick noticed that Collins was using his own, slow and deliberate pace in his delivery, so as to watch Nick ever so closely.

Collins continued. "There are several directions we can go with our thinking here. We can either believe that what you have said so far is true, and DiMarko told you something directly or indirectly that led you to believe that Garcia has some connection to what happened. Or, and I'm sure I don't need to tell you, this is the way Agent Bradshaw is leaning, knowing that Garcia and DiMarko have had business dealings in the past, you are working as an intermediary, passing communications and information between the two."

Suddenly from Nick's side Steve jumped into the discussion at hand. "You're forgetting one other option. Nick could have been involved with their drug operations the whole time, and with Frank dead, it's cutting into his and all of theirs profits. He just might be trying to get the business back on its feet. He might even be trying to get DiMarko and Garcia to put him in charge of it all."

The sarcasm was evident to all in the room. None the less, Bradshaw decided to chime in too. "We haven't over looked that option, we just didn't bring it up yet."

"You son of a bitch." Steve moved towards Bradshaw, but was quickly blocked by Collins.

Nick stood and placed his hand on Steve's shoulder from across the table. "Steve, come on, take it easy. You're letting him get to you more than I am, and I'm the one he's after."

"Yeah I know, that's what gets me. I know that you wouldn't be into anything like that and it pisses me off to hear this jerk say it."

"Don't worry about it, I believe we'll get at the truth and he'll owe me an apology. Especially if he's off chasing his tail in the wrong direction." Nick looked over at Bradshaw, making sure to make eye contact with him as if to let him know that he had no fear of him, or his accusations.

"All right, let's everybody back off and calm down. Why don't we get back on the subject, and maybe Nick can give us his explanation?" Collins said.

"Fine." Nick began. "First of all, none of your assumptions, or 'options' as you call them are correct. I was over at Jose Garcia's enlisting his help. I know who and what he is, but I have known him on a social basis for a couple of years now. He and I belong to a group of people that have speedboats, and we get together, usually on weekends and party or make runs over to Bimini and the Bahamas. One rule of the 'club' is that we never talk about business. We're all there to relax and forget about work."

"So you're telling us that you associate with known drug dealers?" Bradshaw jeered.

"I don't think you can legally call him a 'known drug dealer' since neither the D.E.A., or any other agency has been able to indict him on anything illegal. But yes, I have heard rumors as to how he makes his money." Nick returned.

"Okay, let's skip the lesson in semantics. Go on Mr. Thomas." The FBI man wanted to stay on the subject at hand.

"Well, having heard the rumors about Jose Garcia, I broke the club 'rule' and went to ask for his help. I figured he could find out more, quicker than I could. Besides, he had met Julie and Frank when they have come out on my boat, and from watching them interact, I can tell you Jose had no idea who Frank's father was. Although that is why Jose agreed to check into it for me, he said it would give him an inside track in doing business with DiMarko if he helped find out who killed his son."

"And you expect us to believe this line of crap you're trying to feed us?" Bradshaw was getting irritated with Nick's responses.

"Believe what you want, that's obviously the mentality you have anyway." Nick aimed this remark to Bradshaw. "Unless you have something else, I'm leaving now." Nick stood and went towards the door.

"Mr. Thomas, I hope you remember from your time as a police officer, that withholding any pertinent information to this investigation, could be construed as obstruction of justice." Collins was letting Nick know that he expected to be kept informed, as well as telling him that he would still be watched.

"I'll tell the local authorities if I think I find out anything they should know." It was Nick's way of saying that he would tell Steve if he found something out.

Before Nick was even two steps out the door of the conference room, Steve could be heard to say. "He's on our side Bradshaw, whether you believe it or not. And by the way…you're an asshole."

The rest of the detectives in the squad room had also heard Steve's words, and turned to see what was happening. They all knew that Steve was one to say what he meant, and mean what he said. He was not someone you wanted as an enemy.

"Hey Nick, hold up a second." Steve called.

Nick stopped near the doorway to the stairs, making sure he was far enough from the room that the two agents inside could not hear their words. "Yeah Steve, what's up?"

"Nick, I didn't know about the pictures, or even what they wanted to talk to you about." His tone was apologetic.

"Don't worry about it, you did more than you had to by letting me know that I was being watched. I kind of figured they knew about the meeting with DiMarko, since I saw some other feds roaming around the hotel lobby the first time I went to see him." Nick tried to make sure his friend knew he had no hard feelings about what had just transpired. "And I told them the whole truth in there."

"Hey, I have no doubt about that." Steve tried to sound semi insulted by the fact that Nick felt the need to include the remark, but both knew he wanted some reassurance.

"I'll see you around Steve, it seems I now have another vested interest in having this whole thing go away as soon as possible." The two shook hands and went their own way.

Once in his car, Nick sat in the parking lot and took a few deep breaths to calm himself down. He was angry at the accusations aimed at him by the federal agent's just moments before. But more than that, he felt his credibility, his character being questioned. He had never before felt that way; his honor had never been in doubt. He determined that he would get at the truth, and he would also get an apology from Bradshaw when it was all over.

Nick decided to drive to Frank's boat again, he had some insight that he had not had his last visit, and felt the need to look for anything he may have overlooked with the new possibility that Frank had been running drugs.

As he walked towards Frank's boat, a tense feeling began to rise in his stomach. Nick's senses were heightened to every thing around him. The first thing he noticed was that a few things on the deck of the boat were moved from his last visit. Some of the storage lockers Frank used to store diving equipment were open, and the gear within was on the seats.

Someone had been to the boat. The first one to come to mind was Julie. She may have gone to look for something, or just to be with some of Frank's things where he loved to spend so much of his time. But she had not said anything to Nick about going there, and she knew as well as anybody how meticulous Frank was about his boat and everything having a place. Frank always said that it was not only for preference that things should be kept neat, but it was good business to appear organized as well as a safer way to keep the boat. Like most experienced divers, Nick agreed with Frank, it was a matter of safety. They trusted their lives to their equipment.

Next, Nick considered the authorities. Steve or anyone from the local law enforcement would have contact Julie for permission or at least gotten a search warrant, either way, Nick felt he would have heard. Collins and Bradshaw on the other hand, believed they were looking into a gangland hit, and now at least questioned Nick's involvement. They would not have notified Nick, but Steve would have.

Perhaps it was those involved in the drugs with Frank. Maybe they were looking to make sure that there was nothing to tie them into the murder, or link them to drugs. Angelo DiMarko had come down the day before, and his goons were out doing his handiwork before that.

Instead of going on board and seeing to what extent the boat had been gone through, Nick decided to call Steve. Maybe there would be finger-prints or some other evidence that would be found by using the crime lab in Miami, and Nick had no access to that. Besides, after they went through it Nick would be able to check for himself.

Within minutes, Steve, with the agents and many other officers on tow arrived. Once told what Nick knew, they began to work feverishly, going over the boat and its contents with the proverbial fine toothed comb.

The next couple hours Nick just hung around, staying out of the way, but remaining close enough to hear if anything came up. They were being very thorough, asking everybody in the area if they had seen anyone near Frank's boat. No one had. After a while, Nick noticed that John's boat had been in its slip the whole time.

Even if he had no fishing charter planned, John would have been there early in the morning, making sure his boat was ready should he get a call, and just hanging around in case a passer by decided to book one on the spur of the moment. Knowing John, if by nine a.m. he hadn't booked a charter, he would have walked over to the Dive shack and sat at his corner of the bar. Nick decided he would check out this new idea.

As Nick walked into the Dive Shack he saw that the lunch shift was in full swing. Many of the customers tried to greet him, but once he saw John in his regular place, drinking a beer, he went directly over and joined him.

"John, how's it going?" Nick asked.

John turned, "Hey Nick, I saw you over by all the commotion. What's going on over there? Does it have to do with Frank's murder?"

"I think so. Someone went on his boat, and tore the place apart looking for something. That's why I'm here. Did you see anyone over there this morning?" Nick asked with some sense of urgency.

"As a matter of fact I did. I just figured they were cops, or something like that."

"Why, were they in uniform?" Nick asked with some hope, although he knew it could not have been the police. They would not be tearing the marina apart if it were.

"No, they were in suits, and you know how rare those are around here. I just heard a rumor that it might have something to do with drugs, so I assumed D.E.A."

Without another word, Nick got up and left. That had been one of the options Nick had considered, DiMarko's men. Now he knew it was them, and he was going to go confront DiMarko himself, without telling Bradshaw and Collins.

Knowing the Sheridan on Islamorada well enough to know where the expensive rooms are, Nick went directly to the elevator and went to the top floor. As he expected, he immediately saw the bodyguard from the Omni, and went for the door.

"Tell DiMarko I'm here, and I want to see him right now!" Nick barked.

The lackey went in, and emerged within thirty seconds. "Go on in…Mr. DiMarko will see you."

Nick entered and saw DiMarko standing on the verandah with a drink in his hand. "What the hell were your guys doing on Frank's boat, and why did they tear it apart? Were they looking to make sure that he hadn't left any incriminating evidence around that would prove he was trafficking in drugs?"

"No, it's nothing like that at all." He replied calmly.

"So you don't deny they were there?" Nick asked.

"Yes, they were there, but they were not the ones who tossed my son's boat. It was searched before they arrived, and they called me as soon as they got on board and made sure whomever had done it was not still there. Once they called, I told them not to touch anything, and to get out of there right away."

Nick knew that even if it were not the truth, it would be the only answer he would get. "I'll take your word for it for now, but if I get one hint that you're lying to me, I'll take whatever information I find straight to the fed.'s." It was basically an empty threat since Nick planned to do that anyway if he found proof of illegal activities.

"I give you my word." DiMarko's tone implied that his word carried a great deal of weight. "And as proof of the fact that I am not holding anything back from you, I have some information that you should look into."

Nick's interest was suddenly piqued, but he tried to not let it show. "Oh, and what might that be?"

"First, let me tell you once again that I have not heard from my son since he left New York, so if it turns out that Francis was involved in something illegal, I had nothing to do with it."

Nick began to think that this was just DiMarko's way of distancing himself from something incriminating that Nick was bound to find out anyway. "Go on."

"Well, it seems that some of the people I do business with have found out that another powerful man in my profession has been seeking information about my son."

As he continued, Nick already knew the name about to be given him.

"His name is Jose Garcia, and some of the people my men have contacted, have reported that he has been asking a lot of questions."

"I know." Nick stated.

"What do you mean you know? You have told me nothing about this mans involvement in my son's murder." DiMarko firmly asked. "You are supposed to be keeping me informed of any information you come up with, that's what I'm paying you for."

"Garcia is not any new information about the case, and your people aren't supposed to be getting involved." Nick replied, noticing that DiMarko was obviously not accustomed to being spoken to in that manner.

"If he is not a new development in the case, how is it that I have not heard his name mentioned by you?'

"Because he is looking into this matter as a favor to me. If he had found something of importance I would have told you about it, or he would have contacted you directly."

"This Garcia is doing this as a favor to you? How is it that you know this man well enough to ask a favor of this type."

Nick could hear the distrust forming in DiMarko's voice. He decided to go ahead and tell DiMarko the truth, although he did not like what the question implied. "I know Jose Garcia on a social level. He and I are part of a group of men who get together and go boating, up until now; we have always made it a policy of the group not to discuss business. We are merely friends that get together to relax and occasionally see who has the faster boat."

"So as a favor to you, Garcia is looking into my son's murder?" DiMarko asked incredulously.

"Yes. I couldn't believe what the feds were saying about Frank, so I went to Jose and asked him to look into it as a favor to me. I had heard rumors about Jose's business dealings, and I crossed the line of our group and he said he would check into it." Nick was not sure how DiMarko was taking all of this, but he felt sure he was about to find out.

"Not being involved in our type of business, I find it hard to believe that Mr. Garcia would admit to it to you and do you this favor?" DiMarko questioned.

"On a social level, Jose Garcia and I are very close. Besides, he didn't admit to anything, he just said he would do it as a favor. He also said that it would be to his advantage to help me." Nick left the remainder of his explanation dangling to draw DiMarko in, trying to regain control of the conversation.

DiMarko looked closely at Nick, then asked. "What do you mean, it would be to his advantage?"

"Without saying specifically what type of business he is in, since he knew that I already knew. He told me that your two organizations had done business in the past. He felt it would put him in a favorable position to do more business in the future, if he were able to find some information that might help me get to the truth." Nick was reading DiMarko's reaction; it seemed he believed what he was being told.

"I'd like to meet this, Garcia." DiMarko said, "Could you set it up?" He asked.

Nick was offended by the question, and decided to let it known. "No, I can't set it up for you, I'm not going to get involved in anything that involves the two of you. The best I can do, is let him know that you want to see him, the next time I speak to him. Beyond that, it's up to you."

"It would seem that you have already become involved with the two of us, you just haven't realized it yet."

"No, I have gotten involved with Jose as far as asking him to do a favor for me. One which I expect he may or may not ask to have repaid someday. However, I think he knows me well enough that he will not ask me to do anything illegal, since he knows that I will not get mixed up in something like that." Nick remained calm and in control. "And as far as you are concerned, you are paying me to find out why your son was killed and who did it. This in no way leaves me obliged to you."

"You just let me hire you as a way to insure yourself access to me, should you need to ask me any more questions." DiMarko spoke as though he was telling Nick that he understood that he was being used in some way.

"And you just hired me as a way to find out what the police were doing about Frank's death, and what they were trying to connect you with down here in south Florida." Nick replied in kind.

The two men sat looking at each other for a moment, knowing that neither had imparted any new information to the other, only that they had clarified their position to one another.

Now that their mutual use was out in the open, Nick decided he would try to lay down a couple of rules. "Now that all is out in the open, I want you to know that I expect you to keep your goons out of this. I don't want to see them anywhere near me, Julie, or anyone having to do with this case."

"I do not think I like the tone you are taking, Mr. Thomas. However, I have already told my associates to stay away from you and anything having to do with what happened. I do not need them getting involved with the police, and having it even appear that we are interfering or trying to cover anything up."

Nick was not sure why, but he believed DiMarko. "Fine, as long as we understand each other, there's nothing further to discuss."

The two said good bye, and Nick decided to go home and see how Julie was doing.

As Nick pulled into his driveway, he saw that Donna's car was there, but Julie's was nowhere to be found. He assumed that the two had probably gone to the bar. As he entered he saw Donna sitting on the back porch with a beer and a magazine.

"Hi Honey, what's going on? Where's Julie at?"

"I'm not sure, she said she had to go out and take care of some things. I think she might have gone to see about making funeral arrangements for Frank." Donna replied as she stood and entered the kitchen.

"What makes you think that's where she is?" Nick asked with a little hint of concern in his voice.

Nobody else would have been able to detect it, but Donna knew him all to well. "Well, this morning, after you left, the police called and asked her who she wanted them to release the body to. They said they had completed their autopsy, and that all they needed to know was the name of the funeral home that would be handling it for her. Why, what's wrong, you seem worried about something?"

"Earlier today, somebody went on to Frank's boat and turned it inside out. I don't know who it was, but I just don't like not knowing where she is, or having her by herself till we know more."

Just then Julie came walking in the front door. "Hey Nick, there you are. Why haven't you answered any of my pages?"

"What are you talking about Jules? My beeper hasn't gone off all day." He relied as he removed it from his waist to check it.

"I think I've called it enough times over the past few years, that even if I had miss-dialed once, I certainly didn't dial wrong all five times I tried to get a hold of you." Julie stated.

"OOPS, I guess you're right." Nick answered looking at the blank screen in his hand. "I guess my battery quit on me, I haven't checked it all day."

Nick walked over to the drawer next to the sink and opened it.

As he did Donna remarked. "You're never going to find anything in there."

Nick glanced back over his shoulder at her with a wink and said. "You just haven't figured out my filing system yet." Referring to the often-remarked on junk drawer Nick was about to delve into.

Donna had on more than one occasion told Nick she was going to go through the drawer and clean it out, only to be told not to, that she did not know what he wanted to keep, and what would be okay to get rid of.

The drawer was on of the largest and deepest in the kitchen, and could hold little more than it already did. Still, Nick reached straight into the back, and deftly removed an open package of AA batteries, from which he took one and tossed the remaining two back in the drawer.

With a smirk on his face, he replaced the old battery with the new, and tossed the old one in the garbage. "See, told ya."

Julie burst into laughter. "He sure did at that, didn't he Donna?"

Donna half-heartedly glared at the two laughing at her expense, then joined in herself. "Very funny. As always, the two of you stick up for each other, and I have no chance."

It was the first time since Frank had disappeared that Julie had truly laughed, and it made Nick feel better. She had such an infectious laugh, that it always lit up a room, and Nick had missed it.

"So what did you need me for Jules?"

Julie became more solemn, she remembered what she had spent the day doing. "I wanted to ask you what kind of arrangements you thought I should make."

"What do you mean, I don't think I should have any say into how you handle this." Nick was not sure what she wanted from him.

"Actually Nick," Donna broke in. "Julie and I had been talking, and we thought that since you were the best friend Frank had, you might be able to tell her what you thought Frank might prefer. You know, give her a guy's opinion."

"It's not exactly the kind of thing guys sit around and talk about. Besides, I think Julie would be the best one to know what Frank would want done."

"Nick, Frank and I haven't been married that long, it's not something we discussed. I just felt that since the two of you were a lot alike..." Suddenly Julie's eyes began to mist. "At least the man I thought I was married to was like you, that's one of the things that attracted me to him at first."

Nick moved to Julie's side and put his arm around her. "I still think we knew the real him. The police have to be wrong about what think happened. I'm even beginning to believe that his father is telling the truth, and that means the only thing Frank lied about is his parents being dead. Which means he was ashamed of his background and doesn't make him a bad person, I probably would have been too if I were in his shoes."

His words seemed to buoy her mood. "Thanks Nick, does that mean you're getting close to finding out what really happened?"

"No, but I think I'm finding out what didn't happen. I think for your piece of mind, that might be just as important." Nick was not sure if he should tell her about the incident on the boat earlier in the day.

"Nick...did you go check out the house like you wanted to?" Julie asked.

"No, I didn't get around to it yet. Besides, I forgot to get your key to the house before I went out this morning."

Julie reached into her purse. "Well, here you go." She said as she tossed him a set of keys. "The police also sent me his personal stuff. The keys to the boat, his office files, and the safe in the bedroom are on there too."

"Are you sure you're okay with this?" Nick asked.

"Of course I am, I'd trust you with my life." She replied. "Actually, if you don't mind, would you do me a favor when you do go?"

"Sure, what is it?"

"In the safe we kept our wills and life insurance papers. Do you think you could bring them back with you? I think I'd like you two to be around when I go through them." She timidly requested.

"Okay, I'll bring them for you. I should get going over there anyway, if I want to do it today." Nick walked over to Donna and gave her a hug and a kiss as he whispered into her ear. "Keep an eye on her, I'm not sure she's taking this as well as she's trying to make us think she is."

"I will." Donna whispered in reply.

"Why don't you try to get some rest Julie?" Nick said as he gave her a hug of support.

"I will, thanks." she said as she kissed him on the cheek.

As Nick drove up the driveway he had visited so many times before, he heard Julie's words in his mind, "You were the best friend Frank had." She was right, Nick had been the best friend to her husband.

Frank had been a loner when they had all met. He would come into the bar and have a few drinks while listening to the conversations around him. Occasionally he began to get drawn into one as the regulars recognized him.

But it was when the Bulls and the Knicks were locked in a fierce playoff battle that Nick and Frank first truly spoke. The two being from Chicago and New York, respectively, were extremely loyal to their hometown teams. Each night of a game they would sit at the corner of the bar right in front of the big screen television, and cheer as the other's team faltered.

There were even times, Nick recalled when Julie would come and sit between them as if to insure that they would not come to blows. She was not a sports fan, and could not understand how they could seemingly be so close to a fist fight, and the next minute after the game, be joking and drinking, regardless of who's team won.

Now as Nick entered the home he had been in so many times before, he felt strange. He looked around the living room knowing that what he was here to find was not in this room, but he stood there none the less, as if he finally realized that he only truly knew one of the people that lived there.

The room was spotless, as it always was. Julie was a fanatic about keeping it that way, and always followed from room to room straightening up, even when she had guests over. Nick knew that if there had been anything out of the ordinary, there or in any other room in the house, Julie would have known, and would have said something to Nick about it, either when she found it, or surely when all of this began. The only exception to her fanatical cleaning was Frank's office. Julie knew that Frank had his own way of knowing where everything was, and would get annoyed at her if she moved anything around, much like Nick and Donna when it came to his "junk drawer" in the kitchen of his own home.

Nick decided to go to Frank's office once again. He had already looked around once, but that was before he knew about the suspicions of the D.E.A. and the FBI No, this time he would approach the office as a new location, not only looking for something to help find Frank, but also looking for something that might prove or disprove the allegations against his friend.

Nick sat at the desk and began going through all the books and maps he had seen on his first trip there. The books and maps that had told him of a hobby Frank had and had never shared with any of them, except Julie, who had never mentioned it. Nick began to wonder if Frank had been using all these things to hide what he had really been up to.

Was it possible that all this was just so she might believe his excuse of going treasure hunting, while he was really out somewhere in his boat picking up drugs to distribute through his father's organization throughout the country?

Nick's stomach began to turn as he remembered the time he spent as a Chicago cop. The times he had to go and inform a parent that their twelve-year-old child had just been found in an alley, dead of an overdose. Or perhaps all the peripheral crime that went along with the drug trade, the gangs that were used on the street level to distribute them, the drive by shootings the gangs used when another crossed them, and the children always shot by the errant bullet meant for another? No, his friend could not be involved in all that.

Even as he thought about Frank, Nick began to realize the hypocrisy he had been living himself. He abhorred drugs, and the violence they brought with them, but he had a "friend" that he had felt close enough with to ask a favor from, Jose Garcia, known to be a major importer, and Nick simply didn't let it enter his thoughts while he spent many a weekend boating and partying with him.

Nick shook those thoughts from his head, deciding that he would deal with that when all this was over, first he had to find the truth about Frank's murder.

As he continued to look at the maps and the books, he began to see that there were far to many notes written on pages marking chapters in the books, and even more navigational markings on the maps. The maps had so many crisscrossing search areas on them that it was apparent to Nick that Frank had truly been interested in this hobby. He had put far too much time and effort into it not to be.

After awhile, Nick came across a picture of a man in one of the books that seemed familiar to him for some reason. He did not know from where, but decided to read more to find out who he was.

The picture was of a man called Rafael Crisanto Colunga, a Spanish captain of the time of the conquistadors. The time when Spain had been stealing the gold and silver of the Incas and the Mayas. The book also said that Colunga was one of the captains to have made the most journeys between Spain and the new world, but that during his final trip, there had been a terrible hurricane and his ship, along with three others returning with him, had been lost at sea. The ships' manifests, which had been filed with the governor of Cuba, had shown that between the four ships lost, they had the largest cargo of gold and other jewels to be sent at a single time back to Spain. Captain Colunga had been chosen to lead the voyage, due to his close ties with the royal family, and his having been one of three knights chosen to a royal order, signified by a very ornate golden cross he wore around his neck, also shown in the picture.

As Nick read on he could understand why Frank had been so interested in the tales of the sunken treasures to be had if one could find them. The book he was reading had been published ten years earlier and still estimated the value of the reported manifests at over five hundred million dollars. By Nick's calculations, that would put its current value at nearer to seven hundred million or more. However, this book, as well as two others Nick had found containing information on Captain Colunga's fleet, all had widely different opinions on where they might have gone down. One had even mentioned the possibility that the trusted Captain may have not been so trustworthy after all, saying that his disappearance was why all future shipments back to Spain, were smaller in scale.

However, Nick had the feeling that Frank's interest might possibly be more on a historical, rather than monetary level. Frank had always been known as a very intelligent man, if somewhat soft spoken about it. He seemed to be well read when topics of politics or history where being tossed around the bar.

Nick sat and remembered the times they would all spend sitting around the bar playing the satellite trivia game. When he and Frank were playing alone, everyone would joke and make bets on which one would win, but as a team they were all but unbeatable, for Nick had a sharp mind when it came to remembering facts and the smallest details. Perhaps, he thought, that is what had made him a pretty good cop and an effective private investigator.

Nick was glad for the diversion reading Frank's books had brought, but that was over now. He spent the next two hours going over every inch of the office. He would not only check the contents of the drawers and filing cabinets, but also pulled out the drawers and examined every nook and cranny of the voids they left. Nick turned over all of the furniture, and pulled every cushion and pillow from the chairs and sofa in the room.

When he finished, he was amazed at the mess he had left behind. It reminded him of the boat he had seen at the harbor earlier in the day. Still he found nothing.

He next went to the bedroom; the first stop was the safe Julie had told him about, hidden in the nightstand next to the bed. He found it easily, and removed the keys she had given him. While he looked for the key to open the safe he saw a key to a safety deposit box, also on the key ring.

Nick assumed that would be where Frank would have kept the money he had taken from his father, or at least part of it.

Looking through the safe, Nick found a small strong box type container. The kind hardware stores sell, with a not so secure lock, but built to keep whatever was inside safe, should there ever be a fire in the home. Nick had also found a small key, which looked like the type this box, would take, and decided to try it. It fit, but Nick did not open the box, instead, he re-locked it choosing to have Julie open it herself. The contents would not lead to the answers surrounding his death, Nick told himself.

Looking at the remainder of what was in the safe, Nick found some business type ledgers, which on first glance seemed to be to Frank's business for the past four years. Nick decided to take them back to his house, along with the small lock box, and a couple of the books he had been reading from Frank's office.

Nick returned home to find Steve's car in the driveway, and Steve himself, sitting on the front porch drinking a beer. Nick checked his watch, and it was half past eight. He had spent several hours at Julie and Frank's home.

"Hey Steve, what brings you here?"

"I agreed to keep you informed on what was happening, I assumed you would want to know what we found on the boat after you left."

"Let me guess, nothing." Nick said as he observed the tired look in Steve's eyes, and the four empty bottles at his side.

"You're a hundred percent correct." Steve leaned back and took a long swallow of beer. "Why don't we go inside and grab another pair of cold ones?"

As they walked in to the house, Nick dropped the items from Julie's on the couch and followed Steve to the refrigerator. As he did, he saw Julie and Donna sitting in the back yard at the picnic table talking.

"So Steve, why were you sitting out front waiting for me?"

"I guess I just felt uncomfortable being around Julie. I get the feeling she sees me as the enemy or something. After all, I'm working with the fed.'s trying to tie her husband into some kind of illicit drug dealing."

"Come on, you don't seriously believe all that crap they're saying, do you?"

"I didn't know him as well as all of you did. He seemed like a nice enough guy, but even his own wife didn't know about his background. Until you or someone else can give me a more logical scenario, or even a possible alternative, that is the way this investigation is going to proceed."

Nick knew he was right. "Believe me, I'm looking for one."

"I know you are, so am I."

"Well, are you going to tell me what you found at Frank's boat?"

"Other than the mess you already know about, nothing. No clues as to who might have done it, but they did take a bunch of finger prints that are being run."

"With all the people that have been on Frank's boat, clients, friends, there probably won't be any help there."

"Maybe, but if we find prints that match up to known drug people, we'll know that there's something going on."

"I guess you're right." Nick grudgingly admitted.

"Well, thanks for the beers." Steve said as he got up, and tossed his empty bottle into the trash. "I just came by to let you know what we found and to see how she was doing."

"You know you're welcome to stay Steve. I'm just going to throw a few steaks on the grill."

"Thanks anyway, I'm just kind of tired. This case is wearing me out, physically and mentally." He walked himself to the door and left.

Nick sat there in the kitchen finishing his beer when Donna and Julie came in. "Hi Nick." They said in tandem.

"Hi girls, what's up? Have you two eaten yet?"

"No, we thought we'd wait for you." Julie replied, motioning to a package of steaks thawing on the counter. "Do you want me to fire up the grill?"

"Sure, that would be great. After dinner we can go through those papers you wanted me to bring, if you'd like."

Julie grew instantly pale, then just as quickly regained her composure. "We can do that later, if it's okay with you? What did Jenkins want?"

"He just came by to let me know what was going on. He didn't have anything new to tell me."

As Julie and Donna prepared the meal, Nick went out onto the back porch with one of the books he had brought back from the house, and began to read some more. He was not looking for any clues, but just an escape from the tension of the situation. Occasionally looking in the kitchen, Nick saw the two most important people in his world, getting along as if they were sisters. One at a difficult time in her life, and the other there giving the support needed to help get through it.

Nick began to think back to the time it all began, a little over one year earlier, just after Julie and Frank's wedding. Nick had been working on a case up in Palm Beach for nearly three weeks. A wealthy land mogul was about to initiate divorce proceedings against his wife, and he had asked Nick to get him some ammunition for court. He was looking to protect himself in what was expected to be a nasty property fight. Nick had told him that he did not like doing that type of investigation, but had been talked into going ahead with the job by a mutual friend Nick knew from his boating excursions, and the fact that he had been offered nearly triple his usual fee.

The first couple of weeks had been uneventful, but after Nick had convinced his client to schedule a trip out of town, Nick had been able to not only catch the man's wife out and about with her secret lover, but once he had found out who he was, Nick had found out that she had been paying for much of the mans living expenses.

Armed with the proof Nick had given him, the man and his attorney promptly confronted the soon-to-be ex-wife. Knowing that she had been exposed, she quickly accepted an agreement. Nick felt that it had been more than generous by her husband, who wanted to keep everything out of the papers, and just get on with his life. The man with an additional bonus that would have been understatedly called generous rewarded Nick. The whole ordeal had left a sour taste in Nick's mouth, and he had known he was right not to be in that type of investigations. Nick quickly returned to Key Largo and the Dive Shack.

Upon his arrival at the bar, he quickly noticed a new face. She was at the far end of the bar, cleaning up after the lunch rush. As she moved around the bar, Nick was unable to take his eyes from her. At five foot eleven inches, blonde hair to her waist, and eyes as blue as the ocean he loved so much, she was captivating. The regulars at the bar along with the staff had greeted Nick on hand, of which he had seen her take notice. However, she must have simply thought he was just another regular, of which there were many, that she had not met yet, otherwise, Nick felt she would have come over and introduced herself, had she known that he was the owner.

Nick sat there having his lunch and drinking a beer as she continued cleaning and taking care of customers. He would keep glancing over to her, making sure that she was not looking and that he was not staring. She was a very athletic type, yet still graceful in her movements.

After a while, she came over to the bar where Nick heard her ask Tony if she could take her lunch break, since her area was clean and nobody was seated there. Tony agreed and went in back to deliver her order to the cook.

As she went around the bar to get herself a soda, she asked Nick if he needed another beer, to which he relied yes, and told her Tony had his tab. She gave him one and came back around to take a seat next to him.

"I saw everybody saying hi to you when you came in, you must be a regular around here." She said.

"I guess you could say that."

"Well, I'm Donna. It's nice to meet you. I've only been here a couple of days, but I'm sure I'll be seeing more of you." She extended her hand to Nick.

As he took her hand, he hesitated, looking deep into her eyes. "I'm sure you will, I'm Nick." He replied, expecting there to be some recognition of who he was. There was none.

"So are you a diver?"

"Occasionally I help out some friends when they have a large group and want an extra guide."

"Sounds like a lot of fun. Julie said she and her husband would teach me, if I decided to learn."

"So where did you work before here?" Nick queried.

"Well, a few years back, I was at the 'Sundays' on Key Biscayne, but my ex-husband didn't like me working there, so I spent the last couple years working as a teller at a bank. Now that I'm divorced, I came down here and decided to go back in the service industry. The money is a lot better, and I've always liked dealing with people."

"And how do you like it here so far?"

"It's really great, the people that work here are really friendly, and the customers all seem to be locals, as opposed to Coconuts, where I was for two weeks before I came here. All the tourists, they're spending money on a room and whatever activities brought them here. They don't tip nearly as well as when you get to build up a relationship with your clients."

"That's certainly true." Nick agreed.

"Oh, have you ever worked in the business?" She asked as Tony returned.

"Yes, I've tended bar on and off for several years." As he answered, he looked at Tony, who was placing a salad in front of Donna, while giving him a sideways glance.

"Really. Well, if you'll excuse me for a couple of minutes, I need to go wash my hands." Donna went to the wash room and disappeared around the corner.

"What are you doing?" Tony asked emphatically.

"Nothing, she introduced herself, and started a conversation with me."

"That's not what I mean, and you know it. Don't try playing some little game with her. She's really nice, a great waitress, and everybody likes her."

"Hey, I told her my name, and I thought she might figure it out from that. If she hasn't, I just see it as a chance to talk with her, and get a true reading on what she's like. Is that so wrong?" Nick asked.

"Just don't piss her off." Tony admonished.

"I won't, here she comes."

"Hey Tony, before I forget. I got him a beer while you were in the kitchen. I didn't put it on his tab because I didn't see it back there."

"Don't worry about it Donna, I'll take care of it." As he answered her, he again looked at Nick with disapproval.

Donna noticed the glance and asked. "Am I missing something here?"

"No, not at all." Nick quickly responded. "So, you were telling me what you thought of this place."

"Like I said, everybody here is great, and from what my friends from Coconut's tell me, I'm really lucky to be here."

"What do you mean by that?" Nick asked intently.

"Well, they say this place doesn't have near the turnover rate of most bars. The people that work here make better than average money, and the management..." Donna glanced at Tony as she continued. "...really knows what it takes to run a successful bar, and how to treat its people."

"Yeah, everybody loves Tony." Nick commented.

"Hey, I just run the place the way the owner wants me to." Tony said as he sipped his coke.

"Tony, you really are great to work with, but everybody says the owner is more of a friend than a boss." Donna added.

Nick sat there for a moment, taking a drink from his beer, and feeling Tony's eyes burning a hole through him.

"Okay, okay." Nick said to Tony, then he turned to Donna. "Actually Donna, I am the boss." He extended his hand once again.

Donna looked somewhat confused, or possibly a little annoyed. "So, is this some kind of game you play with new employees or something?"

"No, not at all. I just thought it would be a good way to do an impromptu interview, and find out a little about you. I'm really sorry if I've made you angry." Nick made sure his sincerity was apparent.

"Whatever!" Donna grabbed her plate off the bar and stormed into the kitchen.

"Way to go Nick. You probably just lost us our best employee other than Julie." Tony admonished.

"So what the hell are you waiting for…. go and patch things up." Nick replied.

A couple of minutes after Tony went after her, Nick saw Julie come through the front door. "Hi Baby, when did you get back?" She asked.

"Oh, just a little while ago. How's Frank?"

"Great. I talked to him this morning. He's out on a charter with two couples from Texas. He took them over to Nassau for a few days, he'll be back tomorrow."

"Good, maybe I'll have a barbecue this weekend."

"So where's Tony, and did you meet the new girl Donna yet? She's really great, I think you'll like her."

"Yes, I met her. Yes, I like her, but the feelings not mutual. And that's where Tony is, making sure she doesn't quit."

"Would you care to elaborate on what you just said." Julie had a tone of disapproval in her voice. She knew she was one of the few people that could get away with it.

Nick took the next few minutes to explain to Julie what had happened. Then excused himself, saying that it would be best if he were not there when and if she emerged from the kitchen.

Julie agreed, and offered one more admonishment, before joining Tony for damage control in the back. "You know I love you Nick, but you have to realize that some people get pissed off when you play with their heads like that."

Later that evening Julie called to tell him that they were able to get her to stay, at least for now. Still, Nick decided to avoid the bar for awhile, saying that he was taking a few days off after his last case. Nick told Julie to invite Frank and a couple of their friends over for a party on Saturday afternoon.

When the day of the party came, Nick was shocked to see Donna arrive with Julie and Frank. As he greeted them, she simply said hello and walked right passed him, following Julie to the kitchen with her chicken salad, which she always brought to Nick's picnics.

"So Nick, I heard you pretty well pissed Donna off, huh." Frank said with a smile.

"Yeah, I guess she doesn't have too great a sense of humor, does she?"

"Julie was none to happy either."

"Why would she be mad? I didn't do anything to her."

"Julie thought Donna would be the perfect girl for you, until you two met anyway. The two of them have become really good friends in a very short time. To be honest, I thought you two would hit it off too."

"To be honest, I am surprised to see her here today. Who else did Julie invite?"

"No one. She's hoping to work things out between you two."

Although nothing went terribly wrong, the afternoon saw Julie and Donna speaking to each other, and Frank and Nick speaking. However

Nick and Donna hardly said two words to one another, and Julie was obviously irritated. The next couple of weeks at the bar went about the same as the party, with the two hardly speaking.

Then one Monday afternoon, Tony needed the day off, and after the lunch crowd had thinned, only Nick and Donna were left in the bar together for a couple hours till the night crew were scheduled. They started doing some work, Nick stocked the bar, and Donna wiped down the tables.

After a while of tension, a man in his mid-twenties came into the bar and headed directly to Donna. Nick could see that she was surprised to see him, but could not here what was being said until she raised her voice to tell him to leave her alone.

"Donna, is everything all right?" Nick asked.

Before she could answer the man did. "Mind your own business, she's my wife."

Nick stopped and watched from the corner of the bar as the two exchanged some words. Suddenly he saw the man grab Donna by the arm and push her up against the wall. With that Nick instantly reacted, grabbing him from behind in a chokehold he had learned at the police academy. The man was quickly at the edge of unconsciousness as Nick dragged him out the front door.

As Nick let go of him he said. "Now, do you want to try putting your hands on a man, or do you only try that with women?"

He instantly took a swing at Nick, which was blocked and countered with a right cross, connecting flush on his jaw, and sent him sprawling to the ground.

"If I ever see you set foot in this bar again, I'll have you arrested." Nick turned and went back inside.

Donna was seated at the table she had been cleaning when the man had first gone over to her. As she stared blankly out the window Nick went over to the bar and grabbed a glass of ice water and a beer before going over to her.

"Here, pick one." He said as he placed the drinks before her. "Are you okay?"

Donna looked Nick in the eyes, the first time since the day they had first met. Her eyes on the verge of tears as she reached for the water. "I will be, thanks."

"Well, I'll leave you alone then."

As Nick went to return to the bar, Donna grasped his wrist. "I mean it, thanks for everything."

"Don't worry about it."

When Nick got back behind the bar, he grabbed a beer for himself. As he continued to watch her for a few minutes he saw her quickly drink down the beer he had taken to her. A moment later she was sitting at the bar, directly across from him.

"So, where do we go from here?" She asked directly.

"I'm not sure I understand what you mean."

"I mean, do I still have a job, or how does this effect my job, what?"

"As far as I'm concerned it has no effect on your job. No man that lays hands on you or any woman in my presence is going to get away with it, and they will never set foot in my bar again. And as far as you are concerned, you had nothing to do with it."

"Well than, could I ask you to do me a favor, and keep this quiet?"

"I'm not going to tell anybody, it's not my place. However, I will ask you to do me a favor."

"What?"

"I'd like you to promise me, that if he ever comes around to bother you again, whether it's here at the bar, or anywhere, you'll let me know immediately." Nick said as he wrote something on a napkin, and folded it in half.

"Why would you want me to do that?" She asked with hesitation.

"Because, whether it's you, or a total stranger, I don't put up with violence towards women." Nick slid the piece of paper across to her. "Here is my pager number, and my home number…do you promise to call if he shows up again?"

"Wow, I guess Julie was right, you really are one in a million. I should probably also say, maybe I overreacted to our first meeting. I'm sorry."

"I take total responsibility for that, but if you'll forgive me, I say we just forget it." Nick said as he offered his hand to her across the bar.

As Donna took his hand her eyes began to well again. "It's a deal. Now if you'll excuse me, I'm going to go freshen my make-up."

Later that evening, as the bar bustled with the usual crowd of regulars, and a sprinkling of tourists. Julie and others began to take notice of the change that had occurred in the interaction between Nick and Donna. The two were now actually speaking to each other, other than just relaying customers' orders. They were even smiling to one another when there was a lull in the action.

During one of these lulls, as Donna and Nick watched the basketball game on the television from the waitress station, Julie could no longer resist the temptation.

"Okay, which one of you is going to tell me what's going on?" Julie asked.

"What are you talking about?" Donna replied.

"What am I talking about? I'm talking about the fact that the two of you haven't said anything to each other since you met. And now, all of a sudden the two of you are as thick as thieves, talking, giggling, and I want to know why." Julie was insistent.

"Oh, that." Nick said as he glanced at Donna, and she looked at him. "Well, this afternoon was really slow, and as we were the only two here, the silence was really bothering me. I talked her into sitting down and hashing this out. I told her that I was really sorry, and that it was just a joke that was in no way intended to offend her."

"And I saw that he was truly sincere in his apology, just like you said he was Julie. So we decided to let bygones be bygones, and start over." Donna was looking back and forth between Nick and Julie as she finished his explanation.

"I've been trying to get the two of you to do that for several weeks now. Why all of a sudden?" Julie pressed.

"I guess it just took a couple of hours of awkward silence, with the two of us stuck, alone in the same room for it to happen." Donna answered.

"Well, it doesn't matter how it happened. I'm just glad it did." Julie reached around the two and gave them each a hug. "I knew that the two of you would get along if you just gave it a chance."

"Good." Nick said as he looked over her shoulder. "Julie, a new group just went over to your station. You want to go get their order? I am trying to make money here you know."

As soon as Julie was out of earshot, Donna reached around the corner of the bar and took Nick's hand to give it a squeeze. "Thanks for not saying anything about this afternoon, I would have been really embarrassed."

"I told you I wouldn't, and I meant it. It's nobody's business anyway." Nick returned the squeeze to ensure her, and returned to taking care of the customers seated at the bar.

The next several weeks saw Nick and Donna becoming very close friends, as well as Donna becoming the forth in the tight knit group which was Nick, Julie, Frank, and now Donna. After about three months of prodding Nick and Donna had become an item, to everyone's delight.

"Honey, dinner is ready." Donna called through the kitchen screen, but Nick did not reply. She opened the door and called again. "Honey…are you okay, dinner's ready."

Nick shook his head as if she had startled him, as he heard her words. "Huh. Oh, yeah, I'll be right in." he said as he gathered his thoughts from the past and put down the book he had been reading.

As Nick sat at the table with the girls, he saw that they had prepared a small feast. There were three different vegetable dishes, including his favorite stir-fry, two salads, and even the steaks he had thought of grilling had been cooked two different ways, broiled and breaded.

"Well you two sure have gone all out tonight. Any special reason?" He asked.

Donna was the first to answer. "I know how hard you've been working, and how the first thing you tend to neglect is eating meals on a regular basis." Donna was a health nut when they had first started dating, but with time, even she began eating red meat once in awhile.

"And I just thought it would be a nice thing to do, sort of to show my thanks for all the work you've been doing on my behalf." Julie added.

"In that case, thank you Donna for being so concerned for my well being, and Julie, a simple thank you with a hug will suffice…once I find out what really happened, that is." Both girls just smiled in reply to his words.

"So Nick, that must have been a very interesting book. Donna called you twice." Julie began.

"You seemed a million miles away." Donna observed.

"Not a million miles away, just a year and a half back in time." The girls seemed confused by his answer. "I was thinking back to when Donna and I first met, and how I almost prevented any of this. And how we finally made up and got together."

"You know, the two of you never told us how you finally resolved your differences." Julie mentioned.

Suddenly Nick and Donna were looking at each other, realizing that, in all this time, neither of them had told Julie the truth about that afternoon in the bar. Donna smiled slightly, knowing that Nick had never broken his promise to her of not telling anybody. And Nick smiled as well, he realized that she had not even confided their secret to her best friend.

Julie's words broke the stare between them. "You know, that's the same look you two got the last time I asked about what happened, and I don't want to know, I just want to say that I'm glad, however it happened, that you two finally got together."

After dinner, Julie approached Nick as he sat at the table drinking a cup of coffee. "Nick, would you mind going through those papers with me in a little while?"

"Sure Jules, just let me know when."

"I'm ready now, if you are?" She replied.

The two friends went into the living room, as Donna, knowing how difficult this would be, excused herself from them, and left the house to take a walk.

Julie sat on the sofa, next to the box Nick had retrieved from her home. She had seen the box before, yet had never looked inside of it. Frank had told her that all their important papers were inside, life insurance, their wills, mortgage papers, as well as other bank papers she would need should anything ever happen to him. They had always thought that day would have been so far off in the future that she always just said, "sure, whatever." They were both so young, and in good health. That the only possibilities that they had considered could take one from the other were, a car wreck, a hurricane, or maybe a freak accident while diving. They were wrong.

Looking at the box, Julie commented. "Nick, I don't have a key to this thing."

"I found one on the key ring you gave me. I already tried it at the house, it's open."

"Oh." She almost seemed to wish it would stay locked. As she opened it and placed it at her side, she removed a letter, which was lying on top. From his seat, directly across from her Nick could see her name clearly written on the front of the envelope. Julie slowly opened the letter and began to examine it.

Looking up at Nick, she said. "It's a letter to me from Frank, and it's dated our wedding day."

As she began to read, seeing that it was a letter of several pages, Nick leaned back and began to watch as she reacted to parts of the letter. A look of shock was the first reaction he saw, followed closely by a tear falling down her cheek. The following twenty minutes saw little reaction from her, until she placed the letter on her lap and began to sob.

"Are you sure you want to go through this Julie?"

"I wasn't, until I just read this letter." Julie took a deep breath before continuing. "He wrote me this letter on our wedding day, before the ceremony. In it, he goes on to tell me that although what he had told me, all of us, about his past, was a lie. He truly does, or did love me."

"I never doubted that for a minute." Nick interjected.

"Neither did I. But he says that he wasn't sure I would be able to love him if I knew what his past was. He goes on to talk about his father, and how although he loved him, he could not be a part of his life knowing what he did for a living, even though his father never tried to get him involved. In fact he says his father kept him as far from that as he could. Isn't that the same thing his father told you?"

"Yes it is, and that just makes me believe that drugs had nothing to do with Frank's death. Is there anything else I should know about in there?"

"Here, you can read it." Julie reached across and handed him the letter.

As Nick took the letter he didn't want to read it, at least not at that moment. "I'll read it later. Would you mind if I made a copy of it to show the police? Maybe then they will start looking for the real reasons behind what happened to him."

"What ever you think is best." Julie said as she reached back into the box of papers. "Let's see what's next, and why don't you come over here so you can see them with me? I don't want to keep anything from you that might help."

Nick moved over to be by her side as she removed an envelope that read "Mortgage". "Must be the bank papers to the house." he commented.

As she opened it, both knew immediately that they were not loan papers, they were the title to the house. "Am I wrong, or does this mean that the house is paid for?" She asked as she looked at Nick.

"That's exactly what it means Julie, and the boat is paid for as well." Nick added.

"You knew about this Nick?"

"I knew about the boat and the equipment for the business, but I only suspected about the house."

"Why would you 'suspect' that the house was paid for?" She asked, now somewhat wary that he had been holding back information from her.

Nick went on to tell her about what he had learned at the supply house, and the boat dealership, as well as what Angelo DiMarko had told him. "Well, that would explain why Frank always insisted on paying the bills and handling the money and all. Is there anything else you've not been telling me?"

"Just one thing. Frank's father asked me to see if you would be willing to meet with him. He'd like to meet the woman his son married. I told him that I didn't think now was a good time for that, I wanted to get to the truth and make sure he wasn't involved before the two of you met, I thought it would be safer for you."

"I know you did what you thought was best, but after reading the letter, I know that Frank wasn't involved in anything illegal. I think I want to meet him too."

"I'll tell you what, I'll let him know about the services for Frank, and tell him you'd like him to be there. After that, you two can decide if you want to speak more later."

"Okay, I'm sure he would want to be there anyway."

The next thing to come out of the box was a financial ledger that Julie said she had never seen before. Along with the monthly deposits from the business, and the household withdrawals, Frank had kept close accounting of an account from what seemed to be a bank in the Cayman Islands. Known as an alternative to Swiss bank accounts, the Cayman banks also offered private numbered accounts, with little questioning of large movements of cash. Also in the ledger, was a legal document giving Julie access to the account, should anything happen to Frank. It was drawn up by a lawyer in Grand Cayman, and Nick thought to himself that he should check out both the lawyer and the bank, and soon. Also attached to the ledger were a couple receipts for the rent on a safety deposit box, for which Nick had found a key on the key chain Julie had given him. Nothing else remained in the box, and Julie excused herself for the evening, saying she was going to take a shower and go to bed.

Nick stayed in the living room and read the letter Frank had left for his wife. It was just what Julie had told him it was, an apology to her for lying to her, and a statement of his love for her. On his second time through it, Donna entered through the front door. "Hi babe, how was your walk?"

"It would have been better if you were with me, but it was okay. How did things go here?" She asked as she sat down with him.

"Well, all in all, it went pretty good. Now I'm positive that the only lies Frank was living, was about his parents, he had nothing to do with drugs." Nick said as he handed her the letter. "And tomorrow, I'm going to take this letter and shove it down that D.E.A. agent's throat."

The following morning Nick woke up around seven a.m., and was showered and out the door by seven thirty. His first stop was the Dive Shack, where he quickly ran off two copies of the letter Frank had written to Julie. He planned on giving one to the police, and after a little thought, he decided to give one to Angelo DiMarko as well. Julie would probably not mind, and upon the belief that Frank had not been involved in illegal activities, Nick felt that Frank's father would appreciate reading something his son had written, in which he told his wife how much he loved his father.

By eight fifteen, Nick had arrived at the station, and Steve's car was in the parking lot. Nick proceeded directly up to the squad room on the second floor. As he entered he saw Steve talking to the two federal agents.

Steve, noticing Nick out of the corner of his eye, turned and began to meet him half way. "What's up Nick, you're here awfully early this morning. Have you got something?" He asked, reacting to the look in Nick's eyes.

"Don't bother meeting me over here Steve, what I have to say is for all of you." Nick said as he marched right up to the men standing around the table. "This may not be a death bed statement, but as far as I'm concerned, it carries even more weight."

"What is it?" Asked the FBI agent, Collins.

Nick tossed the envelope holding the copy on to the table. "It's a letter Frank wrote to his wife, two years ago, on their wedding day."

Collins quickly picked it up and began to open it as he asked. "What does it say, and where did you get it?"

"Julie, Frank's wife, asked me to go to her house and get some papers out of the safe Frank kept in their bedroom. Their will, insurance, and bank papers. Now that you released his body, she felt she would need them to make arrangements, and start to get her life in order. When we opened a little lock box that was inside, this was sitting in it addressed to her. It tells her the truth about Frank's past, everything from who his father is, to how, even though he loved him, he could not live with him because of how he made a living." Nick's attitude was more than one of "I told you so".

"If this stands up to our handwriting analysis, it will throw a new light on our investigation." Said Collins.

"I'm not so sure." interjected Bradshaw. "It could have been written just to make it look like he was not involved with his father."

Nick simply ignored Bradshaw's statement, and continued with Jenkins and Collins. "Now, maybe you'll begin to look into finding out why he was really killed."

"Unfortunately, if what you say is true, and Frank's murder doesn't involve DiMarko or drugs, it goes back to being a local investigation, and Bradshaw and myself will in all likelihood be taken off the case." Collins stated.

"You know that I'll do everything I can to find out, Nick. I didn't know him as well as you did, but I've always had my doubts about what they suspected." Steve approached Nick and extended his right hand. "And I want to thank you, in front of all these guys who had their doubts about you, for bringing this to us as soon as you had it."

"I told you I would cooperate in any way I could." Nick said this more for the others than for Steve to whom he spoke. "Now, if you will excuse me, I have some other things to take care of."

Nick left the station and went directly to the Sheridan on Islamorada, where he planned to give Angelo DiMarko a copy of his son's letter. He felt that perhaps his attitude toward the elder DiMarko should change, perhaps soften somewhat. Even though he did not approve of the man's "business", Nick couldn't help but feel compassion now for his loss, Nick knew what it was like to lose his parents, But he had always heard that the worst loss was that of ones child. Nick could only imagine what that was like.

Nick watched as DiMarko read, and reread the letter. Nick was somewhat confused. Frank's father seemed unaffected by what he was reading, no emotions were there, at least, none that Nick could see.

"Who else has seen this letter?" DiMarko asked.

"Julie, and the police. Why." Nick had no idea why these were the first words to come to DiMarko's lips.

"I just wanted to be sure that you took it to the fed.'s, so that maybe now they might try to find out what really happened to my son." He now showed some of the emotion Nick had expected to see.

"Well, we'll have to leave that up to the local authorities, the fed.'s said that if it doesn't involve you or drugs, they will be called off the case. But I can assure you that the officer heading the investigation is quite capable, and I have no intention of letting go either." Nick watched as his words seemed to go right past DiMarko. "I also wanted to inform you that I spoke to Julie about your wish to meet her."

Suddenly, DiMarko was far more interested in what Nick had to say. "And…when would she like to get together?"

"It's not quite that simple. She has some reservations about all this, and isn't exactly sure what you expect from her."

"I expect nothing. I told you I merely want to meet the woman my son married, and maybe get to know her a little."

"Well, I can only relay her message. She asked me to tell you that she would like you to be there at the services she is planning, and she will speak with you there." Nick could see that DiMarko was becoming angry with this. "After she speaks with you there, she will decide whether or not she will speak with you beyond that."

"When and where will the services be?" He asked angrily.

"The plans have not been finalized yet, but I will call you later today with that information. Would you like me to tell her you will be there?"

"Of course I will. I would also like you to tell her to spare no expense, I will pay for whatever she wants."

"It's not necessary, but I will tell her of the offer."

As the sunlight streamed into the room, Nick could feel the warmth of Donna's body beside him. Just knowing that she was there gave him a sense of security. Today was the day that he would help Julie bury her husband, and he wondered how she must feel waking up alone after having shared her life as well as her bed with Frank.

It seemed to Nick that Julie had been a little more at ease the past few days, since they had found the letter which had apparently put to rest the notion that Frank had been involved in something illegal. Although, Nick felt that it was just a temporary calm, Julie was probably just feeling a sense of relief to know that Frank had truly loved her, and not just been using her.

Nick looked over at the clock to see the time, it was only just past six, and the services were not set to begin until ten. He was surprised that he felt as awake as he did, he had last looked at the clock at about two a.m., while trying to fall asleep.

Knowing that it would be useless to try and go back to sleep for another couple hours, Nick carefully got out of the bed, so as not to awaken Donna. As he stood looking at her face, glowing in the warm morning sun, he couldn't help but feel so lucky to have her in his life.

Donna had had such a calming effect on him since she entered his life. Although he had been successful at opening his bar, and turning it into what he had dreamed it would be, his personal life had had its ups and downs. Nick had spent a lot of nights out partying with his friends, and woken up the following mornings regretting the night before. He had not been in a steady or healthy relationship since he had left Chicago, going out night after night with so many different women, that he couldn't even remember half their names. He remembered how Julie had often remarked on that being one of his major character flaws that she had difficulty overlooking, even stating that it may have been a factor in why the two of them had never been more than friends. But now Donna had changed all that, Nick, although never saying it out loud, had even begun to think about what it would be like to be married to her. Wondering what their children would be like, and whether or not he would make a good father.

Nick quietly left the bedroom, closing the door behind him. As he approached the kitchen, he smelled the coffee brewing. Turning the corner he saw Julie sitting with her back to him at the table. He hesitated to go further, wondering if he would be intruding on her private time on this most difficult of days.

Julie, sensing his presence, turned to look at him. "Morning, would you like some coffee? I hope I didn't wake you."

"You didn't. I just couldn't sleep." He said as he took a cup from the hooks over the sink, and joined her at the table.

"You know, this may sound strange, but the last two nights, even with what we're going to do today…" She could not bring herself to mention the funeral. "I've slept better than I have since this all began. Ever since we found Frank's letter, it's like a weight has been lifted from me."

Nick knew exactly of what she spoke, even though he had promised her that he would find out what happened to Frank, he had dreaded the possibility that he would have to tell her that he had indeed been using her in some way to cover some illegal activities. Except for Julie, nobody could have been more relieved by the letter Frank had left her. Now Nick was beginning to feel a new pressure. He had absolutely no idea why Frank had been killed. Although it could have been an act of random violence, Nick's instincts told him it was not. Sitting there across from Julie, Nick silently vowed to her and to himself that the day after the funeral, he would not stop until he knew what had truly occurred.

"Nick, by the way, I wanted to thank you again for setting up the gathering after the burial. It was really sweet of you to close the bar and take care of all the arrangements." Julie said as she looked into his eyes.

"You're my best friend Jules, I'll do whatever it takes to help you get through this. You know that, so let's just let it drop." She was referring to the fact that Nick had made arrangements to have a gathering of their friends and other mourners over to the bar after the funeral. Again, trying to make this as easy as he could for Julie, he did not want her to have to worry about going to the house and having people over. She had been staying with him because it was too much for her to go home knowing that Frank would not be there. However, Nick did not like the thought of all those people going to his home. Nick, Julie, and Frank shared almost all of the same friends, but many of Franks business associates would also be going, and it was only a select circle of friends that Nick would let into his private world, his home.

As Nick dressed for the day, in the obligatory dark suit, his mind drifted back to the last funeral he had attended. Just over five years earlier in the cold Chicago winter, it had been nearly twenty degrees below zero with the wind chill, that January morning. The pain of losing a parent had been magnified exponentially for him. He had lost both parents at the same time, suddenly, in a car crash. Twenty-five years old, and suddenly, the two people he had lived his life for were gone.

There were times when Nick had thought that he had been lucky. Perhaps, he thought, it would have been more difficult if one of his parents had been ill for an extended period of time. What if he would have had to watch, as the vibrant, loving person he had known, slowly became incapacitated? And how hard would it have been on the other parent, watching the one person they had chosen to spend the rest of their life with, wither away, and how hard would it have been to carry on without that life to share?

Although, he thought, he would have had the chance to reconcile his emotions, and been able to say some of the things he wanted to say to them. He could have thanked them for instilling the morals and respect for others, which had led him to be a cop in the first place. He could have told them one last time that he loved them, even though he knew they understood that he did.

"What do you think…does this look okay?" Donna asked as she stood in the doorway from the bathroom to the bedroom. She was wearing a plain black dress that came just above her knees, with a wide black hat framing her flowing golden hair, and bronze face.

"You look beautiful, Honey." Even as he spoke those words, Nick could see the look in her eyes. She had not wanted to here that; she wanted to be told that she looked appropriate.

Without a word, Donna quickly retreated to the bathroom and closed the door behind her. Nick stood there unable to explain to her why he had said what he did. Unable to tell her that he had been thinking of his parents, and that seeing her at that moment, regardless of what she was wearing, she looked beautiful to him.

In the past, there had been times that she would catch him deep in thought, when he was thinking about his parents. Early on she would try to get him to talk about it, trying to share his emotions, but that was one area he could not let her or anyone else into.

Donna, knowing how close Nick and Julie were, even asked Julie what she knew about his parents, and was told that it was not something he would ever talk about. From then on, she would just walk away and leave Nick with his thoughts, or sit beside him silently until he left that painful area in his mind. Nick had respected her wishes, and not pressed for information about her past marriage, and she knew that when he replied, "just thinking" that he didn't want to talk.

Nick's reluctance to speak about his parent's deaths was probably why neither Julie, Nick, nor Donna had ever really questioned Frank about his parents, once he had told them they were both dead, Nick thought to himself.

Now, as Nick sat alone in the kitchen waiting for Julie and Donna, drinking coffee, Donna entered once again. Now her hair was pulled back tightly, and she wore a veil attached to the front of her hat, which hid her face, except for the basic outline of her features.

"How's this?" She hesitantly asked again.

"Honey, you misunderstood my comment, I was referring more to how you looked to me in general, at that moment, not to how you looked in what you wore. You looked fine before, and you look fine now." Nick said as he gently took her hand in his.

"It's just that the way you said it, made it sound as though I had been getting ready for a night on the town. I don't want to look like I'm going to a party or something." Donna looked questioningly at him.

"I know honey. I guess I was just feeling depressed, and alone until you came in, then I was just so glad to see you and realize that I wasn't alone."

"Everybody feels depressed around funerals, but that's usually when they see that they have friends and family to lean on." As she spoke the word family, she saw in his eyes that she had hit a nerve. That instant, it was clear to her what had been going through his mind. "That's it, isn't it? You were thinking about your parents when I came into the bedroom, weren't you."

"Yes, I was." Nick looked away, and then at the floor as he answered her.

"I know that you don't like to talk about it, it's okay."

As Nick just stood there, he began to wonder why he couldn't talk about this with her. He shared every other aspect of his life with her, why not this? He felt as close to her as he had felt with anybody. Perhaps it was just his last defense from being hurt. Maybe keeping this one thing to himself was the last wall between them, the one that if something went wrong in their relationship, he could use to tell himself that it wasn't that important. She couldn't hurt him; she didn't even know him. He had never shared that pain that scared him so deeply.

"Thanks, maybe we'll talk about it later." Nick responded, as he had so many times before.

Donna also recognized this standard response, she knew that there would be no "later" this where topic was concerned. She and Julie had spoken about it many times before; she would just let it go.

"Good morning." Came the words from Julie's mouth, as she rounded the corned into the kitchen.

Dressed in a black pantsuit, looking quite businesslike. She never really liked to wear dresses or skirts, even though, on the rare occasion that she did, she looked fabulous. She had a very athletic body that looked great dressed up, or dressed down in an old faded pair of jeans and a tee shirt. Her eyes were red and puffy from a full night of tears, but now she would be the strong widow, for she did not want the pity of those who would come to pay their last respects to her husband.

Nick and Donna knew Julie would put on a brave face for all to see. The two of them were the two closest people in her life now, and she could share her true self with them, but she would rely on their strength to help her get through the day that lay ahead.

As the two watched her practice her outward appearance of strength, they could see a slight hint of emotion as her eyes began to well up. Julie walked up to the two and embraced them together.

"I know that I don't need to say it, but I want to thank both of you. I couldn't get through any of this with out either of you. I love the both of you." As she spoke her voice trembled, and they could feel her shudder as she squeezed even harder with each word.

As the three friends walked from the car to the small group of people that had already gathered at the cemetery plot, Julie firmly took Nick's left arm and whispered in his ear. "Please, don't leave my side!"

"I won't." Was his only reply.

Donna only heard Nick's answer, but instinctively knew what it was about. She gave his right hand a gentle squeeze, and gave him a kiss on the cheek as he turned to look at her.

The bright mid morning sun was casting long shadows from the trees and those that had already gathered. Everyone wore dark sunglasses to shield their eyes from the intense light, and Nick was not happy about that fact. Now that he and the authorities were convinced that Frank was killed for something other than drugs, Nick felt deep down in his gut, that the killer or killers would be here.

He would carefully watch everyone there, looking for some sign of guilt, stress, or unease that could not be explained by the circumstances that brought them together here. It would not be easy, whomever he was looking for would be hiding behind the shield of dark glass, the same shield he would use to observe the crowd, and it was becoming a crowd.

Many of the early arrivals were familiar to Nick. The employees from the bar, some of the regulars who were very fond of Julie and Frank, and some of the charter captains from the marina. Both fishing and diving operators from the marina were a relatively close group. They all made their livelihoods on the water with their boats, and shared any information that would help one another do good business. On occasion, they would even loan parts to keep boats running, knowing that the favor would be repaid, if the occasion ever arose.

As they reached the chairs that had been set up around the grave sight, the priest Julie had asked to preside over the service approached them. "Mrs. Marks, Mr. Thomas, how are you doing so far?"

"I guess I'm holding up all right, thank you, Father." Julie responded as Nick merely tilted his head.

"Unless you know of anybody running late, I think we can start in about ten minutes, as we planned."

"That will be fine, Father. Nick and some other friends have agreed to be the pall bearers, and they are already here."

"That's good, the casket is right there in the car, and I'll let you know exactly when to go over to it." He said to Nick. He then left them to go speak with some of the others.

"I'm going to go tell Tony and the others what we need to do. Why don't the two of you go take your seats? I think it would be a way to let everyone come over to you to express his or her regrets. They keep looking over to see if they should come." Nick told the girls as he gestured to the small groups that were speaking among themselves while keeping an eye on the three of them.

Nick stood there alone for a moment as Julie and Donna walked over to the chairs and were approached by a couple of the mourners. He reached into his coat pocket and took out his cigarettes and lighter. Suddenly he felt a hand on his shoulder.

"Hey buddy, how are you holding up." The voice came from behind him.

Nick turned to see Tony, his bar manager, and good friend. "I'm doing fine. Why?"

"Just asking. I know how close you are to Julie, and being one of your friends, I know how much you try to do to help, if you can. With this situation, you're not only there for her emotionally, but you are trying to find out what really happened, and that has to be putting you under a lot of stress."

"It's nothing I can't handle." Nick answered sharply.

"I didn't mean to imply that you couldn't, I just was trying to let you know that you're not alone. You can count on me, and all your friends, for anything you need."

Nick felt kind of bad for being short with Tony. As he took a long puff off his cigarette before tossing it aside, he turned and looked directly into Tony's eyes. "I know I can count on you. I'm sorry I snapped at you."

"No apology needed." Tony said as he slapped Nick on the shoulder. "Just keep it in mind."

After the six men carried the casket to the hole that had been dug in the earth, Nick resumed his place at Julie's side. Looking around at the large assembly, he saw Angelo DiMarko and his entourage seated over to the left. Mr. DiMarko was flanked by no less then eight men, all dressed in expensive dark suits and wearing sunglasses.

Nick recognized the two bodyguards seated on either side of their boss, but the other six, four of whom were standing behind them, were new to him. They were all keeping alert, watching what was going on. Watching all in attendance and those in the area visiting nearby gravesites, as well as an occasional glance at a sedan that had parked near the funeral.

Nick assumed that they knew as well as he who was in that car. He had found out from Steve that even though Collins and Bradshaw had been taken off the case, due to the fact that it was no longer considered in their realm of influence, the two federal agents had received permission to remain in the area as long as Angelo DiMarko stayed. Nick had approached the two to ask them to respect Julie's grief, and stay away from the service. Although they had refused, they did agree to try to remain as inconspicuous as possible. They had apparently done so, Nick did not think anyone other than himself and DiMarko's people had noticed the car.

The way the chairs were arranged, Nick had a view of every face there, except for Donna, Julie, and the priest. As he continued to scan the faces for any clues, he was occasionally distracted by the pressure Julie would apply to his arm. That was about the only time Nick would hear the priest's words as he delivered a basic Roman Catholic service, much like the one at his parent's funeral.

Still, Nick wished he could see the eyes of those gathered. He knew he would have that opportunity at the bar, when they would gather after the burial.

Now at the bar, Nick, Julie, and Donna were the first to arrive. As they entered, Nick was glad to see that Tony had taken care of everything, just as he had promised. Two new waitresses that had started just last week were seated at the bar, waiting for the crowd to arrive.

Julie and Donna immediately excused themselves to the ladies room, and the two waitresses approached Nick. "Hi Mr. Thomas, it's all set the way Tony told us to have it." They said as they directed his attention to a buffet that was set out.

Nick knew that the "Mr. Thomas" was due to their newness to the Dive Shack. He had seen them only a couple of times since they had started, and he had been very distant and formal, mostly due to the current circumstances. "It all looks fine, girls, but do me a favor and lose the Mr. Thomas. The name is Nick, and I prefer to be informal with those who work here, okay."

Both immediately seemed to loosen up a little. "Sounds great. Tony told us how close you were to Frank, just let us know if there is anything else you need."

Nick looked at both of them as he reached into his pocket for his wallet. Nick pulled out two hundred-dollar bills and handed each of them one. "Here, this is for working today, and for all the extra shifts Tony tells me you have been working to cover for Julie and Donna.

"That's not necessary, Tony already took care of today," said one. "And we're happy to help out with the shifts." Finished the other.

"Just do me a favor and take it. Consider it a tip." Nick insisted.

"Okay." They said as they put the money in their pockets. "Is there anything we can get you?"

"As a matter of fact, you can mix up three rum and Cokes." Nick replied, as he saw the girls returning from the bathroom.

"Coming right up." They said as they left for the bar.

Donna left Julie's side and went over to the bar. Julie came directly to Nick, and once again took his hand.

"How are you holding up Jules?"

"All right, I guess. Nobody has really said anything to me yet."

"They were just giving you some space, I'm sure that will change here." He said as he saw the people beginning to arrive. "It was the same way at my parent's funeral. Nobody said very much until we got back to the house. Once they saw that I wasn't having a nervous break down, they felt comfortable extending their regrets."

Julie's expression showed her shock at Nick's discussing his parent's funeral. It was the first time he had ever mentioned it to her, and it made her feel better, knowing that he shared some of the feelings she was experiencing. She also knew that was the purpose behind his words. "Thanks, but still, don't leave my side."

"Here, I think we can all use these." Donna said as she held out the drinks Nick had ordered.

"I know I can." Julie remarked.

As the front door of the bar opened again, Nick's attention was drawn to it because of the size of the group now entering. It was Mr. DiMarko and his bodyguards. As he watched, Nick felt the squeezing of his hand by Julie's increase.

"Honey, if you don't want him here, just say the word."

"No, it's not that. It's just that when he took off his sunglasses, I realized how much he looks like Frank."

Nick had realized the same thing the first time they met. And now Angelo DiMarko was coming over to meet his daughter-in-law for the first time.

As his men dispersed throughout the bar, DiMarko crossed the room to where they stood. In his fifties, he was as elegant in motion as one half his age. "Julie…" he paused as he extended his hand to her, "I wish we could have met under different circumstances."

Julie slowly took his hand, as if she were unsure how to react to this man. "So do I." Was her reply?

DiMarko saw that Nick was watching him closely. Obviously making sure that he would not unduly upset his friend. "I realize this is not the time or place, but I would like to get together with you to speak, if we could, before I return to New York."

"Like you said, I don't think this is the time or place, but I think I would like to know Frank's father a little better. His letter showed that he loved you very much." She hesitated for a moment, as if she were unsure that she meant what she had said. "Why don't you give me a call tomorrow, and we'll set something up. I am staying over at Nick's."

"I'll do that." He said, then leaving without another word.

"Are you all right?" Nick asked, as his words seemed to intrude on her thoughts.

"Yes, I guess he's just not quite what I expected. He doesn't seem like some big time mobster."

"Nowadays, they never do. It's not in their best interest to advertise, or live up to the old stereotypes. "Nick thought back to his days as a Chicago cop. Most of the country still thought of the days of Al Capone when they heard, Chicago mob boss, but Nick had lived there and seen it up close.

"Then how do you explain Garcia?" Julie asked as motioned to Nick with her eyes.

When Nick followed her glance, he saw Jose and his men, standing over in the corner of the bar, near the dartboards. Looking and acting very much the part of drug lord. "It's totally different, they're not the Mafia. The Cubans are still relatively new, they still feel the need to show who they are to get respect from others, and use brutality to guarantee loyalty, even more than the Italians ever did."

"Excuse me, Mrs. Marks." Came a woman's voice from behind them.

As Nick turned, he saw Jake Phillips and his daughter. "Julie, this is Jake Phillips and his daughter Karen."

Karen immediately extended her hand, as well as her sympathies. "I am very sorry for your loss Mrs. Marks. I know that we haven't met before, but I feel as if I know you. Frank always spoke of you, and of all his friends here at the Dive Shack"

"I know what you mean, Frank told me about all the times that you had helped him with his research. And please, call me Julie."

"Okay Julie." Karen then turned towards Nick. "It's nice to see you again Nick, and from Frank's description, you have got to be Donna."

"Why yes, I am. Although I don't recall Frank ever speaking of you, I'm sorry to say." Donna replied as politely as her curiosity of this part of Frank's life would allow her.

"No, I don't suppose he would have. Frank seemed as though he wasn't the type to talk much about his treasure hunting." Karen answered, knowing that Donna and the others were curious.

"Unless you've made a big find like I have, or you are doing it as a business like Michaels, most people look down on you, or make fun of you like you're crazy." Jake chimed in.

Nick took some offense to that remark, and decided to let it be known. "I don't think you know Frank, or our friendship well enough to make a crack like that."

"I think I know what he means, Nick. Until we were married, Frank never told me about it either. I think he felt like it was his hobby, and since none of us shared it, he never talked about it not even with me."

"I wasn't speaking of him exactly. As you know, I only met him once, I was speaking in general terms, and remembering not only how my friends, but even my family reacted." Phillips responded. "When I first told them that I was interested in sunken treasure, they thought it was some kind of joke. Then when they saw that I was serious, none of them said it directly, but I could tell that they thought I was kind of nuts."

Nick knew that his explanation was sincere, and that he had over reacted. "Sorry, I didn't mean to jump down your throat. I guess I'm just a little edgy today."

As Nick spoke, Julie gave his hand a squeeze, and Donna placed her arm around him and said. "We all are honey."

As the afternoon progressed into early evening, Julie seemed to relax, at least somewhat. She had already received the initial condolences from all in attendance, and by then most had broken into small groups throughout the bar, associating with those they had known prior to the days gathering.

As the time and the alcohol flowed, many were able to have conversations with her about topics other than Frank, and the small talk seemed to be easier on Julie.

"Donna, I'm going to step outside to the beer garden for some air and a smoke. Will you stay here with Julie?" Nick said as he leaned over and whispered into Donna's ear.

"Sure Babe, go take some time for yourself." She replied as she rubbed her hand on his shoulder.

Nick awoke suddenly. Something in his dreams had given him the answer to Frank's death, but now it alluded him. He was stuck at that point when one first awakes, knowing that something important has just been revealed in a dream. Yet it somehow remains just beyond one's grasp, locked in the subconscious from which it has emerged.

He lay in bed, very still, trying not to fully awaken, for then he might lose contact with this revelation from his sleep. He hoped he might even fall back asleep, thinking it might return to him, or perhaps knowing now of its importance he could will himself to remember the details the next time he woke. Nick began to realize that all his focus had merely served to bring him completely to consciousness, and the tension in his stomach told him that he was on the verge of something very important. He had learned to trust his instincts, his gut feelings. They were tools that man had developed over centuries, but had since begun to discount, but Nick had learned to trust his, and use them as a tool.

Nick began to think back to one case in particular, from his days back in Chicago. Although he did not know the Jackson family prior to being dispatched to their home to take a missing persons report, over the course of the investigation he did grow close to them.

His first meeting with them had the mother Kathy in hysterics, and the father Tom, trying to be the pillar that supported the family with his strength. Although he gave a valiant effort, Nick could see the pain, and fear, in his eyes each time his daughter's name was mentioned.

Jill was a twenty-one, third year student at DePaul. She lived at home and worked forty hours at the Gap, while maintaining a 3.8 G.P.A. at a demanding college full time. Now, without any possible explanation that they could think of, she had disappeared without a trace, two days earlier. She had left for class at nine in the morning, like she did every Tuesday, and now at eight o'clock on Thursday night, she had not shown up or even called. Nick was informed that Jill was a very responsible girl that would call home if she were going to be as much as five minutes late, for anything.

Even as he questioned her friends, co-workers, and classmates, Nick continued to here them all sing the praises of the perfect girl. Yet, either they were fooled into believing her act, or something terrible had befallen her.

Nick had determined that Jill had stopped at a Starbucks coffee, as he had been told she did every morning, whether on her way to class or work. The employees that had taken care of her noted that she was her usual upbeat self, and had ordered her usual grande vanilla latte. It did however, seem as though she were in a hurry, she would often take fifteen minutes or so to chat with some of the staff, one of whom she had gone to high school with. That day had been different, she had entered somewhat hurriedly, and told them that she did not have time to stop and talk, when they tried to engage her inn the usual chitchat. But that was the only thing that had seemed even slightly out of the ordinary.

For about two weeks following his first meeting with the family, Nick had devoted more time to that case than any other. It was partly due to the Jackson family staying in daily contact with the department, Nick specifically. They were aware that he was doing everything he could to bring their daughter home to them, even double-checking the work of other officers, on his days off.

At first the Jackson's had questioned why he had gone so far as to give them his home and pager numbers. As Nick considered his reply, he found himself realizing that in only three years on the force, he had already become as jaded as some of the fifteen or twenty year veterans. The only answer he could give the family, was that he was so accustomed to dealing with the dregs of society, that the thought of something happening to someone like their daughter, simply seemed to be driving him, even without his realizing it.

Finally, after a night of restless sleep, Nick awoke with an unexplainable feeling, deep in the pit of his stomach. As the day progressed, he continually tried to focus his mind on whatever he was doing. Yet, still he could not shake the feeling, and he somehow knew that something bad was going to happen that day. Nick was so certain of his feeling that he had spent his lunch calling his mother to make sure that she and his father were both all right.

"Everything's fine here, and your father is doing fine too. He's still not smoking, and I wish you would do the same." She answered in a half scolding tone that only a mother could use with a son, followed by one of concern. "I think you're working to hard on this Jackson case, it's all you think or talk about lately, and it has got to be catching up with you."

He knew that she was referring to the way he had acted a few nights earlier, when he had gone over for their weekly family dinner. From the outset, she had commented on how tired he looked, and how stressed. He had tried to explain to her, the situation of the missing Jackson girl. But knowing how caring and compassionate a son she had raised, it had only served to have her watch him more closely. She had spent the rest of the night driving him nuts, as only his mother could, commenting every time his thoughts seemed to wonder, and telling him that he should leave the work at work. The thing that had driven him the craziest, was that she had been 100% right, every time she thought that she had caught him thinking about the case.

By four in the afternoon, Nick had begun to believe his mother had been right, that it was just stress, even though the feeling was still with him. Then, for some reason unknown to him, a call came over the radio for him to go immediately to the station and meet with someone. Before the dispatcher had even finished, Nick knew that this would explain his tension of the day. As he drove to the station his anxiety grew with each block, he wanted to know who was waiting for him, and why. But he knew it would be useless for him to ask the dispatch center, for they had merely relayed a message.

Upon entering, Nick was immediately summoned to the shift supervisor's office. Sergeant Swanson was well liked and admired by those above and below him. He had long since made it known that he would not test for the position of lieutenant, he felt that he was more effective on the streets with his men, and would retire before accepting a desk job. He felt his place was with his men, and they all appreciated having him there.

"Nick, this is Kane County Sheriff's deputy, Green." Swanson offered.

"Hi, it's nice to meet you." The deputy said as he extended his hand.

Nick took his hand firmly as he inquired as to why he had been summoned. "What can I do for you?"

"Well, it has to do with a missing persons report we received over the wire from you guys. Your sergeant here, tells me that it's your case, it's about the Jackson girl."

"Yeah, that's mine. Have you got something on it for me?" He asked with hope, yet expecting the worst.

"We found a body that fits the description, late last night. It was in a quarry in Batavia." The deputy answered, as he produced a picture from the file in his hand.

As he looked at the photograph in his hand, Nick had the urge to vomit. Although he had seen his share of dead bodies, both in person and in pictures, many in worse condition than Jill's. He had somehow become connected to this girl that he had never met. Through speaking with her friends and family, he too felt a sense of loss.

It was from that day on, that Nick had learned to trust and rely on his gut feelings, and instincts, and they had never been wrong since. The images from Chicago, and the Jackson family, were now stuck in his mind.

As Nick poured himself another cup of coffee, he realized that he had sat there and drank nearly the whole pot, by himself. With as strong as he made coffee, he knew that he had enough caffeine in his system to stay awake through an entire midnight shift on the force. He looked over at the clock on the oven, and saw that it was almost four a.m., the sun would be up in about an hour.

With no hope of sleep, and not wanting to wake up the girls after the funeral, Nick went over to the dryer and removed a pair of jeans and a sweatshirt. He quickly got dressed, and left a note on the counter.

> Donna,
> couldn't sleep, decided to go for a drive.
>
> > Love,
> > Nick

As he drove out of the driveway in his jeep, Nick could feel the cool, dampness the overnight dew had deposited on his seats, and in the air. The morning sun would not take very long to burn off the moisture, or the freshness the night had left.

Without even thinking about his destination, Nick found himself parked in his usual space at the marina. As he looked out at the boats, he saw his, gently bobbing in the small waves the breeze had stirred. He next found himself instinctively looking over at Frank's, as though he expected him to appear on deck and ask Nick to join him out on a charter for the day, or if he had no clients to take out, he would talk Nick into playing hooky from his responsibilities at the bar and go off to find some new dive spot the other services had not yet found.

The tension in his stomach told him none of that was going to happen, so he forced the images from the past out of his thoughts. He knew that he needed to remain alert, for something today would reveal the answers he was searching for. As he made his way to his boat, he could hear some of the fishing charter captains calling their greetings to him. Nick's only response was to glance in the general direction and wave briefly. They all knew what had happened, and most had gone to the service the day before. They would surely understand if Nick did not stop and engage them in conversation.

Nick began throwing switches on the cockpit console before him, starting with two, which were disguised as meaningless marker lights. In fact, they were electrical disconnects, which if not in the proper one of four positions each, nothing on the boat would function. He gave the whirring pumps a couple of minutes to vacate any fumes that may have collected in the engine compartment, and might ignite when the engines were started. While he waited, he watched to see where most of the boats were heading as the left the marina. Depending on who caught what, and where, the day before, the fishing charters would often wind up in the same area. Nick merely wanted to be alone, and would head off in whatever direction seemed to be the most vacant.

As Nick brought his three engines to life, one by one, he saw some movement off to the port side. There should not have been anything out there, his was the last boat down that row. He realized that there was a sailboat anchored about thirty yards out from him.

The sudden roar of his engines had woken someone sleeping on board, and they were on the deck with a flashlight. Nick's engines must have startled them, since the other boats heading out at that time made it a point to be as quiet as possible, and boats such as his were rarely heard before eight or nine in the morning.

Being fifteen miles off shore, with the only sounds to be heard those of the wind and the sea, as he let himself drift in the current, it had not eased any of his thoughts, as he had hoped it might. He checked his watch, and saw that it was half past nine, so he decided to make his way casually back to shore to find out what the rest of the day held for him.

About half way back, Nick's pager went off. It was Julie; she was calling him from her house. He figured she was just calling to see what he was up to, since she had only entered her code of 0-0-1. Nick gave everybody their own code to enter when paging him, so he could tell whom it was, regardless of where they were calling from. They also knew to enter 9-1-1, if it were urgent that he reply. Since she had not done so, Nick decided to wait until he got back to the bar, before he would return her call, he would be there in about forty-five minutes and would call her then.

Just as he was telling himself that he could wait to return Julie's call, his pager began beeping again. This time the code was 1-1-1, 9-1-1, it was Donna, and apparently important. Realizing that his cell phone was down in the cabin, Nick began to stop the boat so that he could retrieve it. In the time it took him to do so, his pager sounded twice more, once from Julie, and once from Tony. Each subsequent beep had a more ominous tone, Nick knew that the sound coming from the beeper had not changed, so it must have been his instincts at work, trying to tell him something. But what was it? The only way to find out was to return the calls. Once his phone was in hand, he decided to make Donna the first call, she had been the only one to include the 9-1-1 code.

"Nick, is that you?" She asked, anticipating that it was.

"Yeah Babe, what's wrong?"

"I don't know, it's Julie. She has been calling here every couple of minutes, trying to get a hold of you, but she hasn't said why. Only that she has to see you. So hang up with me and call her." Before he could even respond, Donna hung up the phone.

Nick immediately dialed Julie's house. "Hello?" She asked.

"Julie, it's me. What's up?"

"Nick, I went to the bank. I found some things in the safety deposit box. I think they're important. Where are you?"

Something in her voice told him not to ask what she had found over the phone. "I'm on the boat, I can be at your house in twenty minutes."

"Okay, I'll be waiting." She hung up on him immediately, as well.

True to his word, Nick arrived in her driveway twenty-one minutes later. Before he could even turn the engine off, Julie came bounding out the front door.

"Nick, what took you so long?" She didn't wait for his reply; she just took him by the arm and led him inside the house.

"All right I'm here, what did you find?" Nick asked as they stood in the living room.

Julie hurried over to the coffee table, where she ripped open a shopping bag, as she answered his question. "I don't know where this stuff came from, or why Frank had it. Something just told me that it was important, and that I should show it to you right away."

It was as if a twenty-pound cinder block had just dropped on his head, Nick was struck with an answer to at least one of his questions. If not the who, he now knew the why Frank had been killed, and he remembered part of his dream.

"Well, what do you think?" Julie asked with such anticipation, she looked like a child waiting for her parents to give her the answer to the meaning of life, or in this case, the death of her husband.

As Nick hesitated to answer, he could feel her eyes burrowing into him. Although she had the right to be told everything he knew, his instincts to protect her, told him not to let her know the truth. After all, possessing these items had led to Frank's murder, and he was not about to let anyone hurt her too.

"I'm not sure, but I think I know who to ask." He was certain she could tell he was lying to her, and that she was going to call him on it.

To his surprise, she didn't. Julie simply returned the items to the bag and handed them to him without question. All she told him was that she was going to go to the bar and work the lunch shift.

Nick was not sure whether she was shocked that she had been so wrong about the importance of the bag, or if she simply decided to let him proceed as he saw fit, and trust him as she always had.

Nick sat in his jeep as Julie drove out of sight, before removing the contents of the bag to look at them more closely.

The first thing to emerge, was a clump of coral, about the size of his fist. Partially encased within the coral, Nick was looking at gold coins that could only be Spanish doubloons.

Next, was something so unique, that even from across the room he had recognized it, although he had only seen a picture of it, a cross, ten inches long and five inches wide. It was heavily adorned with jewels of all types, but mostly diamonds and emeralds. The cross had also caused him to remember his dream, he had been on a ship in the middle of a storm, and was going down fast.

Seeing the cross had made it clear, but there was something wrong. Nick had recognized details of the cross, which he did not remember seeing in the painting in Frank's book. Yet he knew, somehow, that they belonged there. But how?

Nick began to realize that he must have seen another depiction of Captain Colunga's gift from the Queen of Spain.

While Nick drove to Key West, he was unsure of how he would proceed, but he knew the place to start was Jake Phillips. He would be able to tell him if he truly had what he thought he had in his Jeep.

The more he thought about it, the more he began to question showing the artifacts to Phillips. Nick knew that Phillips was the foremost expert in the area, but perhaps Frank had thought similarly, and it had led to his death. No, Nick would need to be more careful about how he approached him, and later Michaels, if Jake and Karen proved not to lead to any answers.

Before arriving at the Phillips' museum, Nick stopped at a department store in Key West. He purchased a Polaroid camera and film to go with it. Next he went to a secluded area, and laid out the items in his possession. So as to try and disguise where and when the pictures were taken, he laid out a blanket from the back of his jeep.

Nick began to take pictures of the cross from every angle, including close-ups of the details he had not seen in the book. He hoped he could get some insight about Jake, and or Karen, by their reactions to them. Or perhaps they could at least confirm what he had. He could not believe that this man, who had sympathized with Frank's position of keeping his hobby to himself, at the bar after the funeral, could be the cause of Frank's death.

And Karen, she had displayed a deep sense of loss, and expressed a closeness, or friendship that Nick thought was out of line. Until Julie, who could sense his unease with her words, had told him that Frank had spoken much the same way about Karen. She told him that she could understand the friendship they had, that it was an intellectual one, that stemmed from many long hours working together towards a common goal of finding a historic find under the sea. Besides, Frank had been very understanding of Nick and Julie's friendship, when he had first become involved with her.

Nick decided to take the piece of coral itself in with him. He thought it might help prove that Frank had not merely duplicated, somehow, a cross he had seen depicted somewhere.

When he entered the museum, he saw Karen seated at a desk in the library area. Her back was turned to him, so she continued to tap away at the keyboard of her computer, as he approached.

The only others he saw in the place, was a married couple with two children. The children clamored loudly, asking questions at each display. The parents indulged the inquisitive kids, while occasionally checking to see that they were not disturbing anyone else. With a smile to the parents, and towards the children, they were reassured that Nick did not mind the commotion.

As he approached Karen from behind her left shoulder, he could see that she was on the Internet, having a conversation with somebody. "Excuse me Karen, are you busy?"

She turned around somewhat startled. "Oh, Nick. Hi, how are you?"

"Fine. I was wondering if you· or your father could spare me some time?"

"Of course, just give me a minute to wrap this up." As she spoke, she took note of the bag in his left hand.

Nick watched as she told whomever she was on-line with, that she needed to go, and to let her know if they came up with anything.

"Sorry about that, what can I do for you Nick?" She asked, again glancing at the package he carried.

"No, I'm sorry. I should have called to make an appointment first."

"Don't be ridiculous, I'm assuming this has something to do with Frank, and my father and I will help in any way we can. And if it doesn't, you were a friend of his, and that alone makes you welcome here anytime you want." Again her sincerity was unmistakable, or she was a great actress.

"How about your father, is he available? I would really like both your input on this." Nick said, but what he really wanted was to see their reactions at the same time, or to see if one tried to control the others answers. However, if he spoke with them separately, he could see how much their answers varied, or if they were too similar, it could tell him that they had rehearsed the answers.

"I'm sorry, he isn't in yet." Karen glanced at her watch. "But if you don't mind waiting, he usually gets here around one o'clock, and it's quarter till now."

Nick paused for a moment, debating with himself, how to proceed. "Well, I guess growing up with all this around you, you're probably an expert yourself."

"Growing up with the father I have, I probably knew more than most people on the subject of sunken treasures, but I am an expert because I have degrees in history, and a Ph.D. in European studies." She stated confidently. "Although my father is "THE" expert around here, he has the education, the practical knowledge, and the reputation." She concluded.

Nick heard the pride in her voice as she spoke of her father. "I guess your education is why you're in charge of the library here."

"I run the library because I enjoy it. The only reason I don't have the practical, is that my father and I haven't found a wreck in the books, with a high enough likelihood of being found. Sooner or later we will, then I'll get my chance."

"So why do people like Frank, or Craig Michaels, continue to search the way they do?" He asked, watching her closely, trying to get a feel for her, so he could judge the truthfulness of answers to come.

"Don't even think about putting Frank in the same category as Michaels. The two of them have absolutely nothing in common." She was clearly annoyed with her perception of his linking the two in some way.

"I'm not sure I understand," Nick said as he sat in the chair next to her desk. Bringing himself down to eye level with her, trying to make the situation more casual, rather than an impromptu interrogation.

"I know, I'm sorry. It's just that I get really pissed, when I here somebody try to put Craig in the same class as my father, or even Frank for that matter." Karen's blood pressure began to recede. "My father and I do what we do in the context of history. We want to find out more about what was happening at the time, and share what we learn. Even the artifacts we bring up, we look at it as sharing the art of that period, with everybody. Craig is in it strictly for profit. He and his consortium of investors, only want to find and sell as much gold and jewels as they possibly can, to whomever they can find to pay the most."

"Look around, your father has done quite well since finding his wreck, and I have never heard anybody say that he was in it just for the money." Nick remarked.

"I never said that my family didn't make quite a bit of money from his find. But look around yourself, everything of historical value is still here, still together. It didn't matter what it was worth, It's all still here." She spoke with a passion that was rare to see in anyone.

At that moment, Nick knew that she was not involved in Frank's murder, and by extension, Jake probably wasn't either. After all, he had instilled his values in his daughter. "So tell me why you don't put Frank in the same category as Michaels? From what little I know from the books I found in his office, Frank was looking for the ship that had the most gold of all."

"Anybody, including me and my father, would love to find that ship. It's the most famous that one could find, it has the most mystery behind it, and it's the one we know the least about. The one that finds that ship will surpass all others in the history books, including my father." She had a strange glint in her eyes as she spoke the last sentence. "As for Frank, he wasn't in it just for the history, he was also interested in the adventure of it all, the glamour. He loved scuba diving, as I'm sure you know, and his searching was an extension of that."

Truer words were never spoken; Frank did love diving. So did Nick, as did most that got the opportunity to practice the sport. Those Nick knew, and dove with from Chicago, spent much of their time, either planning their next dive trip, or reminiscing about their last trip.

"So Frank wasn't as virtuous as you and your father, but he wasn't as evil as Michaels either?"

"That's not at all what I was trying to say. If anything, Frank had the purist motive of all, he was doing it because he loved it." Again, as she spoke, she did so with signs of deep attachment for Frank.

"Hi Honey, hi Nick." Jake said as he leaned in and gave his daughter a kiss on the cheek.

This time it was Nick who had been startled by the voice behind him. "Hey Jake, how are you? Next time, make a little more noise before you come up behind a guy."

"Sorry, you two seemed to be in some deep conversation, I tried not to interrupt until there was a break." He said with a wry grin. "And I agree with Karen, Frank's were the purist of motives. They are the same ones I had when I started. I guess now I like the respect I get from other hunters, and scholars alike."

"Daddy, how long were you back there listening?" Karen asked, unaware how much Nick wanted to know the answer to that same question.

"Oh, just about a minute." He replied.

"Well, now that you're both here, is there any chance of us speaking in private?" Nick had noticed that there were more people milling around the exhibits now. The couple with the two children, now kept them close by their side, and spoke amongst themselves much softer.

"Sure, we can go to my office." Jake suggested.

As Nick and Karen rose to go with him, Nick grabbed the package from the corner of the desk, and instantly noticed Jake's gaze upon the bag, along with the return of Karen's.

"So, are you going to share with us what's in the bag once we get in Dad's office?" She finally asked.

Nick was stunned by the directness of her question, but tried to hide it in a casual response. "What makes you think that there is anything of interest to you in this bag?"

"You are kidding, aren't you?" She asked coyly.

"No…I'm not." Was Nick's only reply.

"Okay, I'll tell you." She began, then pausing, deciding where she should begin. "First of all, you're investigating the murder of someone I know was searching for sunken treasure. Secondly, you seem more interested in that topic than ever before. Next, you carry that bag as though it is very important to you. And finally, the only people that bring things in here are tourists that have been shopping for souvenirs, and don't have a car to leave it in." She stopped briefly to see if her words were registering with him. "You're no tourist, and you drove down here, so you could have left it in your car. The only other people that bring stuff in here want my father to check it out and tell them if they found something of value or importance. Remember, all I do is pour over books, maps, pictures, or anything else, studying every detail over and over, looking for something someone else missed, or didn't think was important. And I'm very good at what I do." Karen concluded firmly.

"Yes, I now know that you are." Nick admitted. "Why don't we go in to the office, and I'll clue the both of you in. Or should I say, have the two of you clue me in?"

The three of them went to Jake's office, and settled themselves in around a large conference table, over in one corner. Jake turned on a bright light that hung over the center of the table, and brought over a large wooden box, before seating himself with the other two.

"All right Nick, lets see what you've got there." Jake said as he began removing things from the box at his side. First, was an assortment of magnifying instruments, everything from a jeweler's eye piece, to a free standing unit with its own light source. What came next, Nick assumed, were the types of tools Frank must have used to clean the coral, and other debris, from the cross and the coins.

As Nick began to reveal the contents of the paper bag before him, he realized that he felt no apprehension over doing so. "Here it is. What can you tell me about it?" He asked as he placed the piece of coral and two loose coins on the table.

"Give us a couple minutes, and we'll let you know." Karen said, as she took the items. First she took a brief glance at the coral, then handed it to Jake. Next, she looked at both coins side by side and quickly realized what Nick already knew; they were identical. She kept one in front of her, and passed the other to her father.

Jake was intently trying to extricate one of the coins from the lump before him. He took a brief look at the loose coin, then went right back to work on the coral.

Nick watched as they worked, studying both to see if they found anything that held their interest. Other than focusing on their tasks before them, he noticed nothing. For the time being, he decided to keep the pictures to himself.

Meanwhile, Karen was flipping through some books she had retrieved from a shelf behind Jake's desk. She occasionally stopped to check something on the coin, then went right back to the books.

"Well, this one is the same as those two. So I figure they came from the same place as those did." Jake finally announced. "What did you come up with?"

"I put them at ten, to twenty years more recent than anything we have from your wreck, dad." She answered.

"That puts us in the right time frame, but several ships went down before, and after. It could be from one of them." Jake observed.

"I know, but that is as good as I can do from just these coins." She turned to Nick now. "Do you know where they were found? That might be of help too."

"No, Julie just found them in Frank's safety deposit box. She didn't even know that he had one, until we found the key for it on his key ring." Nick was not yet ready to reveal more. "If that is all we can get from these, I guess they're not as important as I thought. I'll just take them back to Julie and see what she wants to do with them."

Karen took the to loose coins from Jake, and passed them to Nick. "I'm sorry we couldn't be of more help. If you find anything else you want us to look at, just bring it by. We'll be glad to help anyway we can."

"Well, I'm sorry to have wasted your time." Nick replied as he noticed Jake placing the chunk of coral still in his hand, on a small scale, then punching some numbers into a calculator. "Have you got something, Jake?"

"Not really." Jake double-checked the numbers in the display. "It's just that there are twelve to fifteen more coins in this. I was thinking that if you left it here, I could get them out without damaging them, and who knows, there might even be one that's different, that might tell us something new."

Nick knew that he was going to leave it with them, but he acted as though he weren't sure. "Well, I guess that would be all right."

"Great, leave me your number in case I find something." Jake was genuinely pleased.

Karen walked with Nick to the front door of the museum. "Dad is really excited. It's been a long time since he had the chance to work on something new. Even if they are just some coins stuck in a chunk of coral, they're not any we've worked with before. Anyway, I wish we could have been more help."

Nick began the drive home filled with mixed emotions about the day's events. On the one hand, his gut feeling had proven to be right, in a sense. He had found what he believed to be the actual motive for Frank's murder. On the other hand, he still had no idea who had committed the crime.

He had also wanted to go by and see Craig Michaels, but a call to his offices, had revealed that he was out on his boat, and would not be back for two, or three days. In fact, his secretary informed Nick that he had been out for the past week, and much of the past month, only coming in for a day, or two at the most, to get supplies for the boat.

Something had told Nick that the secretary thought something odd about the information she had just imparted to him. Perhaps it had been something in her voice or inflection. Or perhaps it had been that she had taken it upon herself to include that information, without his asking for it. Maybe she had just included it, as an explanation of sorts, for why her boss had not attended the services for Frank. Nick had personally notified all of Frank's friends, and associates, but only Craig Michaels had not attended, nor sent so much as a card of condolence to Julie.

Nick arrived back at the Dive Shack around six in the evening. He walked in to the usual greetings from his friends and staff, and to Donna behind the bar.

"Hi Baby, where have you been all day?" She greeted, while at the same time, looking past him towards the dartboards.

"I was down talking to the Phillips', having them take a look at some things Julie found today."

"She told me about that. What did you find out, was it something important?"

"Well, sort of." Nick hesitated. "Promise me that you won't say anything."

"Of course I won't, you know that."

But Nick knew the opposite to be true when it came to keeping something from Julie. The two of them were as thick as thieves, and no matter how close he and Donna were, she always told Julie everything. Donna would try to explain it as a kind of bond women shared, but even Julie didn't buy that, for her loyalties always stayed with Nick. She would remind Donna that she had been friends with him long before Donna had entered either of their lives, and had been there for her every time she had needed him.

Perhaps he could use this second hand line of communication to Julie, to his advantage. If Julie had believed him when he had underplayed the significance of the things she had found, it would not matter. However, if she had seen through him, as he suspected she had, Donna might be able to convey the seriousness of why.

"I still have no clue as to who killed Frank, but I am certain of why he was killed."

Donna stood behind the bar, just staring at him with her mouth wide open, aghast at what she had just heard him say. "Nick…you haven't told her that. Why?" She asked angrily. "She said that you acted totally uninterested in what she had found."

"I know." Nick said, feeling ashamed for having lied to Julie, but knowing that he had done the right thing, what was best for her. "Donna, the things she found were the reason Frank was killed. If she knew what they were, or why they were so important, she would be in danger too. I've already lost one important person in my life; I'm not about to let her, or you, come to any harm, especially if I can prevent it. I told you that I have no idea who did it, so let me do it my way, I know what I'm doing." His tone was half scolding, and half pleading.

She knew he was right. "Okay, I'll let it drop, for now." With that said, she turned and walked to the other end of the bar.

Nick simply walked out of the bar, not even acknowledging some who tried to say hello to him. Within minutes, Nick was sitting on the porch at his home with a beer in his hand, looking out over the open sea, letting his mind wander from all the worries that had consumed him the past few weeks.

As each subsequent beer made its way down, Nick was able to remove himself further from his own thoughts, until finally, he dozed off into a restful sleep in the hammock, suspended between two palm trees, out in the back yard.

"Hey, Sleeping Beauty, wake up, or should I kiss you first?"

The familiar voice brought Nick back to the real world from his dreams. "You kiss me, and it will be the last thing you ever do." Nick replied as rolled his head over, seeing Steve looking down at him.

"Come on Nick, if you keep talking like that, I'll start to think that you don't care anymore."

"Whatever." Nick glanced at his watch as he sat up, his head spinning from the alcohol. It was almost midnight, he had slept for about five hours, and Donna would be at the bar for at least two more.

"I have been trying to get in touch with you since eight o'clock. Donna told me you left the bar hours ago, and she thought I should talk to you. She said that you might need help with something." Steve was far more serious now.

Nick wondered how much Donna had told him, she didn't have any details, so it couldn't be much. She must have been worried about him, after he made it so clear that she and Julie were safer if he did not tell them all that was happening. "Well, that depends on who I'm talking to, my friend Steve, or Detective Jenkins of the Monroe County Sheriff's office."

"I would have thought that question wouldn't need to be asked. Wasn't it answered to your satisfaction when I let you know that the feds were following you?" Steve asked with no emotion.

Nick was even surprised at himself for asking what he just had. "You're right, I had no reason to say, or even think, anything like that. I'm sorry." He said as apologetically as he possibly could.

Steve looked down at the ground and kicked one of the half dozen or so beer bottles at his feet. "Enough said, we'll just write it off to the beer, or to all the pressure you have been putting yourself under lately. Don't give it another thought."

He was glad he understood, Donna had been right to send him, Nick was going to need his help to finish this. Nick spent the next two hours telling him everything he knew, and what he believed. When he finally finished, Steve just sat there, taking in, and trying to process everything he had just been told.

"So you're telling me, that Frank Marks, a.k.a., Francis DiMarko, was killed because he found an old Spanish galleon, loaded with treasure?" Steve finally asked.

"That is exactly what I am telling you." He replied firmly.

Steve could hardly believe his ears. "I need a beer." Was the only response he could manage at that time. So he stood up from the tree stump on which he sat, and made his way to the house.

Nick followed right behind him, but did not stop in the kitchen, as Steve went to the refrigerator for a drink. Instead, he went to one of the bedrooms that he had converted into an office, and retrieved the book that held the picture of Captain Colunga and the cross, still in the nondescript paper bag.

As he walked back through the kitchen, Nick saw Steve seated at the picnic table with a six pack, two finished, and the third well on its way.

Steve paused from his next swallow as Nick approached him. "You know, if it were anyone else trying to feed me this theory, I would either say that it was all the beer you had earlier, or that you were grasping at straws trying to resolve this for Julie. But I know you, and God help me, but I believe you."

"I appreciate your faith in me Steve, I really do, but it's not needed. Here is all the proof you'll need." Nick said as he placed the book in front of him, open to where he wanted him to begin reading. "Start here, and read the next six pages." Nick directed.

Steve spent the next half-hour, not just reading, but studying those six pages. "If Frank really had found this wreck, or at least a solid clue as to its whereabouts, I could see a motive for his murder. It's just that this book says there are so few clues, that it will probably never be found."

"It said few clues, not no clues." Nick opened the bag, removed the cross, flipped the pages back to the one with the painting, and laid the cross down on top of it. "Here is your proof. He found it, and that is why he's dead, not because he was Angelo DiMarko's son."

Although the picture did not show all the details of the cross, there was enough for Steve to know that his friend was right. Before Steve could say anything, the door to the kitchen opened, and out came Julie and Donna.

Both women immediately took notice of the book and the cross, but neither said one word about either. They merely said hello to Steve, then in turn, went over to Nick, each giving him a kiss and saying good night. After which they walked back into the house without saying more.

"What the hell was that all about?" Steve asked, completely confused.

Nick was not confused. It was apparent to him that earlier in the evening, Julie must have said something to Donna, who had told her of the conversation at the bar. His alternate line of communication had worked, the trust and love, each had in her own way for him, must have convinced them that he was right, and only acting in the best interest of those he loved. He had earned their trust in so many ways; they would now let him do as he thought. "They know that I think it's safer for them not to know anything."

The two men sat at the table, waiting to see what the other was going to say next. It only took about a minute for Steve to begin. "You know that we now have a list of suspects, which we didn't have yesterday. And it's a short list at that."

"Shorter than you think. I've got a hunch about this, but I am going to need your help to check it out." Nick waited to see Steve's reaction, there was none yet. "And I have to ask you to do something for me as quietly as you can." He needed an important favor, and let his tone convey it.

"As long as it isn't totally, illegal, you can count on me."

"Illegal? No, at least not yet. It maybe a little unethical though. That is to say, your boss will blow a gasket, if and when he ever finds out." Nick said with a slight grin, showing his disdain for the Sheriff.

"Well, now that's not necessarily a bad thing. Is it?" Steve replied. "So tell me what you need me to do."

"For right now, there's only one thing. I need you to get hold of Agent Collins."

"You what?" Steve interrupted, shocked at the request. "You say that we're going to be acting "unethically", and you want to involve an FBI agent? Correction, you want me to involve an FBI agent?" He asked sternly.

With a slight grin, Nick replied. "For right now, that is the unethical part. I need you to do it quietly, and off the record, making sure that nobody else knows. I want you to tell him that I need to see him alone, without Bradshaw. I think he'll do it if you're the one that contacts him, he seems like a reasonable man, but I'm not sure that he trusts me enough to come alone, without at least telling Bradshaw." Nick further explained.

"You're probably right, but what if he doesn't trust me either? I know that Bradshaw has his doubts, because of our friendship."

"Then it's your job to do whatever it takes to convince him, but you have to do it without telling him anything I just told you, I'm not sure how much I want him to know, until we know he's on board with us."

"That could be tough, but I'll do what I can." Steve said, as he began to go over in his head, just what he might need to say to convince the FBI agent. "Where and when do you want me to have him meet us?"

"I want you to have him meet me, on my boat at ten in the morning." Nick had emphasized the word "me" in his statement.

"What the hell do you mean, "meet you on your boat?" I'm going to be there too," Steve snapped back, with no room for question.

"Steve, I haven't worked out all the details yet. I'm trying to keep you away from as much trouble as I can, let me see how it goes with Collins. I know it's your case, and I'll tell you whatever I can, and bring you in if anything comes of what I want to do."

Steve knew that Nick was telling him the truth, and doing it out of friendship. But out of friendship, he was having none of it. "Well, it's like they say, "in for a penny, in for a pound", and you have nothing to say about it."

Nick accepted his friend's offer. He had no choice, and was actually relived by the fact that he had someone he knew and trusted, like a partner. He checked his watch and saw that it was almost three thirty in the morning. "We'd better call it a night Steve. If things go the way I hope they do, we're going to have a couple of long days ahead of us, and if they don't, They'll be even longer."

Without another word spoken between them, the two friends parted, both deep in thought on what the coming hours would produce.

Nine thirty in the morning, Nick sat in the cockpit of his boat, drinking his third cup of coffee. Unable to sleep with anticipation, Nick had arrived at seven a.m., to wait for Steve and agent Collins.

Nick stared wearily at the compartment by his feet where he had locked away the book and the cross. They were the only evidence he had to present to Collins in order to convince him to help. He also felt a little more at ease, knowing that his nine-millimeter was securely on his right hip. He knew that whomever had shot Frank, had savagely beaten him first, trying to find out where he had come across the final resting place of "La Marisabela", her captain, and the untold riches she held. He had seen the evidence of the brutality in the pictures, and read the coroner's report which verified it. He also knew that they had been on Frank's boat looking for what he now had in his possession, not fifty yards from where he now sat.

Ten minutes to ten, Nick could see Steve and the agent approaching. He was glad that they were early, sparing him further anxiety in waiting. As they boarded, Nick could see the doubt in the agent's eyes.

"Okay Mr., Thomas, I'm here. Do you want to tell me what is so important that we have to meet here, and so secret that I can't tell my partner?" He asked in that near military bearing that the FBI often exhibits.

"If you would just indulge me a little longer, I assure you that everything will be explained to your satisfaction, and you won't think this a waste of your time." Was the reply Nick chose to tender. He turned and fired up the boat's engines.

As Nick walked around the boat loosing the mooring lines, he looked over at agent Collins to see if there were anything he could read about him, there wasn't. Next he looked to Steve, who from behind his sunglasses, was looking at Nick with confusion. Nick hadn't mentioned that they were going anywhere, only that they were to meet on the boat. Nick was appreciative that Steve had chosen to question him in silence, rather than verbally. That may have given the agent reason to resist putting out to sea, and Nick wanted to make sure that they were alone, and that the agent had not involved Bradshaw.

The next forty five minutes saw Nick take the boat out of the marina in one direction, change course no less than four times, and finish with a high speed run, which lasted closer to thirty minutes than twenty. After all that, Nick slowed the boat, killed the engines and let them begin to drift in the currents.

"If you were trying me about what direction where we were going, or what direction we traveled? It didn't work. We spent the last twenty eight minutes going due east, with just a bit of north thrown in." The agent observed with a smirk of satisfaction.

"If I truly cared where in the hell we were, and for some reason didn't want you to know where that happened to be, you wouldn't know. I could have blind folded you, taken your watch, and even put you in the cabin so you couldn't tell what side of your face the sun was baking on. I asked you here today to tell you everything I have learned so far, and to ask for your help. You aren't the one I don't trust, it's your partner." Nick replied with his own look of satisfaction.

"Point taken, can we get started now?"

"Sure we can. Hey Steve, why don't you come up here and fill the agent in on what I told you last night?" Nick asked of his friend seated at the rear of the boat. Without waiting for a response, he went to the cabin to get them some drinks.

Upon his return only minutes later, Nick found Steve briefing the agent. Nick handed each one a drink and sat back to listen.

In barely over twenty minutes, Steve had covered all of the major points, then turned to Nick and said. "Is there anything I missed that you want to add?"

Nick was in the midst of taking a drink of his beer. He removed the bottle from his lips and swallowed, then looked to the sky thinking how to answer, making sure that he had nothing to add. "Nope, I think you covered all of the salient issues that he needs to know about." Nick then turned to the agent. "How about you, are there any points that you need clarification on?"

Collins paused before answering, looking back and forth between the other two, trying to gage whether or not they actually believed the story they had just told him.

As Nick watched to see if the agent had any questions, Steve noticed that it was a bottle of beer in Nick's hand. "Hey Nick, what's with the Michelob for you and the coke for us?'

"The two of you are on duty, I'm just a private citizen with nobody to answer to." Nick replied.

"Well, for the next seven days, I'm off duty. I called the station this morning and put in a request for some of the vacation time I have coming. The lieutenant gave it to me, effective immediately, no questions asked." Steve had a slight smirk on his face, letting Nick know that the lieutenant he was referring to was a mutual friend of theirs. So it had only taken the mention that he was helping Nick, to get the time off with such short notice.

"As a matter of fact, there are a few things I would like to talk more about."

Nick returned his attention to Collins. "Sure thing, that's why we're here."

"All right, for starters, where is the proof for all this theory, the cross for instance? Not that I would have a clue in hell, as to what it should look like."

Nick stood from his seat, and went over to the compartment where he had stored the items. He removed them, and stood before Collins once again. "This is the book to which we have referred. The pages of interest start with the one that's dog-eared, and continue through the next six." Next Nick unwrapped the cross, which was now folded into a beach towel to avoid it banging around while the boat was in motion. "As for the cross, the weight of it alone should tell you that it is gold, and it still has some of the coral it was encrusted in, on the back and bottom. You can't do that any quicker than Mother Nature will allow, so that should prove that it has spent quite a bit of time in the ocean."

Collins first looked at the cross, then placed it in his lap as he began to read the pages Nick had marked for him. He would occasionally pick up the cross and examine something about it, returning to the reading without looking at Steve or Nick. Both of who watched the agent intently, for any signs that he may have reached the point at which, he too believed the conclusions the other two had come to.

Finally Collins closed the book, studied the cross on last time and said. "Okay Mr. Thomas, I believe that you probably found the motive for your friend's murder. Do you also know who did it, and what do you need from me that you are telling me all of this?"

Nick reached into his pocket for a piece of paper. On it were written the names Jake and Karen Phillips, Craig Michaels, and the words, and anybody that works for or with them. "I'm betting that someone on this list, or associated with them did it."

"I have to agree with Nick," Steve agreed.

"From what you have told me so far, I would have to agree too. But I still don't know what you need me for, or why I couldn't tell Bradshaw?" Collins queried.

"Let me answer your first question, why we need you."

As Nick was about to begin, Steve stood and stopped him briefly. "Excuse me a minute Nick. I don't want to miss anything, but I want to grab a beer first."

"Sure thing, grab me one too."

"I could use a beer as well, Steve." Collins said, then turned to Nick. "That is if our host, Mr. Thomas doesn't mind."

"The beer I don't mind, The Mr. Thomas, I do, the name is Nick." He said as he extended his hand to the agent.

"All right Nick, I'm Guy." The agent said as he took Nick's hand.

Steve returned quickly with the three beers, and distributed them, and then he joined Guy quietly to hear what his friend had to say.

"The first thing I need you to do, is get as detailed a background check as you can on everyone on that list. I think it will help us determine more clearly who our real suspects are."

"Nick, you don't need me for that, Steve can get that through the station. Their computers will automatically check L.E.A.D.'s and N.C.I.C. in Washington. You should know that, you used to be a cop." Guy observed.

"Yes, I do know that, but what I want, he can't get to. I want anything that you can find out about their business and personal finances and dealings. You know, the IRS." Nick saw the reaction he had expected.

"Wait just a minute. You people at the local level may be able to just punch up anybody you want to check on, but we keep very detailed logs, and have to explain why we want that information. Especially for that type of check, one involving another agency, I can't justify that." He protested.

Nick had put his restless night to good use; he had anticipated every objection, even this one. "I know, now that the 'mobster, DiMarko', isn't involved in some way, or at least drugs, it's not a matter for the feds, right."

"That's right." Guy quipped back.

"I have to agree with him Nick, technically it's my case, since we reported him missing, or Metro Dade could lay some claim to it, since that is where the body was found." Steve joined with the agent from the FBI.

"So without evidence of drugs, organized crime, or at least the crossing of state lines, there isn't anything I can do to help." Guy looked Nick directly in the eyes before continuing. "And if that is why you wanted to talk to me without Bradshaw, because you think I'll break the law, and he won't, you are sadly mistaken. I have been with the FBI for over twenty years, and in that time I may have bent the rules slightly, but I have never violated the public trust!"

Nick waited for a moment, taking a long drink from his beer, hoping to see the indignation in the agent's eyes subside. The anger remained, so he decided to proceed. "In the first place, I thought nothing of the kind about you. If you will give me a chance, and hear me out, I'll prove it. Including, putting this whole thing right into federal jurisdiction without bending, or even stretching it."

"Oh, this I have got to hear, besides, we're in the middle of the damn ocean, where in the hell am I supposed to go?" Guy said sarcastically.

"I've got to admit, I'm kind of curious to see how you pull this one off, not that I doubt you, Nick." Steve added.

"Fine, but first let me tell you why I wanted you here, and not Bradshaw. I got the feeling, by how you handled Julie when you first got the case when you thought it was drug related, that experience had taught you to keep an open mind. And that maybe, following procedures a-b-c, straight out of the manual, every time, was not always the best way to go. That sometimes, it was best to proceed slowly, and carefully. Bradshaw isn't that way, he's too gung-ho, he's too cocky. That is why he's in the D.E.A., straight-ahead full, damn the torpedoes, and results right now. They're all like that, I've worked with them, they think that they're in Miami Vice, or something." Nick stopped as he heard Steve let out a laugh, and saw the anger and contempt slowly leaving Guy's eyes.

"Too funny, Nick." Steve continued to laugh. "But you're right about those D.E.A. guys."

"Okay, you're right about Bradshaw, and about me." Guy conceded, as he looked into Nick's eyes and leaned forward. "Go on, you've got my attention."

Nick settled himself into his seat, about to deliver the statement he had prepared last night, the one he hoped would get the agent before him on their side. "Well Guy, as I understand the duties, and the jurisdiction of the FBI, it's to uphold federal laws, and to look out for the national interests, within the borders of the country and its territories. Is that basically correct?"

"You know it is." The agent replied.

"So I assume that includes the area, international law recognizes as U.S. waters as well."

"Yeah, so?" Guy asked.

Suddenly, it was as though a huge light bulb had turned on over Steve's head. "I think I know where you are headed with this, and if I'm right, it's beautiful, Nick. I never would have thought of it in a million years."

"Well I don't get it." Guy remarked, still in the dark.

"Steve knows where I'm headed, because it was big news in the diving communities, of which the Florida Keys are the biggest in the country." Nick paused to take another drink. "A couple of years back, a group of divers found, what at that time, was the richest sunken treasure to be located. It was said to be worth over three hundred million dollars. What we are looking at in this find, is somewhere around three to five times that."

"Like I said, I believe you about this being the motive for the murder, but I still don't see where the FBI comes in?" Guy interrupted.

"Give me a chance, I'm getting to that. You see, after they found the wreck, they tried to file a legal claim on it. Then from out of nowhere, the government, the federal government, invokes a little known law, that they had quietly passed a couple of years before, but never used. The law states that if it lies in U.S. waters, it belongs to the U.S. government. There have been dozens of suits filed; most of which are still in the courts on appeals. My contention is that, until the law is decided, one way or another, being that there is a good chance that this find is in U.S. waters, or at least the man who found it and died for it, was a U.S. citizen. It might belong to the government, and whomever killed Frank for it, would probably do whatever they had to, to keep the government from finding out, or at least getting their fair share." Nick sat back in his seat, and finished what remained of his beer in one long drink, satisfied and confident that he had presented a compelling case to agent Collins.

The man from the FBI sat there, not saying a word, just trying to process all the information that had been imparted to him.

"Well, what do you think?" Steve finally blurted out.

Guy looked at both men in a precise and calculating stare, which slowly turned into a devilish grin. "I think, that if this gets approval from my boss in Miami, that this is almost as ingenious a use of the law, as going after Capone for tax-evasion instead of his real crimes, like murder."

"Yes!" Nick exclaimed triumphantly.

"Let's not get ahead of ourselves Nick. I said I have to take this up with the station chief in Miami." Guy admonished.

"But do you think that he'll go for it?" Steve asked.

"I think so, but the sooner you get me back to shore, the sooner I can drive up to talk to him."

"A half hour back to shore, at least another hour and a half drive time, no way. I can have us back in Key Biscayne in forty-five minutes. We don't have any speed limits out here." Without waiting for a response, Nick hopped up to the controls and fired up the engines. Steve and Guy settled into the bolsters along side him, and prepared for the high-speed run north.

About thirty minutes into the trip, Nick, ever watchful of all the gages and controls, especially at over eighty miles per hour on the open ocean. He noticed something odd on the radar screen at his left. Controlling a boat at those speeds requires the ability to drive a mile or more, ahead of one's current position. For that reason, Nick carefully watched position, speed, and projected course of any vessel within an eight-mile radius.

One blip in particular caught Nick's attention, when it began acting oddly. It had first appeared on the screen heading south, almost exactly opposite Nick's course, at about thirty miles per hour. It immediately came to a stop, held its position for no more than a minute, and then changed its course to a converging intercept with Nick's own course. Reaching what Nick could only estimate was something over seventy-five miles per hour. Nick was aware of very few boats in the area capable of reaching those speeds. Except for his, and maybe a dozen others in all of south Florida, the only others capable, with the radar needed to spot them, belonged to drug runners, or the authorities, specifically the U.S. customs, the Coast Guard, or the D.E.A.

Knowing that only the three official agencies' boats would have reason to assume an intercept course, Nick decided to call it to the attention of his FBI passenger. "Hey Guy." Nick yelled above the engine's roar. "Take a look at this." Pointing at the screen.

"What am I looking for?" He asked.

"This right here. It's probably official, and thinks that we're doing something illegal. If they stop us and want to do a search, or safety inspection, it could take hours. Is there anything that you can do?" Nick asked.

"I don't know. If we can get them on the radio, maybe."

Nick flipped the switches necessary to transmit on the emergency marine channel, he knew they would be monitoring. "Attention vessel heading northeast, eight miles off the coast. Please respond and identify yourself, this is the "Sea-Czar", the boat you are attempting to intercept."

There was no immediate reply to his call, they had probably not expected to make contact until they were in visual range, about another five minutes. They now knew that Nick was aware of their presence, and intention to intercept. He hoped they would respond, and after another moment they did.

"This is the U.S. Customs, bring your vessel to a stop, cut your engines, and prepare to be boarded." Came the order.

"Like hell." Guy said as he snatched the microphone away from Nick. "This is special agent Collins, of the FBI we are on official business, and request you terminate your pursuit immediately."

"If you are who you say you are, you should know that we cannot do that without verification of your authority, or confirmation of your identity." Crackled the response from the radio, defiantly.

"If you want to board this boat, you can do so at the marina, located at Sundays, on Key Biscayne. As for my authority, call the FBI office in Miami. And as a matter of fact, you can tell them to dispatch a car to meet us at Sundays, for transport back to the office, ASAP." The agent replied sternly.

There was no further communication from the boat following them. Within minutes Nick saw the boat, and passed about two hundred yards in front of them as they turned to follow. Within moments, it was apparent that they could not match Nick's eighty-five miles per hour, so Nick eased off the throttles, bringing them to sixty m.p.h.

Realizing what Nick had done, the customs agents came back on the radio. "We appreciate your not trying to run, and are awaiting confirmation. We will follow you in, and not try to interfere, so long as you do not try to escape."

"Well that's mighty nice of them, considering you slowed down to let them keep up." Guy commented, joined by Steve in a hearty chuckle.

"It is, pretty nice of them." Nick observed, not sharing their ebullience. "Look over there." He motioned for his passengers to look off to their right. About a mile away, and slightly ahead of them, flew a Coast Guard helicopter.

"He can do more than just keep pace with us." Nick observed pointedly, seeing his passenger's demeanor change rapidly.

Just before they entered the inter-coastal waterway, where Nick would have to slow down for safety, the chopper peeled off, and the Customs boat slowed nearly to a stop. At that moment the radio crackled once again. "Sea-Czar, this is foxtrot-sierra-three. Confirmation received, terminating pursuit. Just doing our jobs."

"Foxtrot-sierra-three, this is Sea-Czar. Understood, sorry about any trouble." Guy answered.

"No trouble. By the way, a car will be waiting for you when you arrive." Again the radio fell silent.

As Nick maneuvered the boat for docking, they could see two men in suits, obviously out of place in the mid-day sun, and surrounded by tourists.

"Hell of a way to call for a ride Guy." One of the agents said with a grin.

"It wasn't planned, Mike. I need to get to the office and talk to the station chief." He said, basically ignoring the second agent, who seemed quite young.

"Let's go then. Are your friends coming along?"

"No, it would probably be better if I went alone." Guy said, not only to the other agent, but also to Nick and Steve.

Nick reached down and grabbed the cross and the book. "That's fine, I think I'm a little under dressed anyway." He said, looking down at his cut off shorts, and the over sized sweatshirt he wore to conceal his gun. "But you had better take these with you. They might help you convince him."

Nick and Steve remained at Sunday's, where they took a table and ordered some food, while they waited for what they hoped would be good news.

Less than an hour later, Nick saw Guy appear with the agent from the dock, at his side. Nick felt that the news had to be bad. As soon as Guy began to explain Nick's theory, his boss must have thought it crazy, and sent him packing.

"Hey guys, this is Mike Davis. How's the food here, I'm starving?" Gut asked.

Nick could not help but be surprised at the joviality with which Guy addressed them. "That was quick. Did you get shot down without even telling them what we had?"

"No, as a matter of fact, I gave the station chief a quick ten minute overview, made the request to have the searches done that you asked for, and asked to have Mike here, assigned to the case with me." He replied, as though he was offended at the thought of his failing to bring the FBI on board this case of theirs. Although it was clearly feigned.

"It sounds like you made them think we might not help them, Guy?" The second agent inquired.

"What are you talking about?" Steve asked of the newcomer, to their impromptu team.

The two agents sat down at the table, as Davis began his comments. "Guy here could have told the chief that he wanted to investigate a UFO sighting, and he would have said okay."

"Excuse me?" Nick asked.

"Oh sure. Guy here, is a pretty big deal at the Bureau. Not only does he have over twenty years on the job, but also he has spent a lot of time on the organized crime task force, working on big high profile cases. He spent two years teaching at Quantico, and could be the station chief, anywhere he wants, but he likes the task force. Actually, the station chief here, was one of his students at the academy." Agent Davis informed them.

"Well somebody hasn't been showing all the cards in their hand, have they?" Nick directed towards Guy.

"I get the feeling you haven't disclosed everything either, Nick" He responded to the charge.

"Everything that I can prove, I have. The rest is merely my own speculation, and I want you guys to be open minded, and free to draw your own conclusions. Free from my theories. Hopefully, if I missed something, one of you will find it." Nick stated with genuine humility.

"That sounds more than fair to me, Guy. So let's all just cool off for tonight, and see what turns up in the files tomorrow." Mike offered.

"You're right, both of you. By the way Nick, I tagged all the requests, need to know only, authorized by me alone."

"Why would you do that, Guy?" Nick was confused.

"Just an added precaution. This way, it doesn't even circulate at the office, what we're working on. It's the type of thing someone might tell their spouse about, or discuss with other agents while at lunch, in public. I figure, if this gets out, we get swamped by every treasure hunting wannabe in the area. My way, as all the research is done, it is placed in sealed envelopes, and delivered straight to me. The agents doing the research are in Washington, and have no reason to know, or even care why it's being done." Guy explained. "Anyway, we should be getting the first of the files, in the morning, but I requested that they be delivered to me, at noon tomorrow, at your bar."

Nick didn't understand the reasoning for that. "Why at my bar?"

"I can't have them sent to the hotel I'm at, Bradshaw is there. They can't go to Steve at the station, he's on vacation, and they think that we're off the case. I thought about your home, but with Donna and Julie there, I didn't think you would want them involved The only option I could think of was the Dive Shack, it has a big enough office for all of us to work in, and a safe secure enough for us to store the files in over night." As he spoke, Guy saw new questions appearing in Nick's eyes. "Sorry Nick, we know about all that, from when we thought you might be involved in something dirty. We checked you out pretty well."

Nick remained calm, and said. "I guess you did, but I feel like I should return the microscope you shoved up my ass."

The four men laughed. There was now an understanding of where they all stood, and they could now get on with the job at hand.

Upon their return to the keys, it was decided that agent Davis would stay with Steve at his home, that way neither Bradshaw nor the girls would know what was going on. They would all meet at the bar around eleven a.m., to wait for the files.

"Where have you been all day?" Donna asked before Nick even had both feet inside the doorway.

"We were worried sick, until we called to talk to Steve, and they said that he had suddenly taken a week of vacation. Julie added, sounding like his mother, when he had been an hour late for his curfew in high school.

"I'm sorry." It was all Nick could say, considering what Julie had recently been through, and Donna by extension. "It was thoughtless of me."

With his apology, the two women let the issue drop. They knew that it would be pointless to expect him to keep them apprised of his where-abouts all the time, and he is capable of taking care of himself. After all, he had taken care of them on more than one occasion. Now that they knew Steve would be helping him, it eased their minds; the two of them together were nearly invincible in their eyes.

Ten thirty the next morning and the bar was already beginning to buzz. The spring season was about to start, with spring break only a week away. With the exception of Key West, every couple of years, the rest of the keys were not the major destination for most college students. However, enough of them had already discovered the sport of diving that it did get instantly busy, and was an important gauge of how the rest of the coming season would be for business.

Nick simply sat at the bar watching, as Tony and the staff worked around him. As he drank his orange juice, he knew his business was in good hands, for he had decided that he and Donna, and Julie if she chose to join them, we're going to get away and relax once all this was settled, anywhere.

Maybe they would go to Chicago. Nick kind of missed the windy city, the way hot dogs should be, and those deep-dish pizzas.

"Hey Nick, where are you?"

"Huh, what?" Nick was startled.

"You seemed like you were a million miles away. Are you all right?" Steve asked, with agent Davis at his side.

"Not a million, just over a thousand." Nick replied.

"What does that mean?" Davis inquired.

"I'm from Chicago. I was just thinking of going up there with the girls, after all this was over." As Nick spoke, they all saw Guy entering with a large box in his arms.

"That's a whole lot of box for some files." Steve said.

"It's not the files. I stopped by your station on my way in, and picked up the stuff we took from the boat after it was ransacked. I figured that we should go through it again. Last time we were looking for something to connect him to drugs, we might have missed something." Guy informed them.

"Good thinking. Give it here, I'll take it to the office." Nick took the box from him, and turned toward the back of the restaurant. "Why don't you guys order some lunch while we wait? Tell Tony it's on me."

As Nick carried the box, he used his chin to lift one of the flaps that was folded over the top, and peered in at the contents. There before him, he saw many of the books and maps that he had seen on his first search of Frank's boat. He began to wonder about them, until he realized that he was beating himself up over them. He could not have known then that they were connected to Frank's murder. It was useless to dwell on it, and would only be counterproductive. Nick placed the box on his desk, and returned to the others.

As he rounded the corner from the kitchen to the bar, he saw two men shaking Guy's hand, then turn and leave. Steve and agent Davis were standing there with an armload of files each.

"Hey Nick, we're going to take these to the office, too. Why don't you have them send the food in there, so we can get started?" Steve asked.

"Go ahead, I heard him." Tony called from behind the bar. "Do you want me to tell anyone that asks, that you're not here?"

"If it has to do with the bar, yes. You deal with it. Otherwise, use your own judgment as to how important you think it is."

The four men began to settle themselves into Nick's office, for what they all knew would be several hours, probably days. For the office of a restaurant/bar, it would be considered huge. Guy had been right, they would be quite comfortable there.

Guy told them that it was only the first of many files to come. He had told those doing the research not to wait until they had all that he had requested, but to send it along as it was compiled.

The first sets were on Jake and Karen Phillips, soon to be followed by those on their employees, and business. Next would come Craig Michaels, his business, and employees. Finally followed by any businesses or people in related fields, in the keys. Collins had figured that order would also follow an ascending order of the quantities of files each grouping would have. The Phillips', including themselves, only had five people working at the museum and guided dive service of their wreck. Michaels had at least fifteen, and as many as twenty-five, plus numerous investors.

About four in the afternoon, Nick's pager sounded. He was not expecting anyone to be trying to reach him, and knew that the girls were at the bar. They had poked their heads in earlier to say hello, or to see whom Nick and Steve had in the office with them. Julie had instantly recognized agent Collins, but was clearly unsure what to make of his presence.

As he checked the number on the display, he was more confused. Not only was it not a number he recognized, nor did it have a code that he issued to most of whom he gave the number, but it was a Miami area code entered.

"Guy, did you give anyone at your office my pager number?" Nick asked, looking oddly at the device.

"No, why would I?" He replied, as he showed Nick his own pager.

"I don't know. It's a Miami number, and everybody I know up there has a code to enter so that I know who it is." Still befuddled.

"There's only one way to find out, Nick, call the number." Steve coached.

"Gee, yak think?" Nick used the sarcastic reply and tone; he reserved only for a close friend, stating the obvious.

"Ha-ha. Just dial the damn phone, would you?" Steve answered, as he threw the cordless phone to Nick.

As he dialed, the others returned to the files. Nick was glad for the interruption, regardless of who it was from. After the first couple files had confirmed what he already believed about the Phillips', he had spent most of the past four hours, trying to read the other three faces in the room, looking for some sign that they had come to the same conclusions.

"Hello, Nick?"

The voice on the other end seemed familiar to him, though he could not place it. "Yes, who's this?"

"It's Karen Phillips."

"What are you doing in Miami?"

"My dad and I thought that I should come up here and check out a few things. I'm at the campus, in Coral Gables."

"What kind of things did you need to check out, You have your own reference library? I thought the two of you were the experts?" Nick asked quizzically.

"Maybe when it comes to the gold, or the artifacts, but not when it's about marine biology. The University of Miami has one of the best departments in the country, and the top Ph.D's in the field." She explained further.

"I don't understand what marine biology has to do with anything that's going on right now." Nick admitted. "Maybe I'm just being dense?"

"No, you're not being dense. It doesn't normally come into play in our type of work, if it did, I would have studied it in school."

"What makes this time different?"

"We're trying to find something, somebody else already found. We have the coins, proving that Frank found something, even if we don't know what ship it was. Although we didn't get anything definitive from the coins themselves, dad thought I should bring some of the coral he cleaned off of them, up here to someone he knows."

"Some types of corals grow only in certain areas, or conditions. Depending on the temperature, some types may tell us they need warmer water than others, or some of them may need more light to grow, so that might tell us how deep the water is where it sank. This is the first time we have ever tried to re-find something, so we thought it might help to try something new." Karen concluded.

Nick waited to see if she was going to report any finding to him. It was clear that she was waiting for him to speak. "Well, did you get anything?"

"Nothing definite yet. He said it would take a couple days to run all of the tests. He's also trying to see if there is any water trapped in the coral, that he might be able to test." She said, hoping he approved of her actions.

"That's good thinking by you two. I appreciate all the trouble you're going to." Nick did appreciate it, and without discussing it with the other three men in the room with him, he decided that he was going to act on the trust he had for the Phillips'.

"Karen, are you going to wait there for the results of the tests?"

"I wasn't planning on it. I thought that he could just call me, or fax them over. Why, would you like me to wait for them?" She questioned.

"No, not at all. I was actually hoping that you would stop by the Dive Shack on your way back home." Nick paused; he could feel the others watching him, wondering why he had wanted her there. "I've got some things here, that I would like you to take back with you, for you and your father to take a look at."

As he continued, he could feel the questions forming in the room. He probably should have consulted with his new partners, but they might have gotten in his way, he told himself as he finished up the call.

"What things are you having her take back to her father?" Guy immediately asked as the phone was hung up.

"I thought that we could let them see the books and charts from Frank's boat. We don't know what to look for in them, and they aren't going to help us find Frank's killer, but they might help Jake and Karen find the ship we're looking for, and that might help us find the killer." Nick watched to see which of them was going to argue with him. None did, that knew he was right.

Nick spent the next half-hour telling them why he trusted the Phillips', and how this most recent call had merely served to reinforce that trust. Another twenty minutes was spent while the others bounced their remaining concerns off him and each other.

In the end, it was agreed that the Phillips' were not considered suspects by any of them, although they gently reprimanded Nick for proceeding with out consulting them, especially the agents, whom he had brought in to help with this investigation. They had also decided that they would tell them about the FBI involvement, but only to emphasize the importance of their keeping quiet. In fact they would be cautioned as to the possibilities of being charged with obstruction of justice, if they were to reveal what they were searching for and why.

Nick felt that the threat was a bit much, but he deemed it to be a price he would have to pay since it had been he that brought in the feds. Besides, they had not quarreled with his decision after he had explained it to them. They had also, all agreed that the files showed the Phillips' to be exactly as they appeared to be.

By seven o'clock, the second batch of files had arrived, though it was much smaller than the first. It was explained to Nick and Steve, that over the night was when the most information could be extracted from the computers in Washington. During the day, so many different people were in the network, that a check that would take only ten minutes at night, could take over three hours during regular business hours.

"At least they were the start of the files looking into Michaels." Nick thought to himself, for he was Nick's prime suspect. If pressed for a reason why he suspected him, Nick would only be able to respond with, "I just have a feeling." and although he knew each of the others had acted on feeling, or instinct, or whatever they chose to call it. He knew that it was not enough to bring someone to court with, or even enough to get a legal search warrant.

Each man had gone through each of the files on the twenty-one people associated with Michaels' Salvage, and had come up with nothing. These files were merely criminal checks, which except for some DUI's, and a couple of marijuana convictions for some of his hired divers, showed nothing of major interest. Although, Nick read into the backgrounds of some of those Michaels had hired, at least the potential for accomplice, to something illegal.

It was ten thirty, before they all decided to call it a night, agreeing to meet again tomorrow, at the same time, then going out to the bar to knock some back and unwind.

The second day, Nick arrived at twelve thirty. As he entered, the others were knee-deep in the files that had just been delivered. "Sorry guys, but I won't be able to help you go through these today, I've got to go down to Key West for awhile."

"Jumping ship while we drown in this sea of paper, huh?" Agent Davis remarked sarcastically.

"Yeah, what makes you so special?" Steve added. "You started this whole thing."

Collins felt that the other two had the sarcasm covered, so he got right to the point. "What's up Nick, did the Phillips' find something"

"No, nothing like that. I got a call from Craig Michaels' secretary. She told him that I stopped in a couple days ago to see him, and he is of course, curious as to why. She said that he wants to see me, but it has to be today. He is only going to be in until tomorrow morning while he gets new supplies for the boat. Once he goes out again, he won't be back for at least a week" Nick informed the others.

"Okay, then lets get going." Davis responded as he removed his car keys from his pocket.

"Lets get going where?" Nick asked. "I'm only going down to ask him what he thought about these." He added, revealing the two gold coins that had been found with the cross.

"It may not be necessary, but if you are going down to meet with our prime suspect, I'll be damned if I am going to let you go by yourself." Guy spoke vehemently, as it was clear that the three others were in complete agreement on this.

"If I show up with even one of you guys, he'll know that something is going on." Nick protested.

"You're right, so we'll just have to make certain that he doesn't know that we are there. You'll just have to wear a wire, that way if he tries anything hinkey, we'll be right there to back you up." Steve said.

"Yeah, we'll tape it, and have it sent to the lab for stress analysis on his voice." As Davis spoke, it was clear that he had no intention of being left behind.

"Well, I'm the lead on this case, so there is no way that I am not going to be there. So it looks like we all go." Collins observed.

"If that's your plan, you're forgetting one very important thing. I have to meet with him today, or wait at least a week for him to come back again." Nick reminded them. "We don't have the time for you to get all the equipment needed for all of this."

"We don't have to go anywhere to get the equipment. We have everything that we will need at the station, including a small camper that is loaded with receiving and recording equipment." Steve said, much to the annoyance of his friend. But it was because of their friendship that he was unwilling to allow him to go alone.

"But you're on vacation, Steve." Nick pointed out to his friend.

"That doesn't matter. The Sheriff said that we could have whatever we needed, and he has no idea that we were ever off the case in the first place." Guy informed Nick.

"Fine…get whatever it is you need, but hurry up and get back here. I'm not going to wait around all day." Nick conceded, but added a note of agitation.

"It would probably be best if I didn't go with you to the station. The Sheriff might be a pain if he figures out that we are working with Nick on this thing." Steve told the two FBI agents.

"I gathered as much when we first arrived." Guy said to Steve, then turned to Nick. "He doesn't much like you, does he?"

"That's because he's an arrogant tight-ass, but it's also a long story, which we don't have the time for. So get going before I leave without you guys." Nick replied.

About an hour later, the two men returned with a large metallic briefcase filled with all sorts of electronics, which they laid out on Nick's desk.

"You people have some really great toys here." Agent Davis remarked to Steve.

"Nothing but the best, paid for by the local drug dealers, of course." Steve said as he began to get the items that they would need.

"Okay…what the hell is going on here?" Bradshaw shouted as he stormed through the office door. His eyes grew even wider as he saw the files and electronics laid out all over the place.

"None of your business! So unless you have a warrant, get the hell out of my office." Nick shouted in response.

"Like hell, that is my partner, and this is my case too." Bradshaw countered in reply.

Collins walked out from behind the desk, carefully placed the receiver in his hand on the desk, and calmly began to speak to the DEA agent standing before him. "First of all, our case was terminated when we found out that this had nothing to do with DiMarko, or drugs. I've been reassigned to this case, which has nothing to do with the task force. It's purely FBI, so I suggest that you turn around, don't say anything to anybody, and stay out of our way. Because if you don't, I am certain that deputy Jenkins here, will gladly place you under arrest for trespassing on Mr. Thomas' property, for which I will gladly be a witness."

Bradshaw's mouth began to widen as the senior agent continued.

"And if you say one word to anybody, I will personally bring you up on federal obstruction charges. Now get the hell out of my face!" Guy concluded with one small burst of anger at the younger agent.

Collins could not have been any clearer, and Bradshaw simply turned around and left.

"Well, remind me to never get in his way, or to piss him off." Nick commented to Steve, and Davis.

"Why…I never raised my voice to him?" Guy asked with a note of sarcasm.

"You didn't have to." Davis observed.

"Good." Guy said to Davis, then he turned to Nick. "What you said about him on the boat was right, he is a cocky little prick, and I never liked him anyway."

Two and a half-hours later, the four men stood in a parking lot five minutes from their final destination, Michaels' Salvage. They checked their watches and agreed upon how they would proceed. Nick would wait there for fifteen minutes, giving the others a chance to get into position. They would park the camper in the marina's parking lot, turn on the necessary equipment, and one of them would move around to the back of the building.

As Nick finally drove his Jeep to the open parking space near the front of the building, he spoke to himself, giving the others one last opportunity to set the recording equipment to the proper levels before he entered.

"Hi, I'm Nick Thomas. I believe that Mr. Michaels is expecting me." Nick said to the receptionist seated at her desk.

"Yes he is Mr. Thomas, I remember you from your last visit. Please go on into his office, I will tell him that you're here."

Nick opened the door to the office and began to enter. Suddenly he was hit by a wave of enlightenment…he knew why he had been so certain of Michaels' involvement in Frank's murder, as well as how he recognized the details he had seen when he held the cross in his hands. The details that were not there in the only known portrait of the cross.

He knew that he was now not in the proper frame of mind to conduct this 'interrogation', he could not look this man in the face without revealing the contempt that filled his entire being. Nick knew that he had to get out of there.

As Nick turned to leave, the receptionist stood right before him. "Mr. Thomas, are you all right? You look very pale."

"I am fine, I just remembered another appointment I have." Nick was lying, and if he was pale enough for her to notice, then Michaels would as well, and that might tip him off to Nick's suspicions.

"Well that's okay, they just told me that Mr. Michaels went out to run some errands, and won't be back for a couple of hours. Would you like me to tell him to expect you later?" She asked.

"I'm not sure how long my other appointment will take. Tell him it was not important, but I will try to get back to see him before he leaves." Nick could feel the perspiration forming on his brow, and knew that he had to get out of there quickly before he said or did something that she might relay to Michaels, tipping him off to his being a suspect.

Nick made his way to the door; it took a conscious effort to stop himself from rushing out. As he returned to the daylight, he saw agent Davis rounding the corner of the building with a look of concern that must have either been brought on by Nick's words, or perhaps his tone, which Davis was surely experienced enough to pick up on.

Nick jumped into his Jeep and sped out of the parking area, he knew that the others would not further jeopardize the situation by following him quickly, so he spoke into the microphone taped to his chest. "I know I screwed up back there. I'm going to go meet with Jake and Karen, meet me there as soon as you guys can, without being noticed." His tone relayed the urgency of his request.

Within ten minutes the camper joined Nick in the parking lot for the Phillips' Museum. Before the camper could even come to a complete stop, Steve and Guy jumped from the side door.

"What the hell happened back there?" Steve asked as he placed his hands upon Nick's shoulders.

As Nick took a deep breath before beginning, anger finally took the place of the shock that had come over him in that doorway, only minutes before. "Michaels did it, I'm positive of that. I think I have seen the proof, but I won't be certain until I speak with Jake and Karen."

"What proof, there in his office?" The two men asked almost in unison.

Nick reached into the console of his jeep, and removed the pictures of the cross that he had taken before his last visit there. "Do you guys remember the painting of the captain, the one in the book with him wearing the cross?"

"Of course we do." Guy answered.

"Do you see these engravings, these little ones here?" Nick asked with some forcefulness. "Do you remember that they aren't in the painting?"

"Right. It would be really difficult to get that kind of detail. So what are you driving at?" Guy answered again.

"Okay, then how did we know that it is the same cross that is in the painting?" Nick pressed further.

"There is enough detail in it to be a reasonable assumption that they are the same. It even states in that book that there were only two commissioned by the Queen of Spain, and the other was melted down sometime in the seventeen hundreds." Steve answered this time, and the two FBI agents agreed.

"That may be right for the three of you, but I knew they belonged there, I had seen them there. I have seen a drawing of the cross showing them, in detail. Only I didn't remember it until I walked into that office back there. When I saw it, Frank was merely missing, and it had no meaning. But as soon as I walked in there I remembered the whole thing." Nick attempted to explain.

"Okay, so he had a better picture of the cross, with more detail. I believe you that he is involved, but he is in the same line of work, it could be a coincidence that he found one that shows more." Steve attempted to reason.

"No...I didn't say that I saw a picture! I said that I saw a DRAWING! It was an original sketch, not even a photocopy, and it was next to a picture of the same painting that we have seen." Nick emphasized.

The three men standing before Nick, listening to his words, slowly began to realize what he was driving at. "So for him to have drawn it, he would have had to have seen the cross, which we know was in Frank's safety deposit box at the bank?" Davis questioned for clarity.

"Or, since not even Julie knew about the cross at the bank, Frank probably drew it himself. He would have taken it to Michaels, since he thought he could trust him after all his work with him, and being allowed to borrow the electronics. But instead, Michaels got greedy and tried to get the information about where he got it, and when Frank wouldn't tell him, he killed him." Nick went on.

"Your friend may have even told him, and that is why he was killed. Michaels would not be able to keep him alive and still take the credit for the find." Steve added as well.

"Either way, Jake and Karen Phillips are our best resource to find out if the drawing I saw could have been a compilation of several sources of information, or if it whoever drew it had to see the real thing." Nick said as he began towards the door. "So let's quit wasting time out here talking, and go find out."

Entering, the four men were immediately greeted by Karen as she crossed from the library to Jake's office with an armload of books. "Hiya Nick, what's going on, the four of you look like you're after something important?"

"I guess we are. We'd like to speak with you and your father." Nick's words were a politely phrased order.

"Sure thing. I was just bringing these to him." She said referring to the books she carried.

As they followed her, Nick hung back with the other three men and whispered to them. "I want to tell them everything"

All three nodded in agreement, and would allow him to do the talking, unless they felt he was leaving something out.

Nick began by introducing Jake to the men with him. "Jake, I believe you met Steve at the services for Frank, and these other two men are FBI agents that have gone out of their way to help too."

Once all the greetings were exchanged, Nick directed all to the conference table where he had first involved the Phillips'. "Jake, Karen, we need to ask you for your help, but this time it is official, so I can tell you everything we know."

"We'll do anything we can to help find out what really happened to Frank. You know that!" Karen responded instinctively.

Nick spent the next thirty minutes telling them all that they knew to this point, saving the information of the cross for last, which they were still unaware that he had in his possession. Finally Nick removed the pictures from his pocket and placed them before the two.

All four men watched carefully, hoping to see confirmation of what they already believed to be true.

"What do you think of these?" Nick asked as he fanned them out like a deck of cards.

The recognition I their eyes was instant, as was the shock, both obviously sincere. They both sat there for almost a full minute, eyes locked on the most tangible clue to the most elusive discovery in their field.

Finally Karen reached out and carefully took one of the pictures into her hands, almost as if the photograph itself were as old as the item it depicted. "Oh my God!" was the only words she seemed to be able to force from her mouth.

Jake stood and retrieved a book from the shelf behind his desk. "You have your proof…Frank found La Marisabela." He said as he placed the book in front of all, open to a page with the painting that they had all seen before.

Although it was a different book, it was the same painting. When Nick asked as to why that was, Jake told him that it was the only known depiction of it, and was painted just before the captain's last journey, the one that lost the La Marisabela. Jake did also mention that there were writings that spoke of the ornate engravings, but not in any detail that they could have been replicated by anyone. Drawing the conclusion that the cross in the picture had to be an original.

Nick began by telling Jake how and where he had found the cross, and that he had seen a sketch of it nearly a week prior to its discovery, to which Jake replied. "If it is as accurate as you seem to say it was, including the engravings, the person had to have studied the real thing, it's the only way to have done it. Where did you see this drawing?"

"In the office of Craig Michaels."

Jake's response to the answer was not at all what any had expected. Turned immediately to his daughter, and looked with a great deal of pain at her.

"That bastard!" Karen said as a single tear escaped from the corner of her eye.

"Is there something we should be told here?" Davis asked the obvious question, the one that they all wanted an answer to.

"I was engaged to marry him a few years back, but I haven't spoken one word to him in at least two. If that is what you're asking? I broke it off with him when I found out that he was using my father's name and reputation to get investors for his company." It was clear that she had been hurt by him deeply, but it was equally clear that all she now felt for him was hatred and contempt, compounded by what she was now being told that he had done.

"So are you saying that he is capable of doing something like this?" Guy asked.

"He is capable of doing anything for money, or fame. Especially this kind of both." Jake answered for his daughter, who simply nodded her head in agreement.

The four men had heard what they had come for, and if any had any doubts about either of the Phillips', they were now gone. This meeting had erased all of those, the reactions that they had witnessed from them, could not have been rehearsed.

They made the drive back up to the bar to plan their next move. For the return trip Guy road with Nick in the Jeep, but neither they, nor the two following in the camper spoke. They were all too busy formulating a plan of action to present to the others once they were back at the office, which served as their "command post".

Nick was the first to put forth his thoughts on the matter of what to do. "I think I should go back and confront him, either late tonight, or first thing in the morning when he least expects it, and is still half asleep."

Collins and Davis thought along the same lines, they wanted to put him under constant surveillance, including having the coast guard track him while he is out to sea. "Give him enough rope to hang himself. He'll make a mistake, and when he does, we'll be right there to take him down." They said. "Put him under that microscope that you joked about earlier

Nick." That was their idea, and what Nick had expected, it was the way the FBI did things.

Steve went last, and his plan had some of the previous two, but with some variations. "As far as confronting him, we should do it by taking what we know to judge here, and I think that he'll be forced to issue us search warrants for his house, his boats, and his business. If the sketch that Nick saw turns up, great. But if it doesn't, Michaels knows he's a suspect, and while he's running scared, he is more likely to slip up."

For the moment the only plan of action that they agreed on, was that Nick would go down and speak with him first thing in the morning, before he got on his boat. Nick would again be wired, and it had taken him a fair amount of talking to convince the others that he should be the one to speak with him. They were not sure that Nick would be able to hide the hatred that had overcome him earlier in the day, but since he was the only one that Michaels had been expecting to see, it might tip their hand even further to be questioned by even one FBI agent, or a Sheriff's deputy.

By five the next morning the men had taken the camper back to its position in the parking lot, and they were glad to see that the lot was already half full with other vehicles, including two other recreational vehicles, probably tourists out for an early morning fishing excursion. The only thing that had set their camper from the others, was that they had Florida plates, which most would not likely notice.

When the FBI agents brought up that fact, Steve had remarked that he would have it looked into, but they had been lucky to that point, that none of the drug dealers in the area had been observant enough to notice.

Nick sat on the hood of his Jeep, waiting for Michaels to arrive. He had not been expecting a very long wait, assuming that Michaels would have wanted to get as early a start as possible, and he realized that he was right, judging by the appearances of those arriving shortly after he had.

Nick could see Michaels' boat, and the men that he assumed were hired divers had obviously made the most of their one night of "shore leave".

Every one of them was moving quite slowly, probably due to too much alcohol, or too little sleep. Nick also overheard a group of four that arrived together, still discussing their conquest of the night before.

It was not until two men in their forties arrived, that Nick first heard anything that might be considered a clue. They were discussing the actions of their boss over the past few weeks, and had used the words relentless, and obsessed, in their descriptions. Nick viewed this as confirmation that he had not yet found, or re-found as it were, the shipwreck that he had killed for.

Just as Nick was about to relay this tidbit of information to the others, a black Lexus with the windows tinted dark, parked next to him, and right in front of the door to the salvage company. It was Nick's query, and all he had to do now was get him into a trap.

"Mr. Thomas, Hi, I assume that you are waiting for me?" His demeanor was weary, not befitting of the friendly tone he had tried to force from his lips. "Good thing you're an early riser, or you might have missed me." He added, revealing some doubt as to the reason for this early morning meeting.

"Actually, I haven't slept yet. Do you think we might be able to talk inside over a cup of coffee?" Nick said. He chose his words carefully, for they served a dual purpose. First, they would let Michaels know that what he wanted to discuss was rather important to him. But it also told Michaels that Nick was very tired, perhaps not as focused as he would normally be, and thus giving Michaels an upper hand in this conversation. A false sense of security to be sure, for Nick was never more focused than when he needed to observe the subtle clues of a person that he was interrogating.

"Sure, come on inside, you look like you missed more than one night's sleep. You have a whole set of luggage under those eyes of yours." He said as he led Nick in, walking directly over to the coffee machine behind the secretary's desk.

The luggage to which Michaels referred, were very pronounced dark circles beneath Nick's eyes. He would have them for the next few days; regardless of how much rest he got.

Back when Nick was in college, he began getting severe migraine headaches, for which the doctors had only been able to find eye stress as a cause, too much reading. Stained eye muscles caused the headaches, as well as the accompanying dark circles.

"So what can I do for you?" Michaels asked as he handed Nick a cup.

Nick revealed the two coins from his pocket, and handed them to Michaels. "What can you tell me about these?"

Michaels showed very little interest in the coins, which he now looked vaguely at. Turning them over, looking at both sides, and comparing one to the other, then handing them back to Nick. "They are Spanish doubloons, and the gold in each one is worth about four hundred dollars. They are in pretty good condition for their age, so you might be able to get an extra hundred for them, but it would have to be from some souvenir hunter on vacation, anyone in this business wouldn't give you much if anything for them." His tone was dismissing, but forced. "With all of the wrecks that have been found around here, and all of the tours that go to them everyday, it isn't that uncommon to have someone come up with an occasional coin or two. It is a real thrill for the tourist that finds it, and if there happens to be a few of them, they might even make enough to pay for their trip down here, but that is about all that those coins are worth.

Jake Phillips brought up thousands of those, and a couple times a year, someone diving his find comes up with some, but he usually buys them, and gets some free publicity in the process. Personally, I think that he plants them down there for that exact reason."

The man before him was lying, and by disparaging the name of Mr. Phillips, he was giving Nick some extra opportunities to see his body language while trying to deceive him. Which Nick knew that his words were, for he knew Jake, and his daughter, would not do anything of which they had just bee accused, if ever so backhandedly.

"Really…I thought that they might have something to do with Frank's murder." Nick did his best to feign disappointment.

"What would make you think that? I thought that it had something to do with drugs, or with the fact that his father is some big time hood from New York, at least that is what the papers have been saying that the police think." Michaels asked.

Those were about the words Nick would have expected from this murderer sitting before him. Nick was having a hard time containing his contempt for this man that had taken Julie's life and torn it to shreds. He began to doubt that Michaels was really going to make a mistake that would bring him to justice, and even more that he was not giving a clue to the fact that he knew of his true guilt.

It had been so long that Nick had been involved in a murder investigation, and the questioning of a suspect, that he was beginning to suspect that the others had been right in their concern that he be the one doing this. Nick decided that he could no longer continue, and would put a stop to this now, before Michaels found out that he was the only suspect, and had a chance to disappear.

"Well Mr. Michaels, I want to thank you for your time. I know that you are a very busy man, and are going out to work for a while, I guess I was on the wrong track." Nick hoped that his words would give this murderer a false sense of security that would have him continue about his plans.

"Not at all, I wish I could have been of more help to you. Frank Marks was a good man, and I considered him a friend. If there is anything I can do to help in the future, please don't hesitate to let me know." Michaels said with as much concern as he could, without sounding too insincere.

Suddenly a thought seemed to flash across Michaels' eyes. "Last night I decided that the area we have been searching was not a viable route for the ship we have been looking for. So if you decide that you need anything else, don't hesitate to come around, I'll be here at the office until we can come up with something else to look at."

Nick had tipped him off, he was certain of it. Michaels must have decided that he did not want to be out on a boat that could be easily tracked. At least on land he had more avenues of escape available to him, even if he did choose to take the boat away from the islands.

Nick felt he had to get out of there before he did any further damage to the case they had begun to build against this scum. "Well, thanks for the offer, but I guess I am on the wrong track as far as motive for Franks murder." Nick said as he stood and made his way to the door.

As soon as Nick started his Jeep, he sped off back towards the Dive Shack. Nick did not even look to see if the others were behind him, for he knew that they were, they would certainly have something to say about how he had handled the meeting, and would not be happy about it.

By the time that Nick made his way into the parking lot of the bar, it was just past nine-thirty in the morning. Although the bar would not be open for another hour and a half, Tony and Donna's cars were there. They would be inside getting ready for the day's lunch crowd.

Immediately upon entering, Nick made his way straight to the bar where he grabbed a glass, filled it with ice, and took a bottle of Scotch with him to the corner of the bar, where he took a seat.

Hearing some unexpected sounds out in the bar, Tony and Donna emerged from the kitchen, as well as did Julie, whom Nick had not thought would be there. Seeing her made it even more difficult to think of what had just happened a short time ago.

Seeing Nick standing there with a glass full of scotch I one hand, and a bottle in the other, Tony was the first to speak, with tones of obvious concern for his employer, and friend. "Nick, what's the matter...what's wrong?"

Nick looked over at the three of them, raised the glass to his lips, and in one swallow, emptied half of what it contained. "I don't want to talk about it." He answered; his voice was raspy due to the burning of the Scotch he had just sent down his throat.

"Nick!" Donna called to him.

"I said that I don't want to talk about it!" Nick repeated, then finished the glass in one more swallow.

With that response Tony and Donna both retreated to the kitchen, they knew when to press Nick, and this was clearly not one of those times.

However Julie had proven time and time again that she could get away with far more than any other, so she made her way to the opposite end of the bar, and took a seat about ten feet from him and lit a cigarette, all without saying a word, or addressing Nick in anyway.

Nick grabbed the bottle and began to refill his glass once more. "What the hell do you think you're doing?" He asked without looking in her direction.

"Just making myself available for you, should you decide to talk to a person instead of that bottle you're holding."

"Don't hold your breath."

"I won't, but don't you think it's a little early for that stuff?" Julie gently asked with no judgment in her voice, merely concern.

"No…I don't." Nick's replied, but he did begin to take smaller swallows of the drink he held tightly in his hand.

About twenty minutes later, the front door opened with Steve and Guy walking through it. "Why don't we go into the office and talk, Nick?" Guy said, looking at the drink in Nick's hand.

"Why? Just go ahead and say it in front of Julie. Just tell her that I screwed up, and now we might not be able to get enough evidence on the man who murdered her husband to get him to court." Nick stated with some evidence of the alcohol that he had consumed coming through in his speech.

"What the hell are you talking about? You handled that perfectly! You showed him the coins, and let him know that we know why Frank was killed, but he still isn't certain that he is the one that we suspect." Steve said calmly.

Nick could see the reflection of Julie's face in the mirror behind the bar, and it was a look of shock and relief, upon hearing that they knew who had done this to her husband. He could also see confusion from the words that he himself had spoken.

"So are you going to arrest him?" Julie asked of the four men.

"I know it must be hard for you Mrs. Marks, but we have to wait until we have enough proof for it to stick, that is why we are going to go before a judge and ask for a search warrant. Maybe we can find something to tie him to the murder…right now all we have is a motive, and some circumstantial evidence that he is somehow connected."

"But you didn't see the look in his eyes the way I did. He knows, and that is why he isn't going out now, he would be stuck on that boat. He is probably getting rid of anything that might tie him to the murder as we speak." Nick further informed them.

"That's exactly why Davis isn't here. We left him down there to keep an eye on him, and we called to Miami to have more agents sent down here. Now we do what the FBI does best, we put him under constant surveillance until he has nowhere to go but straight to jail. No passing go, no collecting on what made him do it." Guy informed him.

Nick could still see that look in Julie's eyes, the one that made him want to have this thing over, once and for all. "Fine, the FBI is on this thing now, I am out of it." Nick stood to leave.

"What do you mean you're out of it? You figured it all out, you are the one that saw the proof, we would have nothing without you. I would have thought that you would want to see this all the way through to the end." Guy questioned, for something did not feel right about all of this, this sudden urge to drop the investigation.

"I have done everything that I can, now I just want to get away from all this and be alone." Nick began to make his way to the door, but Julie was quickly by his side.

"I'll go with you." Julie said as she took his hand. "Let me go get Donna, and we can all get away till they get this thing over with.

"Julie…I'm sorry, but I really need to get away by myself. Please tell Donna I'm sorry too, but you two can be there for each other." Nick said as he pulled his hand from hers, and walked away with her not understanding why he had done so. It was not something she would have ever expected from him, but there was something in his eyes that told her he was not himself.

Julie went to the kitchen and quickly told Donna what Nick had just said to her, and upon hearing the strange behavior, the two went to go stop him and get to the bottom of it. As they walked out into the sunlight, they saw that Nick's Jeep was still in the parking space it always occupied. As if of one mind, they realized that he had gone to the boat, and as they turned to go in that direction, they could see him throttling the boat forward, and leaving the bay.

It had been two weeks since Nick had walked out of the bar and out of the lives of those that meant so much to him. As he sat there on the barstool, as he had for so many days now, it suddenly struck him that it was time to go back. Although he was not sure what he had to go back to, he had changed all that he knew, with one simple action, his life would never be the same.

Now as he returned his boat to its slip at the marina, he knew that everything in his life had changed. He was not the same person he had been, but he had done what he felt was necessary.

As Nick walked into the Dive Shack, he could see all sorts of heads turning in his direction. Some were doing so simply because they had not seen him in so long, while he knew that others were watching for him because they were instructed to. Two men that Nick could tell were obviously federal agents immediately approached him.

"Mr. Thomas, would you please come with us? We need to take you for some questioning." The first one said.

"I kind of figured as much." Was Nick's only reply.

They placed Nick in handcuffs, and lead him to the car they had outside, all to gasps and whispers from those in the bar.

Nick began walking into the station with the two men, and was met just inside the front door by Steve, agent Davis, and agent Collins. "Is this really necessary guys?"

"Absolutely not!" Steve said as he walked behind Nick and removed the restraints. "He is just here to answer some questions, he isn't one of the bad guys." Steve further directed at agent Collins.

"I didn't tell them to do that, but considering what we have to ask him, I probably would have done the same in their position." Guy replied.

"And what exactly is it that you have to ask me?" Nick was getting impatient to hear what he knew was coming.

"We'll do this upstairs, in private, and only after Nick has time to speak with a lawyer." Steve said, looking out for the interests of his friend.

"I don't need a lawyer Steve. I haven't done anything illegal." Nick spoke confidently.

"Nick, I think it would be best if you did talk to an attorney. You don't know what's been going on here, and these guys think you were involved." Steve said with reference to the agents standing beside him.

"We'll just start, and if I decide that I need a lawyer, I am certain that agent Collins and the others will let me stop things until I get one." Nick remarked.

"Of course we will." Guy replied.

"Then let's get on with this." Nick said as he walked himself to the interrogation room with the others following.

Steve, Nick, and the two FBI agents were joined immediately by the Sheriff himself, who never let it be a secret that he was not one of Nick's admirers. "So you finally screwed up enough to get your ass in a sling, huh, Thomas?"

"Okay, let's start with one question by me." Nick began. "Is this an FBI investigation of me, or local?"

"You know this is a federal investigation, you brought us into it." Davis answered.

"Then get this jerk out of here, or I will call a lawyer, and we all know that he will tell me not to say one word." Nick said in reference to the Sheriff.

The Sheriff simply looked at the agent, knowing that there was really nothing that he could say, but his eyes let them all know that he was not pleased with there willingness to go along with Nick's request. "Jenkins, I want to see you in my office as soon as you finish in here!" He ordered to his subordinate.

As soon as the Sheriff left the room, Agent Collins began. "Okay Nick," He said casually, trying to put him at ease. "What can you tell us about the disappearance of Craig Michaels?"

"I have no idea of what you are talking about. Are you telling me that the FBI let him get out from under the surveillance you spoke so highly about?" Nick asked without very much surprise.

"That's right Nick, two days after you took off in your boat from the bar, Michaels just vanished. They had a car following him, and they lost sight of him for about five minutes while he was on his way to his house from the office. At least that is where they thought he was going, but when they got to his home…no car, no Michaels." Steve informed his friend.

"I don't know anything about that, I have been in Bimini since I took off, and just left there a couple of hours ago." Nick answered confidently.

"Is there any way for you to prove what you are saying?" Davis asked.

Nick looked back at them with even more confidence now, for he knew that he did, and that the sources he was going to give them to check, even they could not dispute. "Sure, if you check with the Coast guard you will find out that they stopped me and did one of their famous safety inspections about two hours after I left the bar, just as I was about to leave US waters. Then the Bahamian defense force boat, which also had two US customs agents on board, stopped me about an hour after that, as I was entering their waters into Bimini." As Nick gave his answer he watched Steve's reaction even more than that of the agents, looking to see if he believed what he was hearing. It was apparent that he did. Nick figured that he wanted to hear that his friend was not involved with what they had suspected, and looked past what he would have normally picked up on.

"That tells us when you got there, but it doesn't tell us when you left, or if you were there all the time?" Collins observed, and rightly so.

"Well, you can also check with the same sources about when I left, because they each stopped me again on my way back in. And as far as whether or not I ever left, the Bahamians are based out of the same marina that I stay at, and they can tell you that my boat never left the slip. They saw me everyday, and even waved hello each morning, and then you can check with the people at 'The Bar at the End of the World', because I spent everyday, all day, sitting in there getting drunk!" Nick answered.

Agent Collins looked relieved in some way as he heard Nick's answers. It was not clear that he truly believed him, bit still, his answers and his alibi seemed to be airtight. "Well, Mr. Thomas, if all that you have said here checks out, then there is nothing for you to worry about, but if we find anything that doesn't match up, we will bring you right back here for more questions, so keep yourself available until you hear from us."

"That's it? For this your little storm troopers brought me in to the station wearing handcuffs?" Nick said with a touch of sarcasm. "You should really tell them to be more careful about that, they could open themselves up for a lawsuit."

Nick stood and began to leave, but as he reached the door he felt a hand on his arm.

"Hey Nick, wait for me outside, I really need to talk to you." It was his friend Steve, and Nick simply nodded his head and continued out of the station, where he stood while he lit a cigarette and waited.

Within five minutes Steve emerged and took a cigarette for himself out of the pack in Nick's hand. "Thanks Nick."

The words Nick had just heard did not make any sense to him, thanks for what, he wondered. "What are you talking about?" He finally asked after looking into his friend's eyes for a moment.

"Thanks for having a solid alibi for where you have been. I have been trying to tell them that you wouldn't do anything illegal, but I have to admit that I even had some doubts. You were acting really different at the bar the day you left, and I know how much you want this guy to pay for what he has done to Frank, and by extension, Julie." Steve said with some audible relief in his voice. "I also need you to do something else for me?"

"Name it." Nick said.

"I need you to meet me at my house in one hour, it's very important. I'll be there as soon as I finish talking to the Sheriff." Steve's tone told of the importance that he felt in his request.

"Okay, I'll go as soon as I stop by my place and check in on the girls. I have a feeling I am really in the doghouse with them, and I had better give them the opportunity to get some of it out." Nick had never been out of contact with either of them as long as this, since he had let them into his life.

"You don't need to go to your house to see the girls, they are already at my place waiting to see you. They have been there for the past three days, and I already called them and told them that you were back. I hope you don't mind that I did that?" Steve asked, knowing that Nick would have no objections.

Nick was curious as to what the girls would be doing there, and why they would be there for three days. "Do you think they are in some kind of danger or something?" He asked with a tone of genuine concern.

"Not danger, we all just thought it would be best if they were there until we could talk to you. A lot has happened since you walked out of the Dive Shack, and I need to fill you in on it. But I can't talk about it right now, just go there and you'll find out everything." Steve told him again.

"Okay, I'll go to your place now and wait for you."

"Good…I'll be there as fast as I can." Steve turned and walked back inside the station, leaving Nick standing and wondering what had happened while he was gone.

It took Nick almost twenty minutes to get to Steve's home on Plantation Key, so his friend should be there in about half an hour. As he pulled into the drive, Nick saw Julie and Donna sitting on the front porch waiting for him. Steve must have called ahead and notified them of his impending arrival.

Their eyes welled up with tears as they saw Nick get out of his Jeep. Although both wanted to run to him, it was as though their feet were glued to the porch on which they stood, at least until they heard his voice.

"Hi girls, sorry if I caused you any undue worries." Nick said, trying to sound calm and confident.

His words caused in them the same reaction that a starters' pistol has in a sprinter. Both leapt into his arms, and the tears of joy and relief began to flow. Each wrapped their arms tightly about his neck, and kissed him deeply in turn.

After about a minute or so of that, Julie released her grip of him, and took a step backwards. "Sorry if you caused us any undue concern?" Julie repeated his words sarcastically. "How dare you take off for so long without so much as a word to let us know that you are okay, especially with what just happened to Frank!" She scolded him severely, then as hard as she could, she hit him in the left arm.

Next Donna stepped back, and with as much indignation as she could muster, said. "Yeah Nick, what she said!" Then she proceeded to hit his right arm.

Just as the girls returned to Nick's arms, Steve drove up to the house, and walked to them once he exited his car. "Okay, we're all glad to have him back safe and sound, but let's get inside. We have a lot of things to tell him about."

The girls agreed, and the group of them walked into the house. Once inside, Nick saw Karen seated at the sofa with several gold pieces laid out before her on the coffee table, none of which Nick had ever seen before. "What's all this? Did you find some more things that Frank brought up?"

"Nick, I am glad that you're safe. We were all very worried about you." Karen said as she stood and gave him an embrace of her own. She could see that it caught him by surprise, and that he was not sure what to make of it. "I'm sorry, I guess being here with everyone these past few days, and sharing their concern, I just feel closer to you then you do to me."

"It's not that, I guess with the exception of these two, I am not really the hugs type, but I do appreciate the concern." Nick said gently, but his attention immediately returned to the objects on the table behind her.

Noticing this, Julie took Nick by the arm and led him to a chair to the right of the couch. "Have a seat Nick. That is what we have to talk to you about." She said as she sat next to him on the arm of the chair, holding his hand tightly in hers.

Karen returned to her seat on the couch as Donna took the other arm of the chair in which Nick was seated, and Steve took the chair across from them, on the other side of the table. "Would you guys like me to start?" She asked.

"I wish somebody would!" Nick said impatiently.

"Fine." Karen took it as a yes to her question. "First of all Nick, no, this isn't some of what Frank brought up, my father and I did."

"This stuff isn't from the ship with the cross?" He asked.

"Oh yes, it is from "La Marisabela" all right, but my father and I found it. Or should I say re-found it." Karen said with deference to Julie.

"So you're telling me that after all these years being lost, it has been found twice in barely over a month?" Nick asked.

"Not really. We wouldn't have ever found it if it were not for Frank finding it first, so once we go public with the news, Frank is going to get all the credit for it." Karen spoke modestly.

"No…" Julie interrupted. "Jake and I have already discussed this. Once it goes public, you will share equally in the credit. After all, the wreck would have remained lost if it were not for you, and all the hard work you put into this."

"Since we are on the subject, why don't you tell me how you did re-find it." Nick said with a hint of doubt, suddenly wondering if she could have possibly been involved in all of this with her former fiancé, the infamous "missing" Craig Michaels.

Steve must have realized what had just crossed Nick's mind. "Nick, it's not what you are thinking. At first that went through my thoughts too, but if you listen to it all, you'll understand, and it will all make sense to you."

The others looked oddly at the two of them speaking, not knowing what exactly they were talking about, but Nick knew that Steve and he were on the same page. "Okay...go ahead Karen, I'm listening."

"Okay, I already told you about going to the University of Miami, and having one of my father's friends check out the coral. Well, at first he didn't really give us too much to go on, but he was able to give us a basic temperature range of the water it came from, and he said that this particular coral needed a fair amount of light to thrive. That meant that the piece we had came from no deeper than fifty to sixty feet, shallower then we originally thought. We weren't very happy to hear that. It just multiplied the chances of the wreck being closer to shore, and that would cause more problems with making a claim." Karen paused a moment, making certain that Nick was listening, which he was. "All because of that law that Steve told me you used to bring in the FBI. By the way, I think that was an ingenious way to go about getting their help, even if it did seem to be a problem at the beginning."

"Thanks, but it doesn't sound as though he gave you very much to go on, this expert of yours?" Nick said with some doubt still evident in his voice.

"Not from the coral alone, he didn't. But he took it farther then that, and tried to see if there was any water still in it that had not dried up yet." Karen continued, and with each step, the excitement in her voice grew, this was where the breakthrough came. "That's where he found some microscopic animals, and these little buggers live near the surface, and like it exceptionally warm."

Nick was a bit skeptical, and was about to blow a small hole in this breakthrough. "The water temperature around here is never below sixty-five degrees." Nick observed.

"Right, but that isn't measured at the surface, and these guys live in the top five feet, where the temperature changes quite a bit, depending on the air temperature. They also like it between seventy-five, and ninety degrees." Karen explained.

"Go on." Nick was now getting more interested in her theory.

"Well, Frank was murdered in March, so he found the ship sometime before that. That means it was pretty cool around here, especially at night, so he couldn't have been any further north than Key West to have those specific microbes around. Once I told the professor the time frame we were looking for, he took everything we had so far, the coral, the animals, and everything else, and was able to narrow it down for us." Karen explained further.

"So he was able to tell you where to look?" Nick asked.

"Not really, he was however able to suggest a certain area for us to focus on, due to the limited places that type of coral is found, and going through weather charts for that time of year, we could get a reasonable guess at where to eliminate because of the temperature. He told us to concentrate on the Greater Antilles, Cuba, Puerto Rico, and the Cayman Islands." Karen continued.

"That doesn't sound like it narrowed it down enough to find it as quickly as you did?" Nick said, again with doubt.

"That is why we didn't just hop into a boat and start mapping the ocean floor with electronics." She said with some sarcasm of her own. "Steve remembered that you had mentioned Frank's returning some books to me. Some of those books are very rare, and we don't let very many people take them out of the library, so we keep a record of who takes what, and when they bring it back."

Steve decided to fill in some information of his own. "Jake and I started with the last ones he had, while Karen went and pulled everything he had taken out for the past six months. It was kind of strange that the third book I was going through was the one about Jake's big find, but that is where I found a slip of paper."

Karen once again jumped in. "It was almost like a shopping list, on one of those Post-It things. And the things on the list were all of the electronics that my father had mentioned in his book. They were all the things that my father had figured would have made his search easier, since they were not yet invented when he was out treasure hunting.

The most interesting things on the list were low frequency transmitters and receivers. They could be used to return to an exact location, time and time again. The problem is, unless you know they are there, and what frequency signal they were set to, they aren't of any help."

"Nick, while we were checking on Michaels, his people told us that was one of the things they couldn't figure out. He was using one of those things the whole time they were out, and unless you were the one who put them out, there wasn't any reason to listen for a signal. But whenever they asked, Michaels would just tell them to shut up and do the jobs he was paying them to do." Steve added to Karen's explanation once more. "He must have made Frank tell him everything."

"Everything except the right place to look." Nick said. As he spoke the words, he felt Julie squeeze his hand ever so slightly. The thought of her husband's torture must have been very difficult for her to hear.

"Right, but we still needed to get within one mile to pick up the signal, and we didn't know what frequency to set the receivers for, either." Karen resumed. "It was my father who came up with that. It was thought that the ship was out to sea when it was caught in a hurricane. One of the books that Frank had taken out was about how the captains of many of the ships that were lost had tried to take refuge here in the Keys, from the storms. But father had his own thoughts on this specific captain. He felt that this was a man that saw himself as smarter then all the others, and would not do what they had done. After all, doing what was not expected was what got him noticed by the Queen, and what had earned him that cross." Karen was obviously proud of the fact that her father too, was an original thinker, just as Frank must have been to come up with all of these conclusions, and Frank did not have the added information about the coral, and the depth of water to focus on. "Dad figured that this captain would have tried to go around the western side of Cuba, once he left the harbor in Havana, trying to get around behind the storm. They had no idea back then how large a hurricane could be, or it may have changed course on him, sending him a little wider then he would have wanted.

There are some waters about thirty-five miles west of Cuba that are in the twenty to sixty foot depth range that we knew we were looking for, and they even have the right type of coral. And that is exactly where we found it, and the signal from Frank's transmitters, which Steve was able to pick up by modifying a scanner from the police station."

"Wow...I am really impressed by all of you, but I do have one question?" Nick paused as he took the time to look at each one of them in the eyes. "All of you know how I got the FBI to come into this investigation, and if you have already found the ship outside of their jurisdiction, nowhere near US waters, why are they still here, and looking around?"

The three women in the room looked directly at Steve, who scooted to the edge of the chair in which he sat, and with a wry smile began his explanation. "Well Nick, they were already here, and they were looking for you, which we wanted to find you too. So when Karen showed up two days ago with this news, I convinced everyone to keep quiet until we knew you were safe. Besides, we still want to find Michaels and bring him to justice."

"I have to admit, I am touched by all of your concern for my well being, but you all know that I am more then capable of taking care of myself." With those words Nick returned their smiles, but he wondered what they would really think of him if they were to ever find out the truth about what happened. He also wondered how long it would take Steve and the others to figure out that it had never before taken him more than two hours to get from there to Bimini.

It had suddenly occurred to Nick that someone was conspicuous by his absence. "So where is Jake anyway?"

Julie was the first to respond. "He and I worked out a partnership last night. He is going to finance the recovery of the ship's contents. From whatever we recover, Jake will be reimbursed, and get first choice of what is found."

"And what do you get out of this partnership?" Nick asked of Julie, before turning to Karen. "After all, it was Frank that originally found the wreck, and showed you the way to it?"

Karen leaned forward in her seat, but remained calm because she knew that Nick was simply watching out for the interests of his friend. "Nick, my father and I simply want first pick of what is recovered so that we can keep it all together in one place, just as we have done with the other relics that we have recovered. Keeping them together so that all can enjoy and learn from them in one place. But as far as making certain that Julie is not taken advantage of; we have heard that you are quite an accomplished diver, and would be more than happy if you would come along on the recovery. That way you can see that everything is on the up and up." Karen told him.

Hearing Karen's thoughtful words, Nick felt ashamed of his own hasty ones. "I am sorry about what I just said, but I would like to be a part of the recovery. Not to keep an eye on you, but to be a part of something that historical." His words were true, but he also thought that it would be a good way to be away from Julie and Donna for a while, because he was not sure if he would ever be able to look the two of them in the eyes, not after what he had done.

That night, Nick sat out on the picnic table out behind his house, looking out over the ocean, and wondering where his life was headed. Suddenly he felt a presence behind him, and turned to see Agent Collins standing there. "Well Guy, what can I do for you?"

"Well, we checked out everything that you told us, and they all confirmed your information." Collins said.

But there was more that the agent wanted to say, and Nick could see it clearly in his eyes. "But?" Nick asked.

"But I know you were somehow involved in the disappearance of Michaels. I don't know how, but you either did it, or you got word to DiMarko, and he did it." The agent said.

"If you think I did that, prove it. Check my cell phone, my home phone, the ones at the bar, check whatever you want!" Nick said defensively.

"We already have, and we haven't found anything. You knew that we wouldn't, that is why you suggested it. But I know that someone like you would not have just left this case, not unless you knew that it was going to end very quickly…and you would need to know how it was going to end." Guy spoke confidently.

Nick heard the words, and thought back to the phone call he had made to Garcia. He hoped that his instructions were followed exactly, though he knew they must have, or Collins would not be guessing, he would know. Nick then realized that a man such as this might be able to see something in his eyes, just as he had seen in the eyes of Michaels.

"Well," The agent continued. "Now that we know that the ship is not in US waters, I've been pulled from the case; I am going back to the task force in New York. Take care of yourself, Nick, it was my pleasure to have worked with you. It's a loss to law enforcement to have someone as good as you are not working anymore." Without another word, Guy turned and left Nick sitting there.

Those were not the words Nick expected, and he didn't know what to say. So Nick just sat there alone, looking out over the water, wondering if he would ever find redemption for the actions he had taken in the name of friendship and justice.

The End